Aurora glanced up at Sullivan eventually. Even sitting, he was quite tall and made her feel far too feminine by comparison. She swallowed, assailed by wishes she shouldn't ever have about him. He would never be interested in her that way, and he wanted a wife above everything.

He frowned. "I have a question to ask you."

"Oh?"

He glanced behind him first, and then inched closer to murmur, "You might think me odd to ask this now, but…do you like me?"

She drew back, frowning. "I beg your pardon?"

"It's a simple question. Do. You. Like. Me?"

His stare pierced her own, held her prisoner, as warmth steadily climbed from her chest to her cheeks. Certain her face must be turning pink, she set her cup back on the table carefully and answered without looking at him. "Of course, I like you. Everyone does."

He sighed. "I'm not sure I believe that you do."

Heather Boyd

USA TODAY BESTSELLING AUTHOR

Yours Until Dawn

Distinguished Rogues

The characters and events portrayed in this book are fictitious. Any similarity to real persons, living or dead, is purely coincidental and not intended by the author.

For Morpheous

Chapter One

"Ah, at last," Drew Finch, Lord Sullivan, murmured as Lady Alicia McKenzie-Wellborne appeared in the Castlereagh's London ballroom looking lovely in a white silk and lace gown.

The woman was tall and had a willowy figure but was not exactly as fresh to the marriage market as some. She had caught his eye this past week at another party, and the more he considered her, the more he thought he should know her better.

And not because of some giggle or squeak she'd uttered like the rest of the marriage hopefuls were prone to do. If not for catching sight of Lady Alicia just now, he might have considered leaving the ball already. There was no one else of interest, and that frustrated him.

Drew moved to a better position to see the lady from head to toe. She might just do for him. Not too young, not too short, and quite bright by all reports. Unfortunately, he had not been introduced to the lady yet and only had secondhand information to rely upon about her character. Indeed, they had no connections in common save their host for this evening, but that problem would be easily solved once he found her.

He glanced around, looking for Lady Castlereagh. The matron was nowhere to be found unfortunately at that precise moment to perform any introductions. So, he strolled the perimeter of the dance floor, looking out toward the card room and other places, nodding to women he'd already considered and discarded as potential brides since last season, and drawing ever closer to his quarry.

Lady Alicia's face suddenly turned his way and lit up with a bright smile of welcome. Drew paused, startled that she'd noticed him at all, though pleased, too. He was again hoping for a whisper of a thrill when their eyes met and held. That was all any widow with marriage on his mind could hope for when pursuing a wife. He doubted he could fall as deeply a second time in his lifetime.

A gentleman stepped around him and the connection was lost. Although he tried to catch her eye again, her attention was now diverted to the guests milling about between them.

No matter. Drew would have a better chance once the proper introductions had been made and they spoke. He would ask her to dance immediately.

"Try to smile," Lord Brandestock murmured, stumbling into him. "Your face suggests you've a giant turd wedged up your arse."

"Mind your language," Drew warned, looking to his right where young Brandestock now stood. Perhaps it was a mistake to have encouraged an acquaintance with Brandestock. They were members of the same clubs—White's and Bradshaw's, too—and frequently attended the same tonnish events. But the man's language was as colorful as his taste in garish waistcoats.

"All I'm saying is smile and let the women come to you like I do," Brandestock murmured, smiling widely at a widow of questionable morals as she passed them by. "You're an earl and wealthy and moderately handsome for your age."

"Why thank you," he said dryly.

Brandestock grinned widely. "Nothing more needs to be offered but a little encouragement to enjoy a fine night in some lonely lady's bed."

Drew would have pinched the bridge of his nose in exasperation if he were anywhere else but a ballroom. Brandestock was years younger than him, a bachelor still, but seemed to think Drew needed his advice on courting women. That couldn't be further from the truth. Drew knew exactly how to please a lady, in and out of bed, better than he did.

"Excuse me. But I can tell when I'm desperately needed elsewhere," Brandestock murmured before following after the pretty widow who was beckoning him with just her eyes.

The widow and Brandestock disappeared behind a curtained alcove—as likely a venue for scandalous trysts in any house.

Drew shook his head and shrugged. One of these days Brandestock was going to come undone in the worst ways and pay a heavy price. Like Drew, he had the looks and money to attract dozens of title-hungry women to claim the position of his bride, whether he wanted the woman or not. Not that Brandestock claimed to need a bride yet. Not like Drew seemed to. However, Drew's own vetting of potential spouses seemed to have dismissed a legion of women from contention. Too timid, too talkative, or simply too silly.

He'd no idea he'd become so particular about who he could live with.

But it seemed he had high standards. His approach to his first marriage had been far different from this. He'd not been looking for a bride when he'd first met Clare but had fallen in love with her at first sight. Marrying her was all he thought about from the moment they'd spoken. She'd been graceful, charming, loving, and irreplaceable it seemed. Clare had been the light and love of his life. Drew had looked around society enough now to realize she'd been one of a kind and had set a very high bar for her successor to reach.

Certainly, too high for anyone he'd met so far in London, and every day a little more of his hope of meeting that one special lady whose presence would change his life in an instant faded.

But surely there had to be someone out there for him.

Everyone claimed there was.

He'd been very patient and thorough in his attendance in society's ballrooms and other amusements. Unfortunately, *she* hadn't made herself known to him yet, and he was growing impatient with the endless waiting.

Drew glanced across the room again and saw Lady Alicia on the arm of a slender gentleman. When the fellow leaned down and boldly placed a kiss on her pink lips right there in view of all, no one around them complained. In fact, they damn well near cheered him on.

Lady Alicia blushed and hugged the man's arm a little harder, her smile revealing a distinct partiality, the ring on her finger sparkling in the candlelight.

Drew's heart sank. Clearly, another man had claimed her affections already.

He turned away, acutely disappointed that he'd missed another chance, but thankful he'd not found the hostess to ask her to perform an introduction to an engaged woman. That would have been awkward to say the least.

As he lifted his head, he spotted his father, the Duke of Northport, across the room. Drew scowled that the old man was out in public yet again. That was the third time this month they'd attended the same ball. His father did not usually attend this sort of thing. But there was no mistaking the duke's reasons for moving about in society so much this season.

Drew studied the duke as he moved in that direction. Northport had a long-term mistress, but she was not here tonight. He was engaged in conversation with a young woman, but he kept looking about the chamber. Most likely he was looking for Drew, so *he'd* be forced to talk to the woman. Father was eager to have Drew wed again.

Drew pasted a smile on his face when he recognized the young woman before he got too close to turn away. It was Lady Eloise Barclay again—Northport's friend's youngest daughter.

Unmarried, of course.

Drew would be expected to dance with her, as he had been every other night they'd met at one event or another. He had done so on several prior occasions with no complaint on his part. The Barclays were old friends of the family. Certain courtesies were required, and it was better to get his duty over with now than be berated by the duke for rudeness later.

Lady Eloise was an adequate partner for one dance—but never more than that. As he watched, a gentleman attempted to speak with the young lady, but Father turned her away from the fellow, monopolizing Lady Eloise's attention so the gentleman had no choice but to back away, unspoken to and embarrassed.

Drew groaned under his breath. Was Father attempting to keep Lady Eloise from other men now? Not that Drew would marry her. She was so much younger than himself.

He strolled across to his father, feigning delight to see him.

Drew resembled his sire in many ways. Similar height,

same dark hair that curled in the rain, same blue eyes that many said were remarkably changeable. But the similarity ended there. Drew was much quieter and more circumspect than his father. But then, Drew wasn't a duke yet with designs to control the destiny of members of his family, especially his eldest son.

"Ah, here is Sullivan, too," Father boomed loud enough to be heard in all corners of the ballroom. The Duke of Northport leaned down toward the woman at his side. "I told you he couldn't stay away. My son is as handsome as you remember, isn't he Lady Eloise?"

Drew felt his face grow warm as he extended his hand toward the embarrassed young woman his father had been pushing at him for months. Lady Eloise ranked high on the list created by his family as a potential bride for Drew. Only just eighteen and newly presented to the queen, she had impressed many during her first season. Even him, to a small degree. But there was no thrill, no spark of anticipation, to be felt around her when they met. None at all.

And that lack of attraction was specifically why he could not marry her, or anyone he felt similarly unaffected by.

He smiled politely at the young woman. "A pleasure to see you again, Lady Eloise."

"My lord," she murmured, touching her fingers to his for the briefest of handshakes. Father beamed them both a smile. To Father and many in the family, it was an inevitable match. Lady Eloise knew the family well enough that she had attended Drew's wedding to his first wife—as a flower girl tossing petals in the air, for heaven's sake.

Since Clare's death, Lady Eloise had often been invited to visit the Northport estate while Drew was there. Father had made his preference quite clear. Drew suspected his father had also been secretly preparing Lady Eloise for the day when Drew and his bride would become duke and duchess of Northport—as Drew's eventual wife would one day.

But there was a wide-eyed innocence to Eloise that made Drew's stomach pit at the thought of bedding her if they ever married, and that was as good a reason as any to turn elsewhere in search of a bride. She was too green for a man of his experience.

Not that he was ancient. He wasn't even thirty years yet. But a lot had happened in the decade between their ages that could not be overlooked. He would not be happy married to someone as young as Lady Eloise. But she was well-educated about current events, she was a duke's daughter, and got along well with his family, so she was always pushed at him. She had a decent dowry, too, and seemed to like talking to him.

Unfortunately, she did not stir him in the way his first wife had done. Lady Eloise might be at the top of a very short list of possibilities, but Drew himself didn't bother writing such a list down of potential brides.

When he eventually discovered a woman he wanted to marry, he was sure he'd know it instantly.

He smiled, and asked Lady Eloise if she had any sets free on her dance card, as he was expected to do.

"I do in fact." Lady Eloise handed him her card to look at. Her next dance was free, as was a number of sets up until the one right before supper. Father had done his work well in monopolizing her time tonight. Her card should have been full by this hour.

"Looks like my timing is perfect."

If he chose the very next dance, Lady Eloise would be free to accept other partners once their set was over. Perhaps she might even sit down to supper with someone she really liked then. Anyone but him, really.

Their dance was announced, and he offered his arm to her to stroll to the dance floor together. He glanced down at the young woman on his arm briefly and decided to make the most of the opportunity to speak with her, hopefully without being overheard. "I must apologize for my father," he whispered.

"He's a dear man," she murmured.

"He's grown fond of you, and hopeful where there is no hope to be found, I'm afraid," he said somewhat bluntly, deciding honesty was the best policy where making a marriage was concerned. He wouldn't have this young woman led on about his intentions toward her another moment more.

She nodded slowly, a frown marring her complexion. "That is what I suspected, but he was adamant that…"

Drew inclined his head. "He's mistaken."

"Oh," she murmured softly. "I see."

Did she? He hoped she was not offended by his disinterest in her.

The music began, and they danced, but Lady Eloise said nothing more after his confession. Had he upset her with his disinterest in marrying her? Could she really be surprised? She'd met his wife. There was very little similarity between the two.

When the dance was over, he found himself steered around with subtle pressure toward a distant doorway, away from his father and her family. Alarmed, he glanced down at her. "What are you doing?"

"Getting what I really want," she said.

Her tight smile was a little unnerving. Had she misunderstood that he wouldn't be offering for her—no matter what she said or did? "Lady Eloise, I don't think you understand…"

Her face lit up in a smile, but it was aimed at a young man ahead of them. She made Drew stop in front of the fellow by digging her heels in and could not be moved. "My lord," she said, beaming. "What a lovely surprise to see you tonight. I feared you'd be dancing with someone else."

The fellow, the very one Father had turned her away from earlier, appeared startled by her appearance, but offered Lady Eloise a genuinely delighted smile and bowed deeply. "Not yet, Lady Eloise. I feared we might never have a chance to speak tonight."

Drew was not introduced, and he stood silent on the sidelines, watching the brief press of fingers, the matching flushed cheeks as the pair revealed all the signs of a budding attachment. The besotted stares as they drank each other in wordlessly for a few minutes was decidedly awkward to watch.

Drew had felt and behaved this exact way around his first wife before he'd blurted out a hasty proposal. Looking on, it was a devastating reminder of what he'd lost.

He would have taken a step back, but Lady Eloise had a manacle grip on his arm. Drew couldn't move away to allow them privacy to speak of their feelings. He had to stay and listen as the pair bumbled through his asking her to dance, and her breathless acceptance when he claimed the supper dance.

When the card was returned, and more halting words were exchanged, Lady Eloise looked up at him suddenly. "You can return me to my family now, my lord."

He inclined his head, bemused by the exchange and by

Lady Eloise ordering him about like he was almost a brother to her. "Of course."

He nodded to the besotted young man and then escorted Lady Eloise back toward her family. "You could have introduced me."

She fluttered her fan before her face. "To whom?"

"To the young man who is clearly smitten with you, and you with him, I suspect," he suggested. "I wonder if I might look forward to seeing him again many times in the years to come."

Lady Eloise blushed prettily and looked over her shoulder. When she turned back, her smile was strained as she whispered, "If you hold me in any affection at all, you will hold your tongue about him. My family…"

"Enough said. I can forget everything I just didn't see," Drew promised without a moment's hesitation. If Lady Eloise's choice was not popular with her family, he was the last man who wanted to meddle. It could be true love, even if the fellow was poor as a church mouse. Only Lady Eloise should have the right to decide who was the man for her. It wouldn't be Drew, and he was very glad she might have someone better in her sights.

He returned her to a married female cousin. Stayed until Lady Eloise was approached by other bachelors and had the remaining spots on her dance card claimed for the later night.

The smitten young fellow was nowhere to be seen now, though. Who exactly had he been? No one Drew had ever met before, certainly. After a time, Drew excused himself from Lady Eloise and left the ballroom, looking for other forms of excitement to be expected at a ball of this size.

He went to the card room, won a small sum eventually,

but in the end returned to the ballroom, biding his time as he waited for the right woman to appear.

His next wife really was taking her sweet time putting in an appearance.

So, he amused himself by discreetly keeping an eye on Lady Eloise as she was being swept around the dance floor by countless well-off gentlemen. When the smitten young man appeared to claim his turn before supper, her family started to whisper among themselves, clearly surprised and more than a little disapproving.

Drew hid a smile as Lady Eloise and her would-be suitor swept past him. They had nothing but eyes for each other as they danced. His blunt words to Lady Eloise had been made at the right time, it seemed. He wanted her to set her sights on someone else, perhaps this young man, by whom she had a better chance of being loved in return. Either way, whatever happened in Lady Eloise's life was none of his concern anymore. It never had been, either.

Drew turned away. He was more than ready for his own match. More than committed now to finding someone who lit a spark in him. He wanted what he had with Clare again. He just hoped when he finally tied the knot, he was granted more wedded bliss than the first time. Fate couldn't be so cruel as to shortchange him twice in his life.

Chapter Two

Aurora Hillcrest accepted her dance card back, said goodbye to the last man who would dance with her tonight, and glanced at her oldest cousin. "There. Satisfied now?"

"Yes. You need to be seen," Mrs. Eugenia Berringer promised, offering an impish smile. "Now the business of the evening is arranged, I have to ask how many times Sylvia tried to get you to go away with them?"

Aurora glanced about to see who was near enough to overhear her answer. "Seven directly, four indirectly when speaking to her husband and the dowager marchioness while I was in the room. And I had already declined," Aurora Hillcrest answered with a grimace for her absent cousin's persistence. "Of course, I would not go. I could have enjoyed two whole weeks away from London, but with one of them spent trapped in a carriage with Sylvia and her husband, and then another spent watching them take the waters in Bath for their health—of which mine is already excellent, by the way —it made the decision to refuse very easy."

Eugenia laughed softly. "A visit to the pump room ensures plenty of conversation might be had by all. They are going for the fresh air. It will be good for all of them to get away from the great city for even that long."

"It will be good for her husband. Wharton's been looking harried of late." Aurora shrugged. "Politics gets him riled up too easily."

"Chasing Sylvia about the house used to do the same thing," Eugenia whispered, drawing close. "I thought some time away would do their marriage good, which is why I was so eager for them to go."

Aurora leaned against her cousin. "If you were trying to inflame their passions, why on earth did you suggest taking the dowager marchioness along with them?"

Eugenia winked. "Wharton has to sleep sometime. Besides, Sylvia would never have left the dowager behind in London. She has old friends there, and I knew she was keen to see them again. She's become nostalgic."

Aurora nodded, understanding why. The dowager was in good health now but early last year, she'd suffered through a dangerous surgery to remove a growth in her breast. She was only now professing to feel like her old self again. "You know, I'm not sure I'd want to travel anywhere with a mother-in-law."

"Only time will tell, and you'd have to be married first to ever know for certain if you would like the experience," Eugenia said, giving her a pointed look that always led to a lecture about her unpopular opinion that she would never marry.

Aurora shook her head quickly, drawing back. "Let's not argue here."

"Very well, but I think it grossly unfair that you deny yourself a chance to be happy."

Aurora would make any man a poor wife indeed. Certainly, for anyone connected to the *ton* where a sterling reputation, family connections and fortune by way of a handsome dowry meant everything.

Aurora glanced down at the costly delicate white silk creation she was wearing tonight. Once upon a time, she'd never have believed she could own something so very fine and elegant. Her cousins' marriages had propelled her into a world she had been and still felt undeserving of.

Aurora winced and lifted her chin. The past could not be changed, and this was her life. Accompanying her cousins about Town to the best events imaginable. She fixed a smile on her face and looked upon the happy guests chattering in the Castlereagh ballroom and tried to imagine she was one of them. Marriage may not be for her. Not ever. But she would never begrudge others their joy.

Aurora could not bear to be an embarrassment to her cousins. She was a lady now. Expected to dance, smile, and be gracious at all times in public. She could no longer flirt with handsome strangers and be swept into a scandalous and brief dalliance. Sadly, of late there were few opportunities to meet anyone beyond the rarified circles she traveled in these days with her cousins.

Once though, before her cousins' marriages, she might have gone out to dance and encouraged anyone who caught her fancy. In these dignified circles, Aurora's choices were severely curtailed. Marriage or scandal were her only options here, and a stolen kiss discovered was a guaranteed path toward a hasty marriage, especially for someone in her position.

"Are you sure I cannot convince you to stay with me?"

Aurora shook her head. "But thank you for the offer. Before I forget, will you be attending the Richmond Ball next week?"

Eugenia sighed. "I am waiting to hear what the duke and duchess' plans are before I make my own."

"As always now," Aurora grumbled under her breath, hiding her disappointment.

Eugenia's social calendar seemed to be set at the whim of the Duke and Duchess of Exeter. Aurora hadn't been able to make any plans with her cousin this season without them being consulted first. Once, Eugenia had been capable of making her own choices. That was the only complaint she had against Eugenia's marriage.

Her cousin looked her way suddenly. "Were *you* invited?"

Aurora hadn't had an invitation to go anywhere herself in a long time, and shook her head. With Sylvia's abrupt departure from Town, she didn't think it likely she'd be remembered at this late stage, either. And since Eugenia hadn't made up her mind to go, she might miss out on what was being feted to be the event of the season, thanks to the tiny number of invitations doled out.

That was how many events in Aurora's life seemed to go of late, unfortunately. She went along with her cousins and nowhere else besides. But she shouldn't complain. Her life had truly only begun to flourish when she'd moved to live with her cousins. That life had been good in the beginning. Adventurous. Just the three of them against the challenges the world doled out. But now her two cousins were married, and so well, there were no hardships to face unless one considered the pain of waiting for the next invitation to arrive.

Aurora glanced at her gloved hands. Hands now so soft they might never have worked a day in her life. But she remembered them red and chafed. Of being poor and made to feel grateful for the roof over her head. Aurora knew firsthand how easily anything good could be taken away. She didn't like to think what would have become of her without her cousins.

At present, she was a perpetual guest of Lady Wharton,

her married cousin Sylvia. And an infrequent visitor to Eugenia's home with the Duke and Duchess of Exeter. Aurora hadn't had a home of her own since she'd been a gullible child.

She shied away from that train of thought quickly and forced a smile for the elegant couples swirling by.

When Aurora looked ahead to the future, she imagined a series of nights similar to this. Yet she often felt uncomfortable. She'd had sufficient time to accept her situation could not be any different. Her freedoms were more restricted than ever. But they chafed.

Aurora wished for excitement. To stage a little rebellion that no one else in society would discover. To follow her heart, not her head, and to hell with the consequences.

But she wanted to belong, too. To give her cousins no reason to regret their support. Rejection, even the idea of it, was a fear that was never far away.

Aurora strolled beside her cousin as they followed behind the duke and duchess, who were making the rounds. Discussing their plans for the season with those they met. Aurora kept silent, having none of her own to offer anyone.

The more she heard, the more aware she became that she could not rely on her cousins' company for the rest of her life. That was probably why they urged her to marry and marry well—like they had. When she had moved in with them years ago, Aurora had, like them, been determined to make the best of whatever came her way. But she had done it without ever defining what she wanted for her own life. Now it seemed her only option was to make them proud with a respectable marriage.

But she could not do that for them. That would be reaching too far.

A small life, where she might do some good, interested her more.

Aurora had always resisted any ambition in her life, choosing to let fate surprise her time and again. Discovering now that she might want more for her life wasn't a feeling she was used to. Or even liked. But something had to be done about her situation, and soon. She couldn't keep following her cousins about like some stray animal they'd taken in.

She had tried her hand at being a companion to an older lady, and while she had enjoyed the experience, she did not want to be at anyone's beck and call. She wanted her own home. Somewhere she might *choose* to stay, the fabrics on the furnishings, the best China on the table, the servants who waited on her, and depended on her too. The time she went to bed and rose hadn't truly been her decision for nearly a year now.

Educating and tutoring bachelors and widows in improving their courtship techniques had not paid well enough to give three women all they'd needed, either.

Could she ever have her own home? A place that was just hers, where she could be happy again, away from all this nonsense.

She would rather remain in London, too, where she'd be near her cousins for at least half the year until they returned to their respective country estates. They were already living largely separate lives. But even a simple life in London would not come cheaply. She would likely have to work at something to create an income to support herself.

They reached an open space in the ballroom, and Aurora was urged to take a place near the Duke of Exeter to look over the crowd.

The crowd looked back, as usual.

Aurora's skin crawled to be under such marked scrutiny all the time.

She edged a little farther away from her cousin and the duke, and immediately bumped into another guest. Aurora glanced up into Lord Scarsdale's smiling eyes, and nearly groaned out loud.

"Don't mind me, Miss Hillcrest," he murmured.

"My apologies, my lord. I did not see you standing there," she replied.

He laughed loudly. "My dear Miss Hillcrest, you wound me. I thought I loomed large enough not to be overlooked by you."

"I'm sure you're not overlooked by someone of greater importance," she assured him, hoping no one heard him boasting again. Scarsdale was the last man she wanted to match wits with tonight, in her current mood. She had more important things to do than humoring his need for constant attention and praise. She was on the cusp of understanding what she really wanted for her life.

"But you are the most important guest of all," he assured her with a teasing wink.

She groaned under her breath and did not rise to the bait.

He lowered his head closer and whispered, "Is everything all right? You seem… I don't know. Distracted, and not in a good way."

"I am the same as ever," Aurora assured him. She snapped out her fan and beat it before her face like every other woman was, pretending the room was too hot for her. But behind its protective screen, she hid a sour expression. Scarsdale was the type of man to linger, even without any encouragement on her part.

"No. You *are* out of sorts and just don't want to admit it

to me," he whispered back. "I've known you too long to mistake that expression in your eyes and assume you are content. Is my flattery lacking its usual flair tonight, or is your mood on account of someone in particular?"

"I don't know what you could mean," she replied, edging away from him, and hoping he'd take the hint to do the same.

He winced. "You are still cross with me, I think, for my pursuit last year. You cannot blame a man for making an effort to charm you. I was in the wrong then, and have only wished to see you smile since."

"It is forgotten," she promised the man. "But I hope your apology has nothing to do with Wharton letting it be known he offered to dower me this season?" Aurora murmured, meeting his gaze. "It was not so long ago that you thought me a foolish, gullible twit only fit to be seduced."

She and Scarsdale were not exactly friends, because of his past behavior. But they were frequent companions at balls and dinner parties this season. If he had been honest, she might have liked him more. But she had first met him as a would-be client of the Hillcrest Academy, an enterprise her cousins had created to earn a living helping gentlemen prepare for a future courtship.

Scarsdale had been immediately taken on because a speech impediment afflicted him around women. But that had turned out to be an entirely made-up excuse for getting past their butler and to meet her in a more private setting.

For a time, she had felt hunted by him. However, someone must have had a severe word in his ear because he had begun uttering endless apologies for his behavior whenever they met.

He winced. "Can you blame a man for doing all he could

to meet a lady as pretty as you? I did apologize to your cousins, too, for my deception when we first met," he said, and then tugged on his waistcoat. "This is a new beginning. A new season, and I will never let you forget that you had much to recommend you then, too."

Aurora nodded to a former client as he passed by with a pretty lady on his arm. Scarsdale ought to be doing the same —looking for a wife for himself instead of trying to charm her into liking him better. "Are you to dance with anyone for the next set?"

Scarsdale grunted and looked sour at the thought. "Lady Eloise. My mother arranged it. Again."

Lady Eloise. Large dowry. Excellent poise and long list of accomplishments that put her atop any list of prospective brides. Aurora liked to keep a catalogue of details about ladies hunting for a husband in her head, in case any one of them might suit a gentleman she knew. She had in the past often relied upon her knowledge to assist the gentlemen clients of the Hillcrest Academy. She did not need to do such things anymore, but old habits die hard.

"Think of her dowry and connections if you must to endure the chore," she suggested quietly, recalling Scarsdale's need to eventually marry well to prop up the family fortune. He was not in desperate need yet, but more blunt would certainly increase his comfort in the coming years.

Aurora had exactly the same need for funds, too, but would never consider marriage just to advance herself and secure a better future. But could matchmaking on her own ever pay her way through life? It was an idea she'd entertained before, but her cousins had dismissed the idea of her earning an income out of hand upon their marriages. Yet, if she did not intend to wed, she should do something worthwhile with her life. Matchmaking was certainly worth serious consideration again.

Scarsdale leaned close, lowering his voice to reply, "While Lady Eloise is lovely to look at, she seems too prim."

Aurora struggled not to roll her eyes. He'd made a promise to dance with a duke's daughter. He must honor it, or the young lady would suffer the ill effects of a careless slight. "Have you spoken to her beyond commenting on the weather and asking her to dance?"

The earl shuffled his feet. "Not exactly."

"That is what I knew you would say." She sucked in a breath. She had never directed any client so boldly before, but if she wanted to make a career of anything, matchmaking was a good place to start. Why not begin with Scarsdale? She hesitated only a moment before offering an opinion. "To have any chance with someone that green, you must make an attempt to get to know her," she advised. "Draw her out. Use words, not your usual leer and wink and head toss technique. That only works on widows and bored wives. Be honest about your interest but go slow."

His cheeks colored but he didn't protest that she misunderstood him. By not speaking, he avoided making promises he didn't want to keep, too.

Aurora had truly enjoyed the time she'd spent helping gentlemen conquer the marriage mart along with her older cousins, but it could be extremely frustrating with some clients.

She had never lost her instincts, and knowing what men need and want were frequently two different things. The men she'd helped had often looked in the wrong direction when pursuing a bride. Scarsdale didn't really need to marry a woman with the largest dowry. A modest fortune would do.

He needed someone smart enough to keep him in line more. Lady Eloise would do for courting practice at the very least, until Aurora found him a better match.

She would enjoy this.

But first she had to sell him on the idea of making a well-considered match. "As the daughter of the Duke of Eastwick, Lady Eloise had respectable suitors aplenty, and a healthy dowry large enough to attract many more scoundrels into her orbit. But she is a bit of an unknown. Outwardly quiet and proper but her calm demeanor does not signify, in my opinion. I know many women who speak one way in public and change their tune markedly in private," she warned him. "Lady Eloise could turn out to be exactly the sort of woman you need in your life."

Scarsdale at least seemed to consider what she had to say.

She turned her head to regard the young lady, standing with her family on the far side of the ballroom. Why couldn't she be for Scarsdale to marry?

The longer Aurora looked, the more she wished to see them standing side by side. She might not be an easy conquest and Scarsdale needed a challenge in his life.

Aurora turned back to Scarsdale and tilted her head in Lady Eloise's direction. "You should not delay approaching her tonight."

Scarsdale glanced across the room again, saw other men loitering around Lady Eloise and grunted, the only acknowledgement that he'd detected potential rivals in the room.

Aurora nodded. "You can tell me how charming you were to Lady Eloise and how she answered you later."

He leveled her with a sour look but stalked off toward the distant beauty with more enthusiasm than expected.

If Scarsdale had begun the pursuit himself, and not had

his mother manipulate him into asking for a dance with the young lady, Aurora might be more hopeful there could be a match in the making.

However, Scarsdale had been given no choice, so of course he would be stubborn and grudgingly go. She held her breath and watched their initial exchange, fingers crossed as the woman turned to him with a smile of welcome.

Aurora would find a way to turn her dream of earning her own way in the world once more into reality—but it might be done one reluctant lord at a time.

"Ah, there you are at last, Miss Hillcrest," a familiar deep voice murmured. "Good evening."

A shiver of unwanted tension raced over Aurora's skin at the carelessly seductive timbre of the man addressing her. Lord Sullivan. She turned and looked up into the familiar face of her former client with a smile of welcome. But inside, she was filled with sadness.

Lord Sullivan had been one of the more frequent callers to the Hillcrest Academy, and perhaps the most difficult for her, personally. He could not easily set aside his grief for the wife he still loved and missed, and the regret his son had died in childbirth haunted him. He was the first and only client Aurora had ever considered a lost cause. She'd tried to avoid him ever since the academy had closed.

"My lord," she answered, lowering her face as she dipped the earl a respectful curtsy. "It is good to see you again."

"And you. I had no idea you were attending. The Castlereaghs are old friends of the family," Sullivan murmured, bowing to her. "Castlereagh attended Clare and Pip's funerals."

Aurora had grown accustomed to hearing Sullivan mention his late wife and son, but it pained her just as much as it always had. The man never failed to bring up their names at least twice in any conversation.

"The Castlereaghs are friends of Exeter's, too, so here I am, as well." She looked away from him, catching sight of Scarsdale doing the pretty by Lady Eloise still, and smiled.

"A lucky circumstance for us all to have your company at any event. I paid my respects to Mrs. Berringer already, and then I saw you standing here alone," Lord Sullivan murmured as he drew closer, and her lungs filled with the scent of his distinctive cologne.

She struggled to breathe for a long moment, choosing silence over a response that might have come out as a moan. Why must such a tempting scent exist and be worn by this man? He must bathe in the cologne several times a day.

She ought not to imagine him bathing naked. Nothing good could come of that wicked speculation. She suppressed another shiver though. "Thank you."

"I wonder if you might do me the honor of a dance tonight, Miss Hillcrest? Perhaps the dance before supper, so we might talk."

She winced. "I'm sorry, but my dance card is full," she apologized.

"Ah, I'm too late again." He smacked his fist into his palm as if severely disappointed by the news. "I should have sought to secure a dance earlier."

She risked a deep sniff of his delicious cologne, a scent that never failed to curl her toes in her slippers, before she answered. "Another time, perhaps. Please don't let me keep you, my lord. Do enjoy your evening."

"Of course, and the same for you." Sullivan inclined his head, but the frown line between his eyes deepened as he met her gaze. "But first, before we part, Miss Hillcrest, perhaps you'd do me the honor of reserving me the supper dance at the next ball we both attend."

Aurora inclined her head graciously. "I should enjoy that very much," she promised as her next partner approached. "The next dance is about to start."

Sullivan sighed heavily before striding off across the room, shoulders back, head turning this way and that as he likely looked for his next dance partner.

Aurora welcomed her own partner and was swept onto the dance floor. Yet, she watched Sullivan's long legs increase the distance between them with a heavy heart. He was handsome and wealthy. A nobleman in every sense of the word. He was good, and deserved to be happy, and Aurora hoped he would pick a bride this season.

But there was something wrong with the earl…a shadow that would forever prevent him achieving true happiness. He was completely and utterly devoted to his dead wife and son still. No woman should have to compete with that.

Chapter Three

Women had to be the most maddening creatures in existence, and Aurora Hillcrest was no different from all the rest. Normally, Drew was accustomed to knowing he could have anything he wanted just by crooking his smallest finger. But not tonight, it seemed. Even the one Hillcrest he most enjoyed dancing with was unavailable to him.

Drew grimaced at another lost opportunity to dance with a woman he admired. But this felt the biggest snub of the evening. Should he care that a woman he'd paid to listen to his deepest, darkest fears seemed intent on avoiding him at every turn this season?

He definitely did tonight.

In the beginning of their acquaintance, Aurora Hillcrest had been so understanding. So helpful in absolving him of any guilt he'd felt over his need to remarry for the sake of his title and family. Did she not like him at all, now there were no funds changing hands? Had her overtures of friendship all been an act?

Drew grimaced and noted the location of his dance partner for the next set, and then turned back to study Aurora Hillcrest once more. He had considered her as good a friend to him as her cousins, Lady Wharton and Mrs. Berringer, still were, but it seemed Aurora didn't feel the same about him. Her married cousins treated his arrival far better, the same way they always had when he'd paid them to do so.

The Hillcrest Academy might be no more, but that changed nothing for him. The Hillcrests were good women he'd expected to keep in his life.

All of them.

But it seemed there was one who was perpetually glad to see the back of him. The way she had brushed him off in favor of dancing with another man set his teeth on edge still.

A hand clapped upon his shoulder, and he was wrenched downward to the right as the shorter Lord Wade's voice boomed in his ear over the din. "Three balls, two dinners, and a picnic in the first month of the season. Please put me out of my misery and tell me you've settled on a bride at last."

Drew shook his head vigorously, rather than shout it out over the din of the crowd for all to hear. Lord Wade was another confidant who knew of his inner struggles. He'd known how remarkable Drew's first wife had been, having met the woman during her first season years ago.

He turned to view his oldest friend. Wade appeared to be in a jolly mood, but Drew regarded him sourly. Probably drunk on love again. "So, you finally left your wife's side, Wade, to remember to talk to your oldest friend?"

"Oh, she's not far away. My love is over there keeping a watchful eye on her sister, Lavinia. They said I was scaring off her suitors by asking too many impertinent questions." Wade laughed. "Is that not my right as a brother-in-law?"

"Oh, absolutely," Drew promised as he turned in that direction and easily spotted Lady Wade, and her vibrant younger sister Lavinia, surrounded by gentlemen vying for her attention. "She's popular."

"Indeed, just like my wife was in her first season, too," Wade boasted with the proud smile of an utterly besotted husband who was sure his wife's affections belonged only to him.

"I remember," Drew murmured.

Drew did not covet other men's wives, but he had been one of Lady Wade's potential suitors for a very short time. He was truly glad he'd not pursued Portia, once he'd discovered the viscount's adoration of a woman he'd believed lost to him.

Lady Wade was undoubtedly good for his friend. Her fortune had rescued Wade's family from destitution, restoring an old family in society in a way the viscount had never dreamed possible. Wade had finally revealed how bad it had been for him and his aunt, over drinks one night long after the marriage had taken place. Hiding from debtors, selling beloved furniture like the billiard table that had held so many good memories, had taken a toll.

But now, gone were the shabby, much-worn evening attire Wade had been sporting when Drew had returned to the marriage mart in search of a second wife. They'd played many a game of billiards together since, once the table had been returned to its rightful owner.

Wade had despaired he would lose Portia to a wealthier but widely unliked duke, too. Portia had eventually chosen a viscount she loved over life as a duchess with a difficult man she might never have learned to care for.

People still talked about the abrupt end of that engage-ment, and her nearly immediate marriage to a mere viscount. It was pleasing to see a good man, and family, reverse their fortunes, and all because he had found love. Though the influx of money had not changed Wade at all. He was still as miserly as ever.

Money had never been a severe problem for Drew. He

was now wealthy enough that he could have anything… except a simple dance with Miss Hillcrest this season, he thought sourly.

She was on the dance floor still, and all the disappointments of the evening seemed amplified by her stunning smile for that other man.

Drew felt a touch of unexpected jealousy sting him. Aurora had been a remarkably good friend, and fit well in his arms the few times they'd twirled together at a ball.

Sixteen times in total.

Sixteen…but the seventeenth occasion was proving impossible to arrange.

Was she really trying to avoid him, or did it just feel that way tonight? But if she was avoiding him, why would she want to?

Had he offended her somehow in the last months? He studied her face, flushed and smiling as she twirled about on the dance floor in another man's arms. She seemed to be enjoying herself with the fellow. And she was that way with everyone she danced with. He knew of several other gentlemen interested in Aurora, too, some honest in their consideration and others far less respectful than she deserved.

Drew's pursuit, however, was not romantic in the way that others were.

But since this season began, since she'd started noticeably avoiding him, he felt slighted. That discomfort had prompted him to make a habit of keeping an eye on her. She had no male relatives from her own family that he'd ever met or heard of to look out for her. There was only Lord Wharton and Mr. Berringer, her cousins by marriage, but they had wives and other responsibilities.

When the dance ended, Aurora and her partner started

toward his corner but suddenly changed direction, their heads bent together. Never once did Aurora glance his way, although he was tall enough to stand out in any crowd. It was almost as if she was trying to avoid even looking at him.

But surely that could not be true. He wasn't hideous. She'd even called him handsome once or twice. She had assured him he'd have no trouble finding a bride. Had her praise just been to ensure he tipped them handsomely?

He turned to Wade. "I have a dance with Lavinia later."

"Yes, the one after supper. Watch yourself," Wade murmured.

Drew raised a brow at the unexpected warning. "What do you mean by that?"

"She likes you a little too much still," Wade complained. "There was considerable excitement after you requested that dance with her. You know the sort." Wade scowled darkly at him. "I won't tolerate any nonsense, even from you."

"You have no cause for concern from me." Drew and Lavinia Hayes got along very well, and they often teased Wade at his home together. He liked Wade's sister-by-marriage. She was funny, smart, and obviously fond of Wade. Drew had spent many a night in Wade's company this season, in the company of all of Wade and Portia's family members, too. But that was as far as his admiration went, or ever would for Lavinia. Lavinia, however, was clearly interested in *him* which worried Wade. "I'll be on my best behavior," he promised. Drew nodded solemnly. "I'm not the man for her."

"Mores the pity," Wade murmured. "But I do understand."

Lavinia Hayes made him feel his years, too. She was all energy and excitement. The consequence of her youth and naivety, perhaps. There was so much of the world she wanted to go out and see. Only after some experience of the world would she be content with what a man like Drew could offer a woman. Stability, affection, and a life of comfort and companionship. Right now, Lavinia needed an energetic young man to come along and sweep her off her feet and turn her world upside down.

Drew was not that man.

He glanced around at all the young women being pushed at any man who might take them off their families' hands, and shuddered. None were what Drew really wanted.

Marriage wasn't what he really wanted yet, either, but if he was to tie the knot with anyone, their bond had to be real. Affection, the beginnings of love perhaps…companionship could be his again if he ever met the right lady. He had not found her yet, so unfortunately, he must continue his search.

Perhaps there was something wrong with him that he couldn't see.

Drew turned toward Aurora Hillcrest again and frowned when he couldn't see her on the dance floor or the perimeter of the ballroom. He couldn't spot her partner for that matter, either, and that concerned him enough to stretch up on his toes for a better view of his surrounds. Aurora ought to be careful with men she didn't know so well. She was too pretty to wander off alone.

He sagged when he finally spotted her standing with a friend not far away and chatting with a pair of rather unremarkable bachelors for a change. She looked to be enjoying herself still, as well. In a way she never did when he was around her. There really was only one conclusion he could come to.

He lowered his eyes. She must not like him at all, and that…hurt.

Wade thumped Drew's shoulder. "Portia is planning another cozy dinner soon. Just the four of us. Will you join us, or can I say you have plans for every Thursday night for the foreseeable future? Or at least until Lavinia is engaged?"

"I'm not sure what my plans are." He usually enjoyed dining with Lord and Lady Wade at their home on Thursdays, but perhaps some distance might be warranted if his attendance had raised expectations beyond that of friendship. "But by all means, tell your wife I'm otherwise engaged for Thursdays, and I will make sure I am," he offered.

Wade nodded. "Thank you. You know it might have been fun to become related," he mused.

Drew shook his head. "As much fun as sharing that room at school used to be, I'd say. Only for so much longer."

Wade pulled a face. "You made school bearable."

"You did the same for me, too," Drew promised.

They stood shoulder to shoulder, talking about their school days and watching the parade of dancers glide past their spot.

He heaved a sigh as Aurora Hillcrest spun past again on the arm of another someone he didn't recognize. "Who's that fellow with Aurora Hillcrest?"

"Old friend of my father-in-law. I'll introduce you later. George Fullerton. New money. Lucky son of a bitch, too. Made his fortune in five years on the 'change. Ambitious. Portia tells me he's hunting an equally wealthy bride this season, but he's still got an eye for all the ladies, if you follow. You'd better stop wasting time, or you'll miss out on your right match."

Drew tore his eyes from Aurora Hillcrest immediately and smiled tightly at Wade. "I'm in no hurry to wed."

"But he is. Asked if hiring a matchmaker to perform introductions to the best families was a done thing," Wade warned.

"He'd only have to ask you for that sort of information," Drew murmured, and let out a heavy sigh. "You know everyone—and their secrets, too."

"He tried to get information from me, of course," Wade murmured, brushing a speck of dust from his lapel and smirking. "But I'm saving all my best advice for my oldest and dearest friend. He needs all my help. And so, I again remind you that women won't wait forever for a man to make the first move. If you see someone you want, go out there and get her."

Drew peered across the room, noticing that Aurora was walking onto the dance floor with another man already. No wonder she could hardly spare him a moment's conversation earlier. "I am in no rush, as I've told you many times before."

"A little urgency on your part wouldn't hurt," Wade murmured. "You're not getting any younger."

Drew sighed, wishing Wade would cease teasing him and offering to meddle in his love life. Wade had undoubtedly played a big part in helping him marry his first wife. He'd done so without being asked, and he had certainly helped set up an opportunity to propose. However, Drew expected he could manage a courtship and second marriage all on his own this time.

"The club? Tomorrow?"

"I suspect I will be there at my usual time," Wade said. "We can discuss your battle plan for the rest of the season."

At last, Aurora finally stood alone. But the fellow who

had just left her turned back once to study her before continuing on his way out of the room.

His interest was plain.

So had Aurora's been, too.

Drew gritted his teeth, annoyed that she was clearly more interested in a new acquaintance's company over that of a gentleman she had known for the last two seasons. He pivoted on his heel to face Wade. "Making a marriage is not a battle."

"But courtship is," Wade warned. "The fighting is always fiercest where conflicting desires are involved."

Drew happened to agree with that sentiment.

A bell tinkled somewhere in the crowd, signifying a new set being formed.

He was expected to dance with a new acquaintance, but found his feet were reluctant to move. He'd much rather look for an opportunity to approach Aurora again and get to the bottom of when and how he'd given her offense.

However, he'd made a promise he had to keep first. Speaking with Aurora Hillcrest would have to wait until another occasion. Only in relative privacy could he ask what he'd done or not done. And then, once he'd aired his grievance and hers, if there was one, he'd get back to his search for the right bride.

Drew excused himself from Wade. "I'd best find my next partner."

Wade nodded slowly. "If we might part with a last word of advice. To catch the right bride, you might have to break a few rules. Clare made it easier than you deserved."

Drew agreed with that, as well, and strode across the room toward his next dance partner. A widow just like him.

Drew smiled at her and extended his hand. He had been

on his best behavior since returning to London in search of a bride. No loose women. No reckless behavior that might harm his chances of making the match he needed. His self-imposed restrictions sometimes chafed, but he was aware that returning to the marriage mart for a second helping set him apart from other men. His first wife had died trying to bear his son. He could imagine another lady might fear the same fate, were they to marry him.

Drew turned the widow into his arms on the dance floor and smiled down on her, dredging from his memory a question about her family situation he wanted to clarify. She answered immediately, and he became tongue tied.

This was not the woman he wanted, either. He hadn't cared for her answer.

He held in his irritation. Wade was right. He hadn't always been a well-behaved fellow. Like everyone else, he'd taken risks with his reputation for the thrill of it, and with a few ladies, too. His first wife had liked his wilder side, but it had almost ended their courtship before it had truly begun.

Marriage had settled him in lots of ways. He knew what he wanted in a woman now and couldn't bear to make the wrong choice. Marriage was forever, or until death caused a separation. Drew intended to reserve his ardor and mischief for chasing his chosen wife around their bedchamber. Until that happy day arrived, he presented his best face to the world.

He faltered mid-step but swiftly recovered with a whispered apology to his partner.

Was *that* Aurora's problem with him? Had she discovered his wicked past and realized he was always wearing a thin mask of respectability in public? They had talked extensively about his life, both married and unmarried. He'd of course left a great deal out of the latter while speaking to her.

Aurora Hillcrest had once made her living working with marriage-shy gentlemen. Had asked many questions about his opinion of women and desire for a second wife. If anyone knew him best of all, it might just be her. And if she did, she might have some insights into why he'd no luck finding a wife still, too.

Perhaps it was time to stop pretending, at least around her, and ask the blunt questions sooner than later.

Chapter Four

Aurora saw endless possibilities for matchmaking when she looked around at her friends and acquaintances. They had a host of familiar likes and dislikes for romantic partners, though a lot were uncomfortable speaking of them out loud.

After the ball, she was yet again a guest of Mr. and Mrs. Berringer, as they presided over a private gathering of friends in the early hours of the morning at the Duke of Exeter's London home. The sideboard to her right nearly groaned under the weight of a hearty repast prepared by efficient servants. A half dozen guests grazed at any one time upon the feast, discussing the latest on-dit overheard during the last week.

Her nights spent at Grafton House with Eugenia were almost as predictable as those at home with Sylvia, not that she'd ever share that opinion with anyone connected to either house. It was the usual crowd, just older than when she'd first come to London.

The truth was, Aurora was so restless tonight she could barely stand herself. She could certainly make a match for anyone here tonight if given the chance. But as it was, she had to be practical. She had limited resources and greater needs. She needed an occupation again. And the best place to start was by working with the unmarried members of the *ton*.

But how to go about approaching them…well, that was a bit of a challenge. Spinsters were likely not the first people recommended to play matchmaker for anyone. She would need someone to do that for her. Maybe Scarsdale could write her a reference if she successfully matched him with a bride. But there were few who took the young lord seriously, and he wasn't exactly keen to tie the knot.

She glanced around. She might need someone with a reputation for sincerity and discerning taste, if she was going to ask for a letter of reference to share about. She had to find just the right bachelor and spinster for her first clients, and likely offer her services to them free of charge.

Aurora's mind was so fixed on what she might make of her life with a matchmaking career that she didn't realize someone had come up to stand beside her. Not until she inhaled the most delicious scent ever to be worn by any man, and sighed out loud.

She closed her eyes, blindsided. Aurora didn't have to look up to know who it was. Her indrawn breath had delivered the scent of Lord Sullivan's distinctive cologne straight to her senses. But eventually, she did look up at him. He was so tall, and Aurora trembled a little to have him looming over her. So close. *Too* close.

She took a step back from him, attempting to regather her wits. "Good evening, my lord."

He frowned at her but then nodded. "Can I interest you in a cup of tea?"

"Yes, in fact I was just about to ask a servant for it," she said, turning away.

"Don't bother. It's in the library, waiting for you now," he told her in a clipped tone she hadn't often heard from him.

She looked around slowly at the earl, wondering if something had upset him, besides the usual of not having a wife anymore. "Ah, thank you for telling me. Exeter's butler has read my mind. Excuse me."

She didn't ask him to join her. She didn't want to become trapped in conversation with him tonight. She had a lot to think about, and the quieter library was actually the perfect place to do that. She could consult the duke's copy of the peerage while she considered her choice of first client, how she approached them. It had to be done with delicacy. She would have to prove there was a very good reason to trust her with their happiness.

Unfortunately, Sullivan *did* follow her into the library of his own accord, and when she sat on one of Exeter's comfortable leather settees closest to the fire, Sullivan sat next to her. Close.

She groaned softly, then instantly wished the sound back into her throat as he glanced her way with a question in his eyes.

He'd heard.

She smiled quickly. "It's been a long night."

"Indeed, yes. I often miss country hours," he murmured.

Any moment now, Sullivan would launch into his usual ramble that involved his late wife, and some long-ago summer evening they'd shared. Aurora sighed inwardly as she reached for the teapot. Sad tales were always better heard with a cup of tea.

Sullivan held up one hand to stop her. "No, no, you must be exhausted after all the dancing you did tonight. Every set. Let me pour you a cup of the tea I asked to be prepared for you."

She gaped at him and glanced out the library doors, wondering why he'd bothered. "Should we wait for the others?"

He shrugged. "I only ordered it for you."

Unwisely, Aurora was touched by the thoughtful gesture. "You didn't have to do that, but thank you."

"Actually, I did. I realized it might be the only way I could claim your attention. I've barely been able to catch your eye all evening, since you refused to dance with me."

"Because my dance card was full." She frowned. "Why were you trying to catch my eye? Is something wrong?"

Sullivan smiled tightly as he poured her tea without answering immediately. She found herself holding her breath as he set the pot back on the table. It was not like Sullivan to be mysterious, so she began to worry about the reason he'd lured her away from the others. They were alone, and that was also unusual.

She picked up her cup, cradling it in her fingers and waiting impatiently for him to get to the point.

Sullivan poured his tea and sat back. "You look preoccupied tonight," he murmured. "Are you regretting you did not join your cousin Sylvia on her journey to Bath?"

She shook her head slowly. "Not at all."

"Travel can be pleasant if you keep an open mind and lower your expectations for the quality of service you receive."

"You've traveled extensively," she murmured, remembering a prior conversation with him. He was perhaps the most widely traveled of her male acquaintances.

"Yes. I sometimes wish I could do it all again, but I have more responsibilities now than ever before."

She grimaced and stared into her cup, watching the steam rise as she tried to imagine all the distant places she'd never have a chance to visit. Not even a successful career in matchmaking might make half as much travel possible for her.

Sullivan turned slightly toward her, and she felt his gaze on her. Yet he took several sips of his tea before he set it aside.

Aurora glanced up at him eventually. Even sitting, he was quite tall and made her feel far too feminine by comparison. She swallowed, assailed by wishes she shouldn't ever have about him. He would never be interested in her that way, and he wanted a wife above everything.

He frowned. "I have a question to ask you."

"Oh?"

He glanced behind him first, and then inched closer to murmur, "You might think me odd to ask this now, but…do you like me?"

She drew back, frowning. "I beg your pardon?"

"It's a simple question. Do. You. Like. Me?"

His stare pierced her own, held her prisoner, as warmth steadily climbed from her chest to her cheeks. Certain her face must be turning pink, she set her cup back on the table carefully and answered without looking at him. "Of course, I like you. Everyone does."

He sighed. "I'm not sure I believe that you do."

Summoning up her usual enthusiasm to appease a fragile man's ego was harder than ever tonight. "Why would you think I do not?"

"Just a feeling. You don't talk to me like you used to. We never dance anymore. You are tense when I'm near, and you relax when I'm going. It's as if you see something in me that no one else does, and it displeases you."

Aurora blinked. "What is it you think I see?"

He raked a hand through his hair. "That I am a man only

pretending to be proper and good for the sake of making a second marriage."

She couldn't help but laugh at that. "You're not pretending anything, my lord. You are the nicest man I've ever met."

"Nice? I'm not *that* nice," he warned. "Not all the time. Certainly not in my thoughts. Especially not around a beautiful woman. You see that wickedness in me, don't you? That's why I make you so uncomfortable."

He shifted in his seat, stretching out his long legs that she couldn't seem to look away from. His words sank in slowly. Was he trying to make her believe he was anything but a proper gentleman?

She let her gaze rise slowly up his body. He was built lean but had none of that coltish awkwardness that younger men often possessed. He was a tree she'd enjoy climbing, again and again, actually, were he anyone else. Many women sighed as he passed them by without a second glance, too, but none of them had been with him. They had no chance against a memory that would not fade as it should.

She didn't think him wicked in any way that might be a detriment. "No. No, I don't think you wicked." Not the way Aurora was. Her mind raced with untold fantasies at the thought of him being wicked now, though. But that would never happen. She took a steadying breath. "It is my understanding that you are looking for a bride this season."

"Yes, of course I am. You've always known that."

"Indeed, I have." It was one of the first things that had come out of his mouth the day they met. His duty to marry. She shook her head, remembering how bleak he'd looked that day. And now too. "But I do often wonder why you are not married already."

He squirmed in his seat. "I've yet to meet the right woman."

"That's not exactly true, is it?" She gave him a soft smile and placed her hand lightly on his arm. "You've met many women who could have made you a suitable wife. You always say you're going to marry again, and yet you do everything to ensure it never happens. Perhaps that is what you think you see in my expression. Disappointment and realization that I could not help you overcome this last hurdle."

He looked down at her hand where it rested on his sleeve, and Aurora withdrew it back to her own lap.

"What hurdle could be left? I came to the Hillcrest Academy. You were there, and if there was anything left to be said then it is your lapse, not mine."

She sighed. There had been limits to what they could tell their clients to do and still be considered respectable ladies. They had offered polite suggestions for improvements and sometimes had to hope the gentleman could read between the lines. "What we spoke of there, you *did* need to hear. Absolution, understanding, and support. A sounding board. But…"

"But?"

"You've not taken care of the other things my cousins were hesitant to mention out loud. We expected you to overcome the last hurdle that would help make a second marriage a satisfying one."

He swiveled to face her fully then. "What exactly do you think I have not done?"

She sighed again. This was not going to come out well, but he'd started this conversation. He would simply have to deal with the embarrassment. "When was the last time you were with a lover?"

Sullivan sprang to his feet and stepped away from her quickly, glancing toward the door. But there was no one there to have overheard, and he let out a long and shaky breath. "Surely that is too personal to discuss with you of all people."

Aurora stood too. She had already known what he would say when she posed her question. There was a wariness about Sullivan. Tension in the set of his shoulders whenever any of his friends boasted of their lovers or wives. Of their intimacy and satisfaction. She knew she shouldn't concern herself with that sort of thing, but Sullivan's reaction to those remarks were very telling. He was as skittish as a virgin.

"If your answer is not yesterday, or last week, or last month, or even during these past two seasons, then how can you ever hope to unlock your heart from the black you still wear around yourself?"

He stepped toward her and lowered his voice. "I am out of mourning."

"Are you?" She searched his face. "When was the last time you even kissed a woman?"

His cheeks were turning an unhealthy shade of red at the question.

She turned away from him briefly to take a deep breath. What she said next would either help him make a match or ensure he never spoke to her again. "It is my opinion, and mine alone, that remaining faithful to a dead woman is preventing you from winning another lady's heart."

"You are mistaken," he snapped.

"You will only make a miserable union if you cannot let her go…and I am sorry about that. You deserve more. You deserve to be happy again, my lord." She walked to the settee, sat down, and picked up her half-drunk teacup.

Sullivan stood where she left him, huffing and puffing, before he suddenly stalked away.

No doubt she'd angered him with her blunt words, but she was only speaking from the heart. He did not pay enough attention to the women he was with. He'd never been close to anyone since Clare died. He was too polite, and she'd never seen him flirt with anyone at a ball, although she knew from their meetings how sweet and charming he could be when he was in the right mood.

She finished the last of her tea, staring at the warm fire a moment longer, sad for Sullivan and more than ready to go home to Wharton House, where at least she might plan out her new business venture in more peace. She'd make a list of all the gentlemen and ladies that might have need of her.

The unfortunate thing was, she might even have been able to help Sullivan make his match if he'd listened. She'd known him a long time, and knew what he wasn't doing to capture a lady's heart.

The first thing, of course, was that he had to cease mentioning his late wife and son so much. Not that he should forget them; she doubted he ever could. But no woman wants to constantly fail to meet the high standards set by her predecessor.

The doors to the library suddenly snapped shut—and she spun around in surprise.

Sullivan was walking back to her, and he looked…well, *furious*, to be completely honest about it.

She put her cup aside quickly. "My lord?"

He was in front of her the next moment, and then beside her again. He leaned toward her. His blue gaze never left her face as he reached for her hand.

Aurora was too stunned to move away from him. "What are you doing?"

"Doing what you suggested."

He released her hand and settled the tips of his fingers on her thigh. His hand flattened possessively. His palm was warm through her gown and petticoats. Heavy.

"I'm not still mourning Clare. I can be as wicked as any of the swains who flirt with you, too. You like that about them, don't you?"

"My lord, please," she whispered, tracking the slow movement of his palm up her thigh.

His eyes widened suddenly. "Were you offended that I *haven't* flirted with you?"

Aurora trembled. "Of course not."

But a slow smile spread over his face as she struggled to breathe. "Tell me to stop, and I will. Say nothing, and I'm going to continue seducing you. I hear from a reliable source it's what I need."

Could he?

Would he?

Aurora could hardly draw a full breath as he slid his hand toward her hip, one delicious inch at a time. She had imagined such a moment in her dreams a thousand times before. But seeing Sullivan's hand skimming her gown caused her heart rate to take off at a gallop and desire to flare.

He paused and deliberately pinched up a bit of her skirts, causing the fabric to slide up her legs to reveal her ankles. He looked down at her feet, but she was sure the fabric was not high enough to be indecent yet. His intent was clear, and the anticipation exquisite.

But he'd done it to unsettle her and prove his point that

he *could* be wicked when he wanted to be. And perhaps prove it to himself, as well.

His breathing was labored and when their gaze met, she saw desire writ large all over his face…but then a familiar expression flashed, and he drew away.

Clare. He'd thought of his late wife, even when he shouldn't have the wits to feel guilt.

He was silent for several minutes, breathing hard, before he cleared his throat. "There, now you've seen the real me, not the more cautious face I present to the world. I hope you understand now why I have not married yet. I've never met anyone I could desire before tonight."

Aurora sat up straighter, smoothed down her skirts and reached for the teapot. She poured herself a second cup with hands that were not quite steady anymore. "I'm sure under the right circumstances you could feel lust for anyone. But I was not speaking of only flirting, but of indulging in a tryst. Take a lover, Sullivan, a mistress, or even pay a whore from the street soon, and perhaps you would not be dreading the very idea of bedding every woman you meet. That is what you're truly worried about, isn't it? Whether you can?"

He stared at her, jaw clenching. "I *was.*"

Of course, he was. She sipped her tea, but then set it aside again. She'd never met so loyal a man as Lord Sullivan. He would take his love for Clare to the grave. But loving his first wife still would not bring satisfaction in the marriage bed with bride number two. "Think carefully about what I said tonight. Sleep on it."

Aurora left him there in the library and returned to her cousin, grappling with a guilty conscience. She'd almost *dared* Sullivan to do what he'd done. She should never have let things go so far. She ought to have stopped him, and because

Sullivan had the ability to fluster her when he touched her body, she had not behaved as a lady was expected. She'd been moments away from doing something truly rash…like climbing into his lap and kissing him witless.

Now *that* would have truly shocked him.

She tugged on Eugenia's sleeve. "I think I am ready to go home to Wharton House."

"Oh, I thought you would stay the night," Eugenia said.

"No. I have something to do very early in the morning. For Sylvia," she lied, uncertain how to explain why she couldn't stay. No one needed to know about Sullivan's attempt at flirtation, or that he was uncommonly good at it, too.

"Oh, very well. I'll have a carriage brought round soon."

Before she could answer, Sullivan cut in. "If I might offer my own carriage to your cousin, Mrs. Berringer. It has already been called and can come back for me."

"Oh, that is very kind of you," Eugenia said, accepting on Aurora's behalf without bothering to ask her opinion.

"When you are ready, Miss Hillcrest," Sullivan murmured, gesturing toward the front hall.

She did not particularly care for Sullivan's offer that would essentially take her away from him, but she would not argue with him in front of others. She bit her tongue, bid Eugenia good night, and headed for the front door. When she looked about to say good night and offer thanks for the use of his carriage, Lord Sullivan was nowhere to be seen.

She felt stung by that snub.

The Exeter butler handed her into Sullivan's comfortable carriage, and she drove off alone, surrounded by darkness and the faintest hint of Sullivan's cologne lingering in the air about her.

It wasn't too far to Wharton House, and it was nicely dark, so she wriggled to get comfortable on the velvet seats and lay back her head to think. At least Sullivan couldn't be too upset, if he would give up his splendid carriage for her use tonight. She dug her fingers into the soft leather seats and sighed, reliving her encounter with the earl.

She did not regret her honesty with him. Sullivan had been given a much-needed prod that there was more to hunting a bride than he currently practiced. She would watch and see if tomorrow or the coming week changed the way he behaved around other women. She would like to see him smile more, and flirt too.

After a few minutes' travel, the carriage suddenly came to an abrupt stop. She was about to complain when a large shape barged through the doorway.

Sullivan, judging by the increase of the scent of his cologne in the air.

He sat beside her in the carriage, forcing her nearer to the window, and had the coachman continue on their way. "I didn't want anyone to know we were alone together," he whispered.

"Why are we?" she whispered back.

"Good question." He let out a heavy sigh. "I don't really know."

Chapter Five

Drew glanced sideways at the woman who'd managed to utterly shock him tonight. Aurora Hillcrest, a friend and confidant for two years, saw far too much about him that had proved to be completely right. He had not indulged in any intimacy since before his wife had passed away. But he'd not made a conscious decision not to. He'd just never met a woman that he wanted to be with in that way.

Not until tonight.

He sighed heavily at the awkwardness of the situation he now found himself in. He had almost kissed Aurora Hillcrest tonight. Had wanted to very much, and still did. He'd managed to pull away from her, but it had not been easy. She was his…he wasn't sure *what* to call her now, but he supposed he was still her client, and she deserved better from him. There were rules about propriety when dealing with a lady of the *ton*, too. He should not have pawed at her the way he did. He should not be here in the carriage now, either. But he'd wanted a chance to set things right between them. "How did you know?"

She inhaled deeply before answering. "I've learned to pay attention to that sort of thing. My work at the academy required me to ask impertinent questions sometimes. How men answer them says a lot about their state of mind. Many men had trouble expressing themselves, and what they fear most."

"But you saw through them. You told them…like you told me tonight."

"No. My cousins would never have permitted such an intimate discussion." She shrugged. "Sometimes they were easy to understand, others were harder to pin down. It depended upon their honesty."

He winced, knowing the answer to his next question. "What was I?"

"Oh, very mysterious indeed," she said, and he heard the tease in her voice that hinted she was trying to spare his feelings.

He shook his head. "You probably understood me the moment I walked in, didn't you?"

She rubbed his arm. "Don't take it badly. That transparency made you easy to understand but also a lot harder to help. There were things you were not ready to hear then. I thought you would have taken a lover of your own accord long before now."

He sighed as he remembered the anxiety of that first meeting, when he'd stepped into her home on Albemarle Street. A terrible row with Northport over remarriage had driven him to the Hillcrest Academy's door in desperation, for sympathy perhaps. From his family, he'd received little by way of understanding or patience. But Eugenia, Sylvia and the woman at his side had been a great help to ease his conscience. Especially Aurora.

"The season's beauties are being snapped up every day. Tonight, I heard Lady Eloise accepted Lord Rushworth's proposal," she confided.

"Who is Rushworth? I don't believe we are acquainted."

"A very nice young man, new to his title. Brown hair, nervous smile. Wharton likes him already and believes he has a sensible head on his shoulders. He was at the Castlereagh Ball. Danced with her there, too. You must have seen him."

Drew knew him then and was relieved at the news Lady Eloise was no longer looking for a husband. "I'll be sure to offer my congratulations the next time I see her."

"You're not disappointed? Lady Eloise married a mere viscount when she could have had anyone she wanted, and with a greater title, like yours."

"No. I'm not disappointed," he promised.

"But you were courting her," she insisted. "You've danced with her often."

He shrugged. "I was being polite. Our families are good friends, and while they might have harbored some hope of a match between us being made, I never did. I'm sure you heard that Berringer encouraged his friends to help young women stand out last season. If my attention to Lady Eloise this season has prompted this viscount to propose sooner than later, I'm very glad to have played a small part."

"Yes, I heard about Berringer's efforts to help wallflowers," she murmured. "I didn't know you were also involved."

"When it suits," he murmured. "I would not ever describe any woman I know as a wallflower. I quite dislike the term."

She looked down at her hands. "Many ladies pretend to be proper but are really just trying to fit in with society's high expectations for them."

"Gentlemen do the same," he freely admitted. "As I've shown you tonight, I'm not the man you thought I was. We men curb our hungers when we need to, so as not to offend delicate sensibilities. Everyone except Brandestock perhaps treads lightly around available ladies."

"You shouldn't have to do that around anyone, but someone should put a gag in Brandestock's mouth some nights. Whatever is in his brain comes directly from his mouth the next moment."

"Oh, I agree with you there." He chuckled softly. "Did you really think me tame, dull and unadventurous?"

After a long moment, she shrugged one shoulder. "I'm afraid I did."

"I played the role too well then." He shuffled closer to her. "I would be more than happy to stop being good around you, if you've no objection."

"You may behave any way you like around me. I'm not the one who needs to be charmed."

He relaxed a little more. "Hopefully a title isn't all a woman needs when making a marriage," he replied.

"Indeed, it is not. Nor is a marriage."

He glanced at her in surprise. There was plenty of interest and speculation about Aurora in certain circles. A line routinely formed around her at the start of any ball to claim all her dances. He should know. He hadn't been able to secure a dance with her all season. "Why haven't *you* married?"

She shivered. "I've no interest in it for myself. But for others, I am glad to be of help. That is why I've decided to become a matchmaker."

He was shocked but only for a moment. "You're all in business again? I'm surprised to hear Wharton will allow his wife to engage in trade."

"It's a recent development but it is only me now, of course. Wharton does not know about my decision yet, and neither does Sylvia, since they are away from Town. I will talk to both of my cousins when the time is right. They are much too busy to engage in commerce, but I have the time and a great interest in the welfare of others."

He covered her hand with his where it still rested on his arm. "You'll do well. You have a way of making a man comfortable."

Her hand withdrew slowly from under his. "I won't just be working with gentlemen but with women, too. There's a lot that can be done to make us all more appealing to a potential spouse."

"Like telling widows to start kissing strangers?"

"Remembering to brush your hand against hers as if by accident to make her notice your interest," she countered. "Smiling more often. There are a thousand ways to capture a woman's heart other than with a hefty purse and lofty title like yours."

Drew reached for her hand again. "You are a kind woman."

She laughed and withdrew from his grip a second time. "Don't think I'll be doing it out of the goodness of my heart. I expect to be paid well for my advice to all of my clients."

"How much?"

"I beg your pardon?"

He needed this woman in his life if he was going to make a match. Her insights were priceless. "How much would you charge to make a match for me?"

She was silent for a long time. "You'd really want me to help you find a wife?"

"Yes. Why not you?" He would do whatever it took to get past this hurdle, to have it over and done with at last.

She shook her head. "It might require many more blunt conversations like the one we had earlier in the library. That moment did not go as well as you expected, did it?"

He gulped at the thought of how well that moment of flirtation *had* gone. But he'd never discussed his sex life, or lack thereof, with a woman who was not sleeping with him first. And even then, there were some topics he'd never shared with his wife. Aurora Hillcrest was not a wife, but she was someone he cared about. She was a matchmaker now, though, and he couldn't imagine her ever being indiscreet with his confidences. He was sure she could help him if he just put his faith in her, as he had before. "Name your price."

Aurora suddenly pressed her hand to the window as she peered into the darkness. "Why haven't we reached Wharton House yet?"

"I asked the driver to take the long way round London first."

He imagined in the silence that followed that she glared at him, thinking the worst. He knew she had when she finally spoke. "That was presumptuous of you, and wicked too."

He shrugged, although she likely couldn't see the gesture. "I was desperate."

She sighed. "You're not desperate, my lord. Only a little misguided."

Drew laughed at that. He'd missed hearing pithy offhand comments like that. He'd missed talking so candidly to her. He'd always felt he could tell her anything…and so he usually had.

"I've yet to hear a price," he reminded her.

"I must be honest with you. You would be my first client as a matchmaker," she confessed softly.

Her business couldn't be that new. "Surely not?"

"The venture was only decided upon today, in fact. I need an occupation that is suited to my expertise and experience, and might pay well one day. But I'm under no illusion it will be easy to meet the right people at the right time in their lives."

He thought about that for a moment. Starting anything new was a challenge. A lot depended on her reputation for delivering results. She could hone her craft on him if they could come to an arrangement about other matters. But to get what he hoped from her, he would need to speak to her with the same brutal honesty as she'd earlier bestowed upon him. He couldn't let politeness come between him and making a second marriage. "Would a letter of recommendation from a satisfied client, along with a handsome payment for services rendered be helpful?"

"Yes, actually. I had already considered asking my first client for a reference."

"Then you will have a glowing character from me. I can write one tonight if you like."

"No, not now. Best to wait until you are safely married," she said quickly. "If you are not happily wed, no one will believe its authenticity."

"I'll have it delivered to you on my wedding day then," he promised, hand on his heart.

"I accept," she promised, and named a substantial sum to be paid on his wedding day, too. He haggled, and enjoyed her rebuttals for a higher fee immensely. He reasoned that being the first client should have some privileges, while she leaned heavily on his already professed desperation in order to increase the cost.

They finally settled on a sum more easily borne for a first-time client and shook hands, each with a sigh of satisfaction.

He wet his lips, certain he was finally on the right path, now he had Aurora on his side again.

But there was still that troubling request he wished to ask of her. It was perhaps well beyond the purview of her services, but he needed confirmation.

He took a deep breath. Asking Aurora to be his first kiss since his wife might come as a surprise to her. But who else would forgive any mistakes he might make when their lips met?

He reached for her fingers and drew her toward him a little more. "Might I kiss you? For practice only. I haven't done it in a while and I'm nervous."

"Oh?" she squeaked, a little breathlessly to his ears.

He winced. "Only you would forgive me if I do it poorly the first time since Clare. Unless that is too much of an imposition or beyond the scope of your new service."

Her silence indicated she definitely thought about refusing, and he waited with his heart in his throat for her eventual reply. He toyed with her fingers, changing his grip until it felt right.

Aurora exhaled slowly and finally squeezed his fingers back. "I...I suppose it couldn't hurt just the once, if you think it might help you."

"Thank you." Drew twined their fingers together tightly, binding them together as the carriage swayed while it rounded a corner. His heart beating fast with anticipation and a little panic for what might happen next between them.

But he bent his head slowly and dropped a gentle kiss on her cheek first. Aurora uttered a little gasp, an encouraging sound to his ears. He dropped another kiss close to the first, and then more. He hoped he wasn't going too fast. But he'd wasted so much time already that he couldn't seem to stop.

Drew lifted his free hand and cradled her face in his palm, drawing her even closer.

Aurora shivered and leaned into his touch.

He took that as permission and continued dropping kisses toward her jaw. He let go of her hand and slid his arm around her body, drawing her into a loose embrace. Aurora was softer than he expected. Delicate and warm. He wanted more of that warmth pressed against his body.

As soon as he thought of it, with a quick lift, she was settled on his lap, her arms twining tightly about his neck. He found that slender column of her throat with his lips and worked his way up to her jaw again.

Aurora moaned and squirmed, seemly lost to passion in his arms. As his mouth wandered lower to rain kisses along her collarbone, Aurora leaned back in his arms to give him space.

He gripped her torso, holding her in place between his hands as they rounded yet another corner that might have unseated her from his lap.

But with the first brush of his thumbs against the underside of her breasts, she was jolted from the spell and struggled out of his reach to sit opposite him, gasping.

She was undoubtedly glaring at him now, and he was in the wrong again.

"I'm sorry," he whispered, his voice rough and vibrating with the need to have her back in his arms. That fierce impulse shocked him.

"You should not have done that," she warned, her voice shaky and raw.

He'd gone too far without realizing he was doing it with *her*. His matchmaker, rather than his match. He steadied his racing heart. "I did warn you, I was only pretending to be good," he said, and then raked a hand through his hair.

"So you did," she whispered. "You were supposed to kiss me."

"I did kiss you," he murmured. "About two dozen of them, actually, not that I could have kept count." He'd been too swept up, knocked off his foundations by a passion he'd planned but not expected.

"On the lips," she complained. "That is where I expected yours to go and stay."

"I got carried away." They both had, though he said nothing of that realization immediately. It had been a very long time since a woman had been so near, or so desirable to him. This particular one he might like to kiss again, too. "I apologize again. I have no excuse for my lapse of control other than I thoroughly enjoyed kissing you."

"Well, at least your loss of control is something positive to come out of our discussion tonight," she said somewhat primly. "I sensed no real hesitation on your part when you kissed me."

He squinted at her in the darkness, annoyed that she sounded so calm when his thoughts were still so chaotic. Their kiss had been a turning point in his life. His first taste of desire since Clare. He wanted more.

"Neither did I."

Aurora cleared her throat. "I'm certain that the next time, matters will proceed even more smoothly. With someone else, of course."

Drew was not sure about someone else, but if it turned out to be Aurora in his arms, and perched on his lap, letting him kiss her, he was certain he would perform admirably. "I hope so."

"The asking was a nice touch, too," she added softly after a moment.

"Thank you," he murmured, and then laughed, feeling awkward again. Had he really doubted his ability to kiss properly before? It wasn't so much the kissing that had concerned him, but rather the emotions of guilt that he'd feared might follow.

Right now, he felt not the least bit guilty about anything.

There were other signs pointing to a good outcome of tonight's conversation, too.

Despite the dark that surround them in the carriage, obscuring her clear view of him, Drew shrugged out of his coat and wisely laid it over his lap to hide the evidence of an erection that would not seem to subside.

Of all the women in London he could have chosen for his first kiss, why had he responded to *her* so strongly? He'd known Aurora for more than a year, for heaven's sake. They were hardly strangers to each other.

And Aurora had reacted to him in a way that surprised him, too, until she'd realized what they were doing was wrong and put an end to his seduction.

"Would you please have the carriage take me home now," Aurora whispered, and then spoke more firmly. "I think your first private lesson has been a great success."

Drew sputtered. That was no lesson. That had been pure lust uncovered. But he told the driver to turn and take them to Wharton House immediately. He would not take any further risks with Aurora's reputation. Not if he wanted her to help him make the right match.

He tapped his fingers on his thigh, puzzled by Aurora Hillcrest as much as himself.

Aurora had reacted to him instinctively, without artifice or calculation, in a purely physical way. Responded in a manner a new lover might to a wanted caress. Breathless, eagerness betraying her desire for more. Willing to play along with anything he might do until he'd gone too fast. But he could not mistake the fierce burst of desire that had awakened him from his stupor.

Earlier in the evening, he had watched over her with other men, telling himself his concern was solely because Berringer and her cousin had been absent from the ballroom for a good long while.

Had he always been envious of every smile she'd bestowed on other men?

There was more to this to be discussed and explored, especially her reaction to him, but that could wait for another day.

He sensed possibilities he'd not considered before. Scandalous ones, too, given that brief tease of passion between them. They were already often thrown into each other's company due to her cousins and their mutual friends.

And as he looked at her in the imperfect clarity of the dark swaying carriage, he yearned to touch her again.

But to what end?

He could not practice on Aurora and then marry someone else later. That would not be fair to Aurora, even if that was exactly what she expected him to do. She insisted he take a lover. Suggested he pick some light-skirt or penny whore from the street corner to grace his cock for a few shillings. But he'd had those opportunities all along and never partaken with strangers. Making love to someone known to him, however, was an entirely different matter.

The driver tapped the carriage, signaling their destination was imminent, and there was no further time for conversation as the carriage started to slow.

Drew sat forward in his seat and put his hand on Aurora's knee.

Her breath caught again. "My lord?"

"I should say good night now, so no one suspects I'm with you. I will not step from the carriage when we reach Wharton House."

"I so appreciate your concern for my reputation *now*," she drawled, and then removed his hand from her body.

Drew couldn't be satisfied parting on bad terms. He probably deserved more of a set down than that, and he would give her the opportunity tomorrow. He had taken liberties, after all. "Words were not how I wanted to say good night."

He tugged her onto his lap again and caught her chin in his hand. Aurora Hillcrest was a fine woman. He'd like to know her much better, too. He smiled quickly and closed the short distance between them to kiss her lips. Aurora tasted sweet, of unimaginable excitement, and he twisted his head, eagerly seeking a deeper taste of her mouth.

But Aurora drew back, moving out of range. "Good night," she said firmly.

This was clearly a woman he could not easily sweep into passion. What surprised him was how much he suddenly wanted to. She'd always seemed the most impulsive of the three cousins. On every other occasion, especially at the academy, where he'd been a client, she'd been an endlessly passionate champion of his chances of making a good second match. But perhaps that enthusiasm did not extend to gentlemen who tried to kiss her in dark carriages. She was a spinster, after all. An innocent.

He winced. He had forgotten that somewhere along the way.

Drew might have a chance to kiss her again someday, or perhaps not. "Good night, Miss Hillcrest," he whispered, as the carriage came to a complete stop in front of Wharton House.

He moved deeper into the shadows when the Wharton butler appeared in the open doorway holding a lantern. Drew's grooms raced to put down the steps to allow Aurora to disembark. She allowed the grooms to steady her on the steps and then she was safely beyond his reach.

Aurora hurried up the stairs of Wharton House and passed inside without looking back even once, leaving him in darkness.

Drew, however, watched the front of Wharton House as the carriage drew away, a familiar disappointment gripping him.

He was going home alone again. He would sleep alone again. He would speak to no one in the morning when he first woke, save his valet.

He closed his eyes and remembered how it felt to be holding a woman in his arms…and particularly Aurora Hillcrest. The moment had been perfectly natural between them, and that was rare in his experience. He truly hoped he dreamed of her tonight.

Chapter Six

Aurora decided to meet Sullivan alone the next day. She had sent for him at dawn, after a troubling sleep recounting the events of the night before. On the surface their kiss should have no lingering consequences. It was never proper for a woman to be alone with a gentleman, though, and yet having anyone overhear there had been a foolish flirtation between them last night wouldn't be, either. So, she waited in the small parlor at Wharton House for Lord Sullivan without a servant attending her.

Although she told herself their meeting today should unfold just like any other had in the past, part of her knew it would be different. Pleasantries would be uttered, a dead wife and son mentioned, and then a continued discussion of his search for his elusive bride could take place—hopefully ignoring last night's amorous encounter.

But first they had to get past any lingering misunderstandings left over from yesterday's carriage ride. It was essential they clear the air if she was to be any help to him. She wanted to make sure he had formed no wrong conclusions about her character, and hopefully he would understand it had been a one-time mistake. Then he could go back to his search for a suitable bride who would accept coming second to a ghost.

She wrinkled her nose. She couldn't really help him unless he was willing to help himself. Clearly, he needed to find an outlet for his pent-up passions if he thought kissing his matchmaker was a good idea.

When the butler announced he had arrived, she believed she was ready. Calm. Perfectly poised like the proper young lady she wanted everyone in society to believe her to be. And she was…until the man strode across the room wearing a huge grin just for her.

Her heart skipped a beat, her knees trembled, along with higher parts that quivered, as he swept into a deep, respectful bow. He rushed forward, reaching for her hand. "Miss Hillcrest, you always look lovely in blue. You must know it's my favorite color?"

Her smile faltered as she stared up into his face, surprised by his lie. But she managed to hold her hands together at her waist and kept them there until his outstretched hand fell. "Your favorite color is green, my lord. You always wear it, or brown."

His eyes sparkled, and her heart lurched again for having mentioned knowing that about him. "So I do, and so clever of you to notice my preference for muted colors. Blue is my favorite color on *you*, though. It brings out the intelligence in your eyes."

She narrowed her eyes on him, unwilling to fall for flattery so early in the day. She was wearing a plain round gown. Nothing too fine for the occasion of their meeting to be considered remarkable. "Then you see something no one else has ever made mention of, without expecting something scandalous in return from me. Most men notice my pretty face and green eyes, and assume there is nothing at all between my ears. Then, of course, they discover I'm not married, and weigh the risks should they be caught misbehaving with me."

That might have been too harsh for so early in the day, but she wanted it clear from the outset that she would remain blunt with him. She would not be mistaken for a woman who expected to be courted with fine words, or was eager for flattery. She'd kissed this man as part of a lesson and nothing more. She had to stop him smiling at her like he currently was.

Sullivan shrugged. "A smart man knows which woman is worth the risk of misbehaving with instinctively." Despite her best efforts, Sullivan was still smiling at her. But it was early yet. He hadn't mentioned his wife. Once he did that, there would be long sighs and the return of that deep cleft between his brows.

She put her hands on her hips and glared, annoyed with him for being so calm in the face of her blunt words. "You and Scarsdale must be quite the pair, or has he started tutoring you, too?"

"Take lessons? From him? Ha. I hardly need the teachings of a man who has never won your favor. He surely must have tried to seduce you by now."

She fought the urge to confide that Scarsdale had sought to tempt her many times. She turned her back on Sullivan, moving toward the window to glance out, but there was nothing to see but brick walls from this room. "Somehow he still does quite well with the ladies."

"Not with a proper one, and he's clearly never been in love to know what he's missing out on by flattering so many so insincerely."

She turned back to the earl and found him closer than she cared for. He was much too tall and handsome today. She too easily remembered his taste, and the warmth of his hands. She moved away from him again, putting a large globe between them. She let her fingers drag over the sphere, making it turn and pretending to be thinking. "I know the answer to this of course, but why do you think he's never loved a woman?"

Sullivan stopped the globe by planting his hand on it. "Because if he had ever been deeply enamored, he'd be married to the woman by now. Even if there were unsurmountable difficulties, he'd have moved heaven and earth to be by her side. Just as I did once before."

There it was. The subtle mention of his enduring first love. She breathed a little easier now. "Some difficulties cannot be overcome," she told him. And a wedding proved nothing. There were some obstacles, stains, that could never be erased to make a marriage a happy one.

Sullivan was suddenly at her side again. He touched her arms, running his bare fingertips up and down her skin lightly. "I see no difficulties here."

Aurora stiffened her spine and walked away from him quickly. Kissing him last night had been a grave mistake. She'd revealed a side of herself she'd never wanted him or anyone in society to see. Aurora had relived their encounter all night…and come to the unpleasant conclusion that he might want to marry *her*, simply because he felt she was compromised.

Aurora hadn't rejected his overtures soon enough, strongly enough, in the carriage to have been convincing. Too stunned by his request to kiss her for rational thought to have taken hold. And because his advances had been welcomed then, he likely assumed they would be today, as well. But she was wrong for him. "For us, do you mean?"

An assent rumbled up his throat. "I like the sound of that. *Us.*"

Aurora clenched her jaw. The earl had wanted her last night, and still did. She'd been right about him having intentions because of what she'd allowed already. He truly might ask her to marry him, and that was unfortunate. She turned to face him, her stomach in knots as she met his gaze. "But I don't. You must never forget why you are here."

"To be with you," he said quickly.

"To marry." She stepped toward him, drawing in a deep breath. For a change, his cologne did not distract her. It gave her strength to resist. "There can never be anything between us, you realize." She stared at Sullivan, waiting for her denial to register.

His face slowly changed as the intent behind her words sank in and a frown appeared on his face. "But last night…"

She shrugged. "I won't deny that I allowed you some liberties a courting man might hope for in a prospective bride. At the time, I did not perceive the very real danger that allowing you a simple favor of a kiss might lead you to assume I have an interest in marriage, too."

"Honor requires a change of course, because it was you I kissed," he said, his brow furrowing until those deep lines were etched between his brows. "I've made no secret of my desire to make a second marriage. I *will* marry you; I promise. You've no need to fear I would toy with your affections with so little regard for your future or reputation."

He would destroy the peace she'd made with her past if she let him too close. "But I will not marry *you*, my lord. If my cousins' marriages have led you to believe I, too, would be grateful for a similarly spectacular match, you are gravely mistaken."

His face brightened, however. "Have you considered me as a potential match for yourself before?"

Aurora's face grew warm. "My cousins and I have discussed dozens of gentlemen and their potential to make a woman happy…or not."

He advanced on her. "Why would you think I could not please you?"

Because Aurora was unlike other women. Not to mention Sullivan still loved a dead wife, and until he put that love firmly aside, no woman could ever live happily with him. Nothing in his demeanor today suggested anything had changed.

He was only speaking of marriage to her now because of how they'd acted together in the carriage last night. He'd kissed her because she'd been convenient, and that was the only real reason. "I won't explain, and you shouldn't ask. I will understand, however, if you would like to disengage my services as a matchmaker for you. If so, do please take your leave and go with my hope of hearing a wedding announcement in the near future."

"Miss Hillcrest. Aurora—" he began.

She held up her hand to stop him talking. "I have not given you leave to address me informally. It is Miss Hillcrest and nothing else."

He grasped her by the arms. "Stop pretending you felt nothing last night when we were together."

"It was…pleasant," she said in as offhand a manner as she could manage. She carefully extricated herself from his grip. "Obviously you are a man of great passion."

She met his gaze to see how he'd taken her words. That was her second mistake when it came to Sullivan, because he was too close yet again.

"I am, and I want more," he said slowly. She knew he

meant it, too. However, when he lowered his head to try to kiss her again, she easily evaded him.

"Enough!" she cried, putting another piece of furniture between them. "Surely you can see that I cannot go around allowing a client to seduce me whenever he pleases? My only interest is to help you make a match."

"You are," he assured her, reaching for her hand again.

"If you cannot behave yourself, my lord, I urge you to leave before it is too late for us to remain on good terms," she told him.

His jaw clenched, and then he dug into his coat pocket and produced a small pouch that he tossed onto a table nearby. The pouch struck with a heavy clink of coin within. "There. As promised. Half now, the rest on my wedding day, and with a letter of recommendation to show others delivered at the same time. Is that all you want?"

"Yes. Thank you for your prompt payment," she murmured, watching as he started to stalk the room. Aurora tucked the money into her pocket, smoothed her skirts over the bulge and winced. Dealing with Sullivan now might be more fraught with tension than before they'd kissed, but she did still think she could help him find a suitable bride. He would simply have to forget their kiss and take the lover he clearly needed from somewhere else.

Aurora glanced about the room. While she had in the past conducted every meeting with a gentleman with a table between them, she urged Lord Sullivan toward a pair of chairs set close together, picking up her journal along the way.

Sullivan was her client. The first of many, she hoped. She must adopt a businesslike demeanor at all times and see this through. "Now, to the business that brings you to me. Tell me who you like best in society at the moment," she asked firmly.

"You," he said instantly, then shook his head when she scowled. He gave a shrug. "There was one woman recently who had caught my eye but before we could even be introduced, I discovered she's newly engaged, so of course…"

"You were too late there, but many others are surely good enough for you," she murmured.

He turned to her then. "It is not a matter of whether they are good enough, but of compatibility. I won't marry someone I don't desire, no matter how well connected their family might be."

"Dowry?"

"Utterly unimportant," he insisted. "I told you and your cousins that before, I'm sure."

"You did, but it doesn't hurt to enquire a second time. Was there anyone else? No? Now, this morning I have written down the names of three ladies with whom I would like you to consider again and pursue a meeting within the coming week."

He scowled. "This morning?"

"Indeed. I rose early, invigorated by the challenge of helping my client make a match." From her journal, she produced a small scrap of paper and handed it to him.

He took it and studied the names. "I am already acquainted with these women."

"Yes, I know. You danced with Miss Firth last month. She sighed heavily as you walked away without looking back. Lady Sophia Peel, you also danced with once, and you seemed to be drawn to her, leaning down whenever she spoke. But you've not danced with her since."

He looked at her sharply. "You must have been watching me very closely to have noticed all that."

Aurora nodded. "Many women become friends of my cousins, and many are hoping to make a match this season, too."

His expression sobered. "Lady Sophia spoke very softly. I couldn't hear hardly anything she said to me over the din."

"She's quite shy but interesting to talk to. Ask her about her new pug when you meet with her, and her tongue will be sure to unravel. She'll speak up about her endless love for the little beast."

Sullivan looked at her sideways. "Beast?"

"He liked my shoes a little too well the last time we met," she admitted sheepishly. "He nearly ruined my favorite half boots. I'm told he was very hungry that day."

"Not well trained then," Sullivan noted with a sour look toward her feet.

"Very young still," Aurora explained, tucking her feet more tightly beneath her skirts.

He winced. "Like his owner."

"Now, I know you've spoken of your own experiences in training your dogs and other animals. I'm sure you've much to discuss on that topic with her, too."

He sighed. "I had discounted Miss Firth and Lady Sophia mostly due to their youth and inexperience of the world."

"Then my third suggestion might be more to your taste." She pointed to the paper, hoping to stir his interest in her last suggestion. "Lady Catherine Jagger, viscountess. Older than the other two by a few years, a widow like yourself, and with a daughter who is the sweetest, most agreeable creature."

Lord Sullivan's face colored. His jaw worked. "The daughter is the same age as Pip might have been this year."

Aurora sighed. "All the more reason to consider getting to know her mother better, then. The child will need a father, someone to look up to and for protection as well."

He folded the paper unnecessarily small and held it clasped in his hand. "So, what do you expect me to do with these women? Seduce them, too?"

Aurora nodded. "If the mood and circumstances are right, why not indulge a little before marriage? But given Miss Firth and Lady Sophia Peel are certainly innocents, you might be wise to wait a while before exploring that possibility. You would not need to be so reserved with a widow, perhaps. If she likes you and wants it, too. But if you are at all desperate for pleasures, and I suspect you are now, there is always the ladies of Bradshaw's to entertain you at night, or by day as well."

He gaped at her, clearly surprised by her extensive knowledge of what went on in a pleasure house like Bradshaw's. "Is there anything about me and my life you *don't* want to talk about?"

She shrugged. "I hear things. It's impossible not to in this house. Wharton remains a member of Bradshaw's since his marriage, as do a number of his friends. I know you attend."

"The food is excellent, as is the company of our friends."

"It wouldn't hurt you," she said softly. "To make love without affection. You might find that a little passion restores your equilibrium."

"My equilibrium is just fine as it is." He burst to his feet. "I know what I want, and what I don't, without having it shoved in my face again."

Aurora stood as well. She'd rattled him yet again, but without intending to this time. She had hoped he was open to discussing his lack of love life. "Perhaps we should call it a day."

He turned to her slowly, face draining of color. "Forgive me. You seem to bring out the worst in my temper with these suggestions of yours."

She smiled quickly and went to him. "There is nothing to forgive. I think this a great step forward that we can speak bluntly and honestly with each other. You have always been far too careful of the words that come out of your mouth around women. We have to be honest with each other if I am to help you make a match."

His jaw tightened, and then he leaned close. "I still want it to be *you* I kiss."

She raised her hand between them. "No."

He held still in front of her, but his breath was fast and loud to her ears. His hand rose toward hers and hovered there, inches away from touching her fingers.

Aurora held her breath until his hand dropped away. "We will speak again in a few days. I'll send a note with a date and location for our next discussion."

"Very well." And then with a strangled growl, he stalked away, closing the doors behind him, his fist clenched around the list of prospective brides she'd given him.

Aurora exhaled and bowed her head. She really hoped Sullivan might try to bed someone before they met again. He was suffering from misplaced lust. And now so was she.

Chapter Seven

Drew strode into his study, tossing aside the book he'd been trying to read all day. He was unable to settle into any task, it seemed. Aurora Hillcrest was very much on his mind. Her passion and her instant rebuff, particularly. He'd known it was too soon to bring up any future with her last week. But at least she knew he was stealing kisses with some thought for her continued good standing in society.

He might have wished she'd been more forthcoming concerning her reasons for declining to become his bride, though. He hoped to learn them that very afternoon.

It had been over a week since he'd seen her. Her note that morning had been brief. A time and date had been suggested for tomorrow, but that unfortunately clashed with other plans he'd already made. Since the reason he could not meet her was to attend an event where one of her choices were sure to be, he had written back, asking for a change to a venue of his choice today.

He had arranged to meet Aurora at an empty house in Conduit Street. She had initially suggested a meeting at Hatchard's Lending Library, a place they both regularly patronized in London that would make it seem to be a chance meeting, no doubt. However, given Drew went there so often, he was not keen to discuss his private affairs in so public a location. Absolutely anyone in society might over-hear them talking about marriage.

Aurora wished him to speak honestly—and bluntly—about his affairs, but he would only do that in private and to her alone. An empty house he was considering purchasing as an investment was as good as anywhere that he could think of.

Thoughts of Aurora—her defiance, the softness of her expression after kissing him—had plagued his mind for days. She confused the devil out of him. He almost hadn't been able to walk away from her the last time without pressing his suit again. He'd wanted to stay and argue the merits of choosing her over another lady. To kiss her rosy lips properly.

But walk away he had.

And after half a week of deliberation, of paying court to other women who failed to excite him half as much with their smiles, he was ready to give up and give in.

He wanted Aurora.

He had managed to meet two out of her three candidates several times each. Pleasant encounters, and all without any stirrings of lust. He had tried. He'd pictured each woman in his arms, under him too, sharing his bed, and not been roused by lust at all.

Given any absence of desire with them, and a great deal more when standing in Aurora Hillcrest's presence, he'd made up his mind. He would not be deterred…but he *would* be patient. He could pursue her under the guise of seeking her advice and few would probably notice, and if they did, he had an excuse to use. She called herself a matchmaker now. There was no reason for anyone to know of his pursuit until Aurora said yes to him at last.

Not even her.

But he would do all he could to support her chosen career. He knew how much help she'd always been to him.

However, he would definitely draw the line at kissing lessons with other clients.

There was a scratch at the door, and he looked up to see a footman hovering. "Yes?"

"Forgive the intrusion, but His Grace's carriage has pulled up outside," a footman told him quickly.

"Northport?"

"Yes, my lord. Thought you'd prefer a moment to prepare," he said before scurrying off.

Drew was surprised and annoyed by the unexpected arrival. He glanced at the clock on the mantle. He had to change and leave to meet Aurora soon. He could not be late, today of all days. Not when he was hoping to make a good impression.

Drew headed out to meet his father. Northport was only just being relieved of his hat and cane at the door when Drew arrived in the hall.

He bowed to his father. "Your Grace, what an unexpected pleasure to have you visit."

"I should not have to make the effort if you lived closer to me," Northport complained, and continued to regard him sourly. "I suppose you've heard the news about Lady Eloise."

"Ah. Quite," Drew said, quickly leading the older man to the library and shutting the door behind them. Northport had likely come to shout at him for dragging his feet where Lady Eloise was concerned. "You've come about the engagement, I take it."

"I've given you a few days to lick your wounds in private, but no more. That damn foolish woman. She has no idea of the disappointment she has inflicted upon her family and ours."

Drew sighed. Father was the one upset. Understandable,

when he'd been rather obvious in his preference for Lady Eloise to make a match with Drew. Though Drew had never given the old man cause to believe he'd any intentions toward Lady Eloise. Still, the duke had persisted in dropping hints in every private conversation they'd had since Christmas just past. "I'm happy for her."

"That is ridiculous. She was meant to be yours!" Northport raged.

"That is not so. I really *am* happy for Eloise. She's chosen, and there is nothing at all to say about the matter now."

Northport rounded on him. "After all the care and interest we've shown in the chit, I should say we are most put out about the matter. What are you going to do about it?"

The only thing Drew might do is help them elope so they were married faster. "I made Lady Eloise no promises." Drew met his father's hard stare. "*You* are the one upset. That's why you're here—to take your frustration out on me."

The duke paced, back straight, hands behind his back. "She is marrying beneath her! Don't think I shall ever invite her to visit us again."

Lady Eloise came from a large, important family, and if she was not invited to join Drew's family for the summer or winter holidays, it might not matter so much in the end. Lady Eloise would have a great many other demands on her time once she was a wife with a new family to answer to. But the Duke of Eastwick was Father's good friend. The pair had regularly visited each other over the years. It might be awkward for a while, but Drew was certain those disappointments would fade in due time.

"I'm sure Lady Eloise knows what she's doing. I cannot claim to know her reasons for her choice, or the character of the man she's chosen to marry. But you know Lady Eloise as well as I do. Probably better. She is aware of her responsibilities to *her* family. She'll have made her choice with her eyes wide open."

Father continued to pace back and forth, puffing. "But to marry a mere viscount when she could have been your duchess when I am gone."

Drew took his father a glass of port and urged him to sit down to drink it. "What does her father say about the match?"

"Eastwick was coy about his opinion at the club yesterday, but concerned for you."

"So, he's not obviously angry?"

"You know Eastwick. He doted on his youngest child. Hoped for a match with our family for many years. When I think of all the plans we made for the future," Northport complained. "It would have been the joining of two great families."

That was no reason to wed anyone. Drew sat forward. "Is it a love match, do you think?"

Northport huffed and puffed, and the upset slowly drained from his face as Drew's suggestion sank in. He scrubbed his jaw, thinking hard. "Perhaps," he conceded in the end. "She did seem particularly keen to dance with the young man, despite her family's disapproval and mine."

"Well, there you have it," Drew exclaimed, sitting back. "You always say nothing can be done to stop a marriage when there is true love involved."

Northport sipped his port, a sullen and frustrated expression on his face. The duke usually had no complaints about even bad matches made because of love. Drew's first marriage had not been accepted at first. But once Father met Clare, and he had seen them together, saw how deeply attached they were to one another, he'd thrown his support behind them as if it had always been that way. Clare and Northport had enjoyed a polite but somewhat formal affection. He'd been deeply saddened by her death, too. He'd even shed a tear over her grave.

But the very next week, Northport had begun to mention acceptable families with daughters of marriageable age to Drew.

"So, you must resume your search," Northport stated, downing his drink in two swallows and setting it aside with a loud bang on the nearest tabletop. "I won't have it said that you're hiding from society and licking your wounds. The Rooney ball, the Gill soiree. You must be at each and monopolize the season's remaining diamonds to keep everyone guessing who you will pick as your bride."

Actually, Drew did not have to do anything anymore. He'd chosen his bride, though Northport could not know it yet. Drew might have forewarned his father of his intentions toward Aurora Hillcrest. However, given her unwillingness to entertain even the idea of making a match for herself, he decided to keep his interest and pursuit quiet for now.

It was clear he and Aurora might be well matched in passion. She just needed time to understand his commitment to her was unbreakable, even now. "Yes, my search is ongoing," he agreed.

"You're not at all disappointed by that, are you?"

"No." He shook his head. "I have always held Lady Eloise in the highest esteem, of course, but she was never the lady to capture my deepest affections."

Northport pulled a face. "That is the trouble with being in love. Once you've had it, nothing else will do for you."

"Nor for you, I imagine." Drew breathed a sigh of relief

the worst was over and turned the conversation to the duke's favorite subject. His longtime mistress. "How is Juliette these days?"

Northport heaved a heavy sigh. "My mistress has taken to collecting curiosities. Little animal figurines. They are everywhere about the town house, and heaven help me if I accidentally knock one over. She acts as if they were alive and cries most piteously, forestalling my leaving by at least an hour, sometimes more."

Juliette had been Northport's mistress for nearly as long as Drew's mother had been duchess. Juliette lived here in Town during the season, and when the duke removed to his country seat, she gladly went with him—living in a little cottage on the edge of the estate so the duke could visit her daily.

It had caused a scandal in the beginning, of course, but the woman made Father happy so what more could be said? Drew knew Juliette quite well by now. She was a warm and jolly sort. Weeping was decidedly out of character for her, as far as he could tell. "Perhaps she's become lonely. You could get her a puppy. Something small that will be content to sit in her lap when you're not there with her."

"I will not share her affections with a snarling mongrel," Northport vowed. He rubbed his jaw and frowned. "But perhaps I *should* do something for Juliette. She's a good woman."

"The very best," he agreed with a small smile, watching the cogs turn in his father's mind. Drew often wondered why Father hadn't married Juliette. He was not getting any younger, and neither was Juliette. They could marry now, live together properly, and likely no one would care at this point.

"What's important is that she still adores you after all these years."

Father grunted. "I wish you would hurry up and wed."

Drew nodded and kept a tight rein on his smile. Happiness was again within reach. He just needed another chance to plead his case.

Drew stretched out his legs, considering a future with Aurora as his bride. He really didn't know why he hadn't considered her before, but he was a fool not to have noticed her appeal. She was bold and intelligent. Insightful, really. She had a kind heart and had proven to be none too shy in the right circumstances.

That made all the difference.

He smiled. No, not at all prim and proper, and he liked that about her even if she denied herself more. It would make wooing her, and their courtship, that much more exciting. He might not have to wait until they wed to satisfy any of their mutual urges his courtship might stir up. He planned to begin seducing her that very afternoon, in fact. He had cleared his schedule for the day and night ahead.

He could not wait to see her again, if only for a chance to kiss her cheek and touch her hand.

He glanced at the clock on his fireplace mantle. Time was finally passing quickly. He'd change the moment the duke was gone and waste no more time going to her.

He tapped the arm of his chair. Impatience for kissing a woman he desired had made him unusually restless. "Where are you bound next, Northport?"

Father raised a brow. "Was there somewhere better you need to be?"

Drew smiled. "Yes, I do, and soon. And I think too that if Juliette is weeping over broken figurines, you'd better do something kind for her sooner rather than later. Perhaps flowers or jewels to begin with?"

"She has had enough flowers from me to plant a garden, and she doesn't wear even half of the jewels I've bestowed on her over the years, either," the duke complained.

"Perhaps a surprise outing is called for then. A trip to the country, or even a holiday by the sea. I remember her saying how much she enjoyed that last trip you took together."

Father grimaced. "That's an excellent idea if I could leave."

"Why can't you?"

"Well," Father started. "I told her I'd not depart London until you were settled in marriage again."

Drew wanted to groan. No wonder Father had been attending the same events. He was trying to be there the moment Drew's decision was made. "No!" he sighed.

"Well, I know it's not easy for you to make a second match. I hoped to hear a wedding date by now, but still nothing." The duke scowled darkly. "I'm starting to suspect I'll have to make the choice for you, and make the proposal as well, too."

Like hell he would. "Why does everyone think I need their help to make a match?"

"You seem to have no idea how to go about it." the duke sat forward eagerly. "You went to that Hilltop Academy, of all places. Everyone knows those women were never going to help you find a bride."

"It was the Hillcrest Academy," Drew murmured, correcting his father's mistake. "And they were very helpful indeed."

Because of them, he'd found his bride. Albeit, he'd been a

little slow to see the light. Spending time with Aurora *had* been one of the highlights of the time he'd spent there.

"Any light-skirt out there could have done the same job as them," Northport grumbled. "Once the first bedding was behind you, the ride is much smoother after that. Don't you agree?"

Drew scowled darkly at his father for assuming he'd bedded anyone since Clare. No matter how often Drew explained it, Father believed the Hillcrest Academy had been a brothel in disguise, no matter what he said to the contrary. As evidence of the women's supposed wickedness, he insisted that two of the Hillcrest cousins had seduced their husbands into marriages above their stations in life. That was not how those marriages had come about. The Hillcrests were fine ladies, one and all.

"I didn't need a whore. I needed to hear a woman's opinion. From someone wholly unconnected to Clare and our family."

"And yet you still remain unmarried," Northport persisted. "They helped with nothing but lightening your pocket as far as I can see. You're too particular. That's always been your problem. Just pick one of the women I've introduced you to and be done with it. All you need is an heir and a spare."

"You've been a widow fifteen years, Father. I don't see you making a second marriage, or even making an honest woman of the one who loves you yet," Drew bit out.

Father stood and pointed a finger at him. "I had my heirs when I engaged Juliette to be my mistress. You don't have that luxury or time to dither about. I never need to marry again, but you certainly do. You lost your heir, so now get another brat on someone, anyone, and soon. After the marriage, you can indulge in such an arrangement as I enjoy with Juliette."

Drew glanced down at his hands, fighting his temper. Father never failed to pour salt on the wound of his failure to ensure his boy had lived.

The duke shuffled his feet. "I didn't mean that the way it came out. I know—"

"I know what you want, *Northport*." Drew stood slowly and faced his father the duke. A man who would likely never understand his eldest son, nor had he ever tried. "You said all you need to say to me today."

"Now, my boy, don't take that tone. I know losing the boy nearly broke you," Northport assured him.

"Losing *them*, Father." He met his father's gaze. "I lost my whole world in one day. Something you don't seem to understand or care about." Father had never outwardly mourned Drew's mother. He'd already had his eye on the younger Juliette by then. "Forgive me if I don't see you out. I have an appointment to view an investment property shortly and must be on my way."

Drew headed for the door.

"Sullivan," Northport called to his back. "*Drew*! Come back here this instant."

Drew didn't stop. He had not expected to be reminded of his loss, today of all days. He needed time alone to rid himself of his sadness before he met with Aurora. It wasn't fair to her to have his attention divided from their new beginning.

Father, however, wasn't done with him and followed Drew all the way to his bedchamber. "Young man, we are not done. Not done at all, I say!"

Drew glared. "Am I not to have a moment's privacy to even change my clothes?"

Father shut the door behind him. He approached Drew slowly, arms spread. "I apologize if you feel I'm being insensitive again."

"Oh, you are," he bit out, starting to undress even with an audience. He strode to his dressing room and selected fresh attire despite his father's glare. He laid out what he would wear to meet Aurora across his bed, and then stood back to decide whether it all seemed too plain for what he hoped would be a momentous occasion.

His second meeting with Aurora called for some ceremony, after all. He was going courting, and would ask her to marry him a second time if the moment was right. Go down on one knee and say the words he'd been practicing in his head since he'd begun his search.

Aurora deserved a properly done proposal, and more time to consider it. Wharton's drawing room had not been the place. He'd rushed to insist he had honorable intentions after their kiss. He'd been swept away by anticipation and hadn't considered how it might look to her.

But today there would be time to do things right. He imagined, hoped, Aurora had had sufficient time to consider the advantages of a marriage to him. She knew him well. He'd told her a great deal over the length of their acquaintance, and only held back revealing his amorous nature.

Desires she urged him to explore with other women.

He was never going to do that.

But she knew him completely. And what could be better than marrying a woman who knew him so well?

Northport cleared his throat. "The decision when to marry has been difficult for you."

"Of course, it is."

"I don't mean to rush you," Northport apologized.

"Oh yes you do," Drew bit out, changing his mind about his brown coat and fetching one in dark green instead.

"I'm not getting any younger," Northport complained.

"And neither am I. I know, I know," he replied, stripping off as he headed for the washbasin.

The water was ice cold, but he hadn't the time to waste waiting for a servant to heat some. He could not be late today. Thankfully, he'd already been shaved that morning and all he had to do was scrub his hands. "We've had this conversation a dozen times, Father. I will marry when and whom I please."

Father blocked his path back to his fresh clothing. "I want to be alive to see it. To know you are wed to someone who deserves to be your duchess."

"I'm sure she will be," he said, dodging around the older man to change his trousers.

"I'm just not sure I will be here," the duke admitted. "I worry about you. I worry that you'll take so long that I might be dead when that day comes, at the rate you go."

Drew turned and really looked at his father's face. "You've the stamina of an ox. The growl of a lion still. It's not your time yet, Father. You will live as long as you want to, I'm sure."

"You've always said that," Father muttered darkly. "But I'm seven and fifty years, you know."

"That isn't that old," Drew promised. "Didn't your father live to be over eighty years?"

"Yes, but I favor my mother more. She died at my age. Suddenly. She was there one day and gone the next. Same as your mother, and you lost Clare and Pip that same way.

Death is inevitable. So, I worry that there will be no one to support you when I'm gone."

Drew stared at his father, speechless for a long moment, and then rushed to finish dressing. When he was decently covered, he pulled his father into a fierce embrace. "I'm as strong as you. I'll be all right, I promise." He quickly sniffed back a tear.

Father remained rigid until Drew released him. "I must know the succession is not in doubt," he warned.

Drew cared little for the succession. His thoughts were for his own future, and he thought he could be happy with Aurora.

Chapter Eight

Aurora sat forward in her hired carriage, watching Lord Sullivan rush up the front stairs of the distant town house where they were supposed to have met earlier that day. She had arrived on time, before him it seemed. Had already knocked on the door to no reply from within.

He had not said the house in Conduit Street was unoccupied. She had expected at least a servant to answer the door to admit her.

Disappointed and slightly embarrassed, she'd rushed away to hail a new carriage, since she'd unwisely sent her last one away. She'd dived inside to hide her flaming face and wondered what to do. She'd assumed Sullivan had given her the wrong address. But just as she'd started to ask the new coachman to take her home, a gleaming black carriage had deposited Sullivan in front of the town house.

He seemed in a great hurry to get inside.

She gulped, unsure whether his rush was a good sign or not.

She could admit to herself that she'd thought of nothing but Sullivan's mouth on her skin since their last meeting a week ago. Seeing him, even from this distance, seemed to affect her greatly.

"Where to, madam?" the coachman called out a second time while she had been sitting here, indecisive.

She had to see Sullivan again, if only to hear of his pursuit of other women. That's what matchmakers do.

With that thought firmly in mind, Aurora stepped out of the carriage, handed over some coin for the coachman's trouble, and headed for the front door of the town house.

The door opened before she could even knock, and she slipped inside. Sullivan shut the door by leaning against it until it closed. "I feared you wouldn't come," he whispered.

She didn't mention he was tardy. "I keep my promises."

"As do I. Come this way," he said before immediately striding into the next room.

Aurora followed more slowly, taking a moment to get her bearings. It seemed she was in a modest town house. Four square chambers below and a narrow staircase splitting the house into two. Upstairs appeared very dark, despite being the middle of the day and sunny outside. But the downstairs drapes had been drawn back in each front room, revealing the house was fully furnished. Many things were under dust cloths.

She followed after Sullivan to discover him uncovering a desk and chairs. "Whose house is this?"

"No one's yet. It is for sale though. It's a rare opportunity indeed. I have the permission of the owner to inspect it this afternoon and take all the time I need. If I like it enough, I might just purchase it."

"An investment?"

"Perhaps. It could be mine, too. The town house I currently live in is a seasonal lease, and my landlord expects more and more each year."

"I see." She glanced around again. "This room at least seems very comfortable."

"That is what I thought, too," he said as he sat down at

the desk as if he planned to work there. "I do like this chamber. What do you think of it as a study?"

"The light is good." She went to the window and peered out. "It has a view of the courtyard but not much else."

"That is all right by me. I would sit here to work most mornings and shouldn't become distracted anyway."

She nodded slowly. "Why did you want to meet me here?"

"It's more private than anywhere else," Sullivan murmured. "Far away from prying eyes and servants, since there are none here."

"None at all?"

"There's only an old fellow who sleeps here each evening to deter thieves, I'm told." He covered up the desk again. "Would you like to talk while we take a look at the rest of the place together?"

"Have you not been here before?"

"Not until today." He caught her hand in his larger one and dragged her from the room with a soft laugh. "The best way to decide about any property, I find, is to imagine living there. Can you help me do that? I would appreciate a woman's point of view."

"Why not? But we will discuss your progress this past week."

Sullivan nodded as he uncovered all the furniture in the drawing room, and once he'd slapped the settee a few times and judged it free of dust, threw himself upon it. "A good length for me. All the furniture would be mine, so it is important to test it all, too."

Aurora looked down at him, stretched out there as if he already owned the place. "I hope your testing will not impede the time you have to spend choosing a bride."

"I should not think so." He jumped up and gestured for her to replace him on the settee. When she sat, he caught up her feet by the ankles and placed her legs along the length of heavy brocade cushions. "A good length for a woman, too. And if I wanted to sit down beside my wife, we could both be very comfortable together."

He plopped himself back down, sitting in the remaining space beside her, and stretched out his legs along hers. "This is quite cozy, isn't it?"

"Indeed." She knocked his feet aside and struggled to sit up properly again. "You were saying?"

"Oh, yes. I happened upon Miss Firth in Hyde park, four and then two days ago, and had a friendly chat with her each time. I mentioned seeing you recently, of course, and she sent along her best wishes for your health and expressed a wish she hoped to see you soon."

Aurora blinked. "I did not imagine you would mention your matchmaker when courting."

"Why not? You are a friend we have in common. It was an excellent way to begin a conversation, too. She had so many good things to say about you, and I agreed with all of them."

Aurora nodded. "When do you see her next?"

"Sadly, she headed out of Town yesterday with her family to visit an ill relative in the countryside," he said, wincing. "I've no idea when she might return."

"Oh," she said, disappointed to hear it. An ill relative in the country might mean that Miss Firth would not be back for some time. She smiled at Sullivan though. "Any other developments."

"I came upon Lady Catherine Jagger riding into Hyde Park the day after I last spoke with you. She was with a trio of other women, and I could do no more than raise my hat to them as they raced past."

"Did you not join them?"

"No. I was leaving, having exercised my horse enough for one day."

She sighed. "That was bad luck. Next time perhaps you will be able to join them."

"Yes," he agreed, before walking off into another chamber. "Dining room, and I believe that there could be a parlor for the lady of the house," he said, looking about with his hands on his hips. "Terrible drapes though. They would have to be replaced."

Aurora shuddered at the color, a shade of burnt orange that hurt the eyes to look at. "Something in a soft green, perhaps?"

"Or blue," he murmured, casting her a cheeky smile and looking her up and down. Aurora's pelisse was blue. "But of course, I would leave that decision up to my wife, since it would be her chamber…her house to decorate to her taste."

"Yes, indeed," Aurora murmured, and walked away from him to return to the front room to hide her annoyance. She hadn't chosen the blue pelisse because he'd said she looked well in it. It was a match for this particular yellow gown. They were a set. "Is that all?"

"Upstairs next," he suggested before filling her in on the details of his week of social engagements. She had to give him credit. He had not shirked his need to meet with other ladies.

They headed upstairs, Aurora lifting her skirts clear of the treads. It was far dustier upstairs than below. Again, there were four square furnished chambers, all accessible from a narrow hallway. One chamber had a small walled-in closet at one end. "The master or lady's chamber, I suppose," Sullivan murmured before crossing the house and disappearing inside a far doorway. "There's another here, too."

"Another what?" she called, rushing after him when she couldn't clearly hear his reply.

"Another closet for clothing, but oddly shaped. Do you think it large enough for a lady?"

Aurora walked inside. "I could fit my entire wardrobe, but perhaps not Sylvia's."

"Ah, well. I'll have to consider whether the space could be enlarged later," he said. "I would want my wife to have the luxury of an extensive wardrobe, too."

Aurora turned. Sullivan was blocking the doorway, his arms extended to each side of the door frame as he leaned in. He offered a grin. "I'm glad I invited you to join me here today."

"To discuss your courtships."

He leaned even farther toward her, his eyes locked on hers. "Yes, but I knew I could count on you for an honest opinion, too. Tell me, would you want to live here?"

"This house is not for me," she said quickly, as her heart started to beat faster at the thought that maybe it might be.

"But imagine if it was, then…"

Aurora ducked under his arm, and out into the open space of the bedchamber. "I could not say, my lord."

She headed for the stairs and went down, leaving him above to inspect the attics alone if he saw fit. She needed a moment to catch her breath. Being alone with Sullivan was too enjoyable, especially when he seemed to care for her opinion. He took his time on the higher floor, coming downstairs adjusting his cuffs. "The attic roof appears sound. I saw no sign of leaks in the highest chambers. Shall we inspect the servants' quarters below together now?"

Aurora considered refusing. She was not there to pass judgement on an investment property but to get him married to someone deserving. "Did you attend Bradshaw's since I saw you last?"

"Yes," he answered as he strolled away. He started down the steps into darkness without saying more though.

"And? Did you…?" she called out, but Sullivan had disappeared.

There was a loud thump but no explanation forthcoming when she called out his name. Concerned, she hurried down herself.

Her foot caught on the second to last step, and she fell forward…into his waiting arms. "I've got you," he promised, holding her close against his chest.

Aurora considered swooning as she inhaled his cologne and felt the warmth and strength of the body holding her up.

"Thank you," she murmured, and then glanced over her shoulder at the steps.

Sullivan gently set her on her feet. "That must be fixed as soon as possible," he announced.

Unsettled by how good it had felt to be held, she led the way down the dimly lit hallway, peeking into every chamber they found. She was accustomed to the curiosities of servants' quarters and judged them adequate before Sullivan could enquire. "The kitchen will need a thorough scrubbing before use but that is all that would need to be done."

She climbed the stairs, Sullivan following close behind, stepping over the wobbly step that could have broken both their necks easily. In the hall again, she glanced at Sullivan.

He was watching her. He unnerved her.

Well, two could play that game today. "Did you take a lover?"

"No," he answered slowly. "I found my imagination fixed upon a certain pretty matchmaker."

Aurora shook her head. "Sullivan."

She was suddenly caged between him and the nearest wall. "Why not have me?"

She meant to push at him. Instead, she caressed his chest. "I cannot tell you."

He caught her eye. "Did I not kiss you with enough passion last time?"

"With a surfeit of it," she promised.

That made him smile. "Then why not let me love you?"

"Make love to me? That was not what you asked for, my lord."

"They are one and the same to me."

"No, Sullivan. They definitely are not the same, even if they are both temporary."

He frowned at her words. "Love is not temporary."

"It always ends, and you, better than anyone, should know that."

He leaned closer. "Love never entirely goes away."

"For many it does," she answered, getting cross with him for being so stubborn. After a week, he ought to have reconciled himself to pursuing another lady. She ducked under his arm again and put some distance between them. "It is not in your nature to want a temporary anything with a lady. Your resistance to taking a lover is proof enough of that."

"I may not have *loved* a woman since we first met," he asked. "But I'm not the same broken man who appeared in your library, am I?"

"No," she conceded. "You've come far since we first met,

because the very idea of marriage once made you nauseous, you said," she murmured. She had always wished he could be a little freer with his affections. That he would not cling so hard to the years-old memory of his first love. He might be happier if he could ever let that love go. The best way to start, in her opinion, was to take up with another lady and make new memories.

But he was not going to do that for himself.

Not unless she gave him a good reason to try.

And the only way to do that, it seemed, was to become his lover…and prove he could enjoy what they shared, even when it could only be for a short time.

She looked up at him, doubting the wisdom of her decision a little longer before deciding it was worth the risk.

She held his gaze, returning to him to boldly caress his broad chest.

His eyes widened a little in surprise. And this time when he drew closer, she didn't try to evade the inevitable. She kissed him first—and then let him have his way.

As his tongue teased the seam of her lips, of their own accord her arms snaked around his neck to pull him closer. All her senses were alert at the warmth of his large body pressed against hers. Her entire body came alive again, vibrated with the need to get close to this man while she could.

Sullivan seemed to feel the same way. He wrapped his long arms about her and with one lift, carried her effortlessly toward the nearest secluded corner of the room. The papered wall was cold against her upper back, but it provided stability as the earl turned her world upside down with his hungry kisses.

Sullivan was no shy gentleman. He was a man of experience who knew just how to draw out their kiss to the utmost limits of decency and endurance. But the kiss had to end eventually, and when it did, he slid sideways to brush his lips against her throat.

"You should always be like this with me. Free."

Aurora struggled to catch up her scattered wits and her breath again. She was utterly undone, despite every thought in her brain focused on how to end the encounter before he thought less of her. But she couldn't seem to untangle her fingers from his dark hair yet.

"No matter what happens between us, I won't marry you," she whispered, struggling for control.

"Very well," he agreed after a long moment of consideration. "So, you will let me kiss you but will not agree to marry me?"

"Yes." She wanted Sullivan. His touch, his kiss, his previously hidden wild side, to be hers to enjoy for just a little while. Why deny herself this one tiny thing just to keep up the pretense of propriety?

Sullivan's hand slid from her shoulder, down her side, and came to a stop on her hip. His grip was tight. Definitely possessive. Aurora felt a thrill that she'd been the one to draw out this side of his nature, even if it was wrong for a matchmaker to be seduced by her client.

But how glorious it was to be chosen as the first woman he wanted since his first wife had passed.

At that thought, she stiffened.

She was second.

Drew seemed to sense her distress and caught her face in his hands, then leaned his cheek against hers to whisper, "Don't pull away from me now. I won't ruin you or get a child on you."

Aurora knew he couldn't ever do that, and she didn't bother to argue the point as his fingers slid round her body and closed over her rear. He pulled her hips to his, yanking her hard against him. He was already becoming aroused, obviously so, too. He pressed his hips against hers, rubbing her sex with his hardness, and Aurora loved it.

Sullivan, however, started to sink, kissing as he went, sliding out of her arms, and she realized he intended to kneel.

Fearing she was about to hear a proposal spill from his lips, she gasped and tried to pull him back up.

Sullivan whispered "trust me," and lowered himself farther, catching the bottom of her gown and lifting the hem of her skirts to her knees.

He grasped her ankle, kissed her stocking-clad calf, and then his head and shoulders disappeared entirely under her skirts.

Aurora whimpered as he moved about under the blue muslin, kissing anywhere and everywhere it seemed he could reach. When he reached her upper thigh, Aurora took a steadying breath and wondered if she should end this madness. She couldn't believe he was about to do what she hoped he might.

He hadn't really seemed the type.

But he widened her legs with impatient hands, and at the first brush of his mouth against the curls at the apex of her thighs, she rose up on her toes. He grabbed her hips and pulled her back down, and tried to throw one of her legs over his shoulder, too. However, the gown she was wearing today made the task difficult unless she helped him.

He growled impatiently against her curls, and a rush of desire pulsed through her entire body. She wanted to hear him make that sound again. To feel the vibration of his frustration and impatience against her skin.

Aurora quickly hiked up her own skirts and put her bare thigh over his shoulder. Nothing should convince him more of her unsuitability to be his wife than this moment of unbridled lust. She accepted her shortcomings. Others would not. She'd become his first lover, and once he'd taken his pleasure with her, she'd turn him to look elsewhere for the proper wife he deserved.

A moan burst from her lips as his tongue swept the length of her sex, and then pushed between her lower lips. Hard and deep. Just the way she liked it. Aurora leaned against the wall for support and captured his head with one hand, holding him there. He lapped at her sex like a man starving for the taste of a woman.

Perhaps he was.

Aurora sighed as his tongue teased her and began to flick over her clitoris repeatedly. Her knees trembled as her pleasure in the moment increased, too fast to stop. He certainly knew what he was about and where to devote his attention.

Aurora lay her head back against the wall, gasping, but an unpleasant thought crossed her mind. Was he pretending he was making love to his late wife, or was he really with *her*?

There was no way to know unless she asked. But if she did so, he would stop the exquisite thing he was doing. She did not want him to stop now, or to hear about Clare today.

Aurora whimpered as he sucked harder on her clitoris. She was going to climax soon, likely scream down the house at the relief of it. She'd occasionally dreamed of a moment like this.

She looked down at him—only to find Sullivan looking

back at her, a bright light in his eyes as his tongue flicked across her clitoris a few more times.

Her climax swept over her, and she shuddered and buck against his face.

She did not scream, but only by the barest thread of control did she hold in the sound. She held fast to Sullivan's head as her world turned giddy, and when it was finally over, she was utterly spent and weak.

Sullivan immediately rose to hold her tight against his chest, and Aurora allowed herself the luxury of basking in his embrace for a short time.

But it had to end.

Everything had an end when it came to Lord Sullivan.

Slowly, reluctantly, she pushed him away, expecting him to be impatient to unbutton his trousers and seek his own satisfaction in her. Sullivan was breathing hard, but he turned out to be in no rush to undress himself, even a little. He merely smiled at her. Appearing decidedly pleased with himself, too.

Aurora unfortunately was not feeling the same, and she straightened from the wall. If he was not willing to make the effort to undress himself, she was not about to do it for him.

Sullivan reached out and brushed his fingers across her cheek softly before he took two steps back. "I hope you won't say that I should not have done that."

"I was going to ask if you feel better," she replied, one brow raised, as if having a man under her skirts happened all the time.

He frowned. "I have no regrets. Do you?"

"No," she assured him, turning toward a mirror to check that her hair was still neatly coiled about her head. Regret would come later, surely, and when it did, he would be the last to hear about it. "I am glad that moment between us is over. You've finally been with another woman, and so you can be certain of yourself with any other, too."

In the reflection, she saw Sullivan had followed her to the mirror, frowning again. "I need no one else. Marry me, Miss Hillcrest. I have surely compromised you now."

She winced. The man still confused lust with love. Aurora did not. "No."

He brushed his lips back and forth across her shoulder as he whispered, "I had to ask. As a gentleman and as your friend. I had to ask you to become my wife today…but I knew it would be too soon for you to say yes to me."

At least he was finally being sensible about something. "I won't change my mind later, I assure you."

"We will see," he murmured, settling his hands lightly on her hips. They lingered there, heavy and warm. "I have a proposition for you now, though," he said. "You've every right to refuse, but I want you to stay for a while with me. Alone like this."

His hands slipped forward, landing one atop the other over her curls, through her skirts. She gulped, startled by the boldness of the gesture. She had thought she'd known Sullivan's character. She'd been so sure he would never act this way around her. But clearly, he possessed an abundance of lust yet to be satisfied. "I'll consider it."

His grip on her tightened until a gasp left her lips. "We could continue our conversation upstairs. In bed, perhaps. I noticed it was somewhat warmer up there."

Aurora was tempted to agree. She weighed the risks carefully. Her cousin Sylvia would be away from Town a few more days yet, and Eugenia was much caught up in her husband's interests. They had no plans to meet today, or tomorrow either.

There was likely no one to notice what she did with her days. Should any servants enquire, she had any number of acquaintances who would cover for her. She had done it before.

Another tryst might once and for all purge the impulse to propose from him, too. "I won't marry you, if you think to persuade me with more passion. Or worse, use today to get what you think you want by telling anyone about us."

"I would never force a marriage between us," he promised, kissing her cheek, and then dropped another on her neck. He kissed her skin and caught her eye in the mirror and stared at her like a wolf who sees something he plans to devour. Her sex responded with a lurch of anticipation, and when his hand rose to cover her breast, she let out a sigh. "You might not want me for a husband today, but you want *this* as much as I do. Stay or think about it and come back tomorrow and kiss me again."

Sullivan squeezed her nipple to encourage her to say yes to his invitation. Given the lusty look in his eye, she would probably climax again very easily. Sullivan's first thought seemed to run toward showering her with attention, rather than taking his own pleasure, and that was a vast improvement over other men Aurora had known. She would not have the worry that she might conceive with him.

She was also starting to appreciate his unpredictable nature more and more. What other secrets would be revealed if she spent a few hours with him?

Aurora believed in equality, in fairness, and giving back in kind. To her mind, she owed Sullivan a release, at least, but nothing more permanent than that. She could not stay today though. She couldn't give in too easily to her own lustful impulses. "Very well. I'll meet you here tomorrow at the same time, and you can tell me how tonight's event went."

"Thank you." He kissed her cheek again, and sauntered away to finish covering up furnishings so he could leave. Aurora slipped away while he wasn't looking.

Chapter Nine

Aurora stood in an upstairs chamber on Conduit Street the next day, astonished by the changes that had been made overnight. Gone were the dust covers over furniture, the dusty floors, too, had been swept and the bed had been freshly made by the look of it. The light streamed through the windows, casting a delicate warmth over her.

And *him*.

Her toes curled in her slippers as Sullivan kissed a path down her throat. His breath was so warm against her skin that she was already aroused. He'd been kissing her since she'd first walked through the door downstairs, half an hour ago, and he seemed incapable of stopping.

"You've been busy," she whispered.

"My valet helped, though he chafed a bit at the chore of improving a room in a house that does not belong to me as yet."

Sullivan was so warm against her, she felt the urge to purr like a cat as she rubbed her body ever closer to his. "Are you going to buy the place?"

Sullivan hands roamed to her waist, then crept up higher, toward her breasts, his breath churning. But he did not touch them, merely teased his thumbs ever closer. "Should I? We could meet here again tomorrow."

Aurora looped her arms about his waist, and then she let

them slip a little toward his rear. Tomorrow was a long way away. "It's not my place to say you should. But…"

"But?"

"As an investment, it is not far from Bond Street, which a woman of the house would appreciate. But it is farther from Hyde Park where you always ride, and where the *ton* gather to show off for the fashionable hour." She met his gaze, noting the blue in his eyes had brightened. Lust did that to him. "Do those things matter enough to make it a bad investment?"

His fingers dug into her hair, the pins spilling to the floor at their feet as he took it down without asking. "Not really. It is hard to come by a place like this for sale without everyone knowing about it, though. Everything else is wrapped up in ninety-nine year leases."

Aurora sighed as he ran his fingers through her long hair, twisting it behind her head and letting it fall down her back. "Then you've already made your decision to buy it, I think."

He pressed his head against hers. "If you thought it a bad idea, I would listen."

She grimaced that he continued to speak as if her opinion really mattered in the long run. She was his lover now. A temporary arrangement between them, even though he kept trying to bind her to his life. Aurora would have him now, enjoy this unexpected affair, and then give him over to another lady's pleasure soon. But she didn't want to think of that now. She just wanted to enjoy being with him. Being her true self.

Aurora slid her hands up his chest, rising up on her toes to claim his lips. She gave herself over to passion, allowed herself this selfish moment with the earl. She knew he wanted more from her, but she couldn't give him the forever he wanted.

There was just this moment to share.

There was no reason to be shy about why she was here. He must know her character wasn't as pristine as that of other spinsters by now, especially after yesterday. She was not here to help him make a match anymore. Her intentions toward him were more carnal.

The earl seemed to need nothing more from her by way of words at the moment, and he kissed her back as if he was starved.

Aurora looked beyond him at the neat square bedchamber facing Conduit Street. It *was* a pretty room. The bedding had been turned back, revealing crisp white linens, and it looked comfortable indeed to spend the afternoon in. She looked forward to lying there upon the bed with the earl over her, having his most immediate needs met.

Sullivan kissed her throat before wrapping her in his arms and lifting her feet from the floor. "I want to hold you for a while," he whispered.

Sullivan was deliciously solid around her, but Aurora shook her head. "That wasn't what I came for, and you know it. Stop trying to be a gentleman."

She knew the signs of a man on the edge of control. He hadn't climaxed with her yesterday, and until he did, she couldn't be satisfied with anything less.

"All right. If you insist. I need you on that bed, and now," he told her.

Aurora shivered in excitement at his demanding tone.

But he lowered her to the ground and lifted her chin to stare into her eyes. "It's natural to feel fear," he whispered.

She returned his stare steadily. "Is there a reason to fear you?"

"No." He looked a little lost for words for a moment. "I promise you will never have one, either. But continuing and increasing intimacy with me might be unsettling at first."

Dear God, he thought she was an innocent still. She closed her eyes, embarrassed momentarily that she wasn't, for *his* sake. But it was a passing feeling. She'd had years to accept she wasn't like the proper young women of the *ton*. The women he'd considered courting before. "I'm not afraid."

"Good."

She gasped as her gown sagged around her body. Sullivan had somehow managed to undo her buttons without her feeling a thing. Her gown was stripped away, and Sullivan took it to carefully arrange it over the only chair in the room. She was grateful for his care, but uncomfortable being the only one standing about in their underclothes.

Sullivan returned quickly, shedding his coat, and he caught her up against him again. His hands swept up her body to capture her breasts. Aurora groaned at how good it felt. *Him* touching her. No fumbling. No hesitation.

No threats.

Sullivan was no novice in the carnal arts. She expected a great deal of pleasure from him after yesterday's generous intimacy.

Her underclothes fell away piece by piece.

"You are horribly efficient at that," she murmured approvingly as he again laid out her underclothes carefully, so they would not be more wrinkled when she put them back on. "Faster than any maid I've known."

"I am quick about it because I want you desperately," he

promised. "You were all I thought about since yesterday. The taste of you on my tongue. Come to the bed, Aurora."

Aurora turned toward it. It was a high bed that required her to climb up. She did it slowly, and Sullivan groaned behind her. Delighted by the sound, she waggled her derriere a little more obviously.

She knew how to tease to speed up proceedings.

Sullivan was immediately pressed against her behind, as she had hoped he would be. Evidence of his arousal poking her through his trousers. His fingers clamped tight on her hips. "You shouldn't provoke a man like that unless you're prepared for the consequences."

Consequences from Sullivan would be easy to bear. He was a gentleman at all times. Respectful of her. But slow to take what he needed without encouragement. He was the type of man who might ask her forgiveness if he got a little too heated between the sheets. "Who says I'm not eagerly anticipating you, my lord?"

"Drew. Call me by my name when we are together like this." Another groan, and fabric rustled as he stripped behind her. Judging by the sound, he was quite rushed. "God, I hope you're ready for what we're about to do."

Aurora was. But she would not drop the use of his name anywhere, even in private. She was not comfortable whispering endearments to men, as some women might do more easily. She had to keep some formality between them, if only on her side.

"Aurora? Where are you?" His lips brushed her back and then his hand gripped her shoulder, trying to pull her around to face him.

"I'm here," she promised, resisting his efforts to turn her over onto her back. "Don't keep me waiting."

Aurora arched her back at the first prod of Sullivan's hot cock between her legs, and she held her breath as he sought her entrance. There would be no barrier to break, no reason to cry out in pain. She would not pretend to be an innocent. He could take her any way he chose today, and she'd enjoy it.

But he proceeded with the bedding slowly, and it was all she could do not to beg for him to get inside her.

Sullivan was mostly seated in her when he reached around and sought to tease her clitoris with gentle fingers. Aurora gasped out loud, unable to hide how enjoyable his touch was there. His attention to her needs wasn't expected but appreciated. He worked his magic against her clit. Strumming her with patience and skill until she was panting and on the verge of a climax.

Only then did he take care of himself. He gripped her hips in his hands and slowly worked himself inside her body, taking his time as he made love to her. No matter how hard Aurora tried to hurry him along, he continued at his own pace, increasing her pleasure into the bargain.

Aurora shut her eyes, her tension increasing as his thrusts became relentless. She clenched the sheets, bracing herself, and realized she would come before him because of the steady pace he'd set.

He thrust into her with a single-mindedness she couldn't complain about. If she had been a virgin, she would have appreciated the control he exerted over his lust where other men she'd known had not bothered.

Aurora, however, had no control over her own lust. She was always impatient for her peak.

She put her hand between her legs and toyed with her clitoris herself. A few strokes might be all that was needed to climax. And then it would be over when Sullivan released his seed.

He sank deep and then stopped, holding still, panting against her upper back. But Aurora's climax was just there, ready to burst from her at any moment. She squirmed and twisted under him, and he allowed her to work herself along his cock, finding those places inside that felt the best and increased her pleasure until she was moaning.

She came much too loudly, but quickly lowered her face into the mattress to mute the sound in case he didn't like to hear a woman lose control.

When it was over, Sullivan finally began to move again. Aurora shamelessly encouraged him, too. She was taken somewhat more vigorously from then on, and Sullivan let out a great bellowing roar that included her own name as he withdrew to spill his seed on the sheets beneath them.

He toppled over her, pinning her down in an awkward position as he panted for breath against the back of her neck.

Aurora bore the extra weight until he got too heavy, and then she wriggled to silently ask for freedom.

He rolled aside immediately. "Marry me?"

Aurora blinked at the unwanted question. She had chosen to remain unburdened by any husband many years ago. She'd not be taken for granted, and certainly their trysts would never change her mind.

She crawled away from Sullivan, and the question he shouldn't have asked of her again. She moved to the very end of the bed, far from him, before glancing back. "No. Again, no. If you're going to ask me to marry you each time we are intimate, then I must leave and will never return."

He laughed, and then propped himself up on one arm, facing her. He was silent a long time, studying her. "So, you want me. Will let me make love to you, but only if it's never to be forever."

She studied the earl with exasperation. He was persistent, she'd give him that.

Unfortunately, he was simply too delicious like this to stay mad with for long. Tousled, sweaty, and vulnerable. Bare-chested and sated suited him very well. He bore no resemblance to the sad and awkward widow who had sought her out, and her cousins, a year ago to engage their counsel on making a second marriage. He seemed happier, which was undoubtedly due to his climax. He had finally been with another woman, and now he could bed someone else, too.

Cautiously, she moved up the bed toward him, lying on her side as she held his gaze. "Yes, that's all I want."

His smile was slow in coming. "I like this, too. But I am in earnest. I want to make an honest woman of you in the end."

Aurora rolled out of bed immediately, annoyed by his stubbornness.

After so many refusals, he should know better by now. He'd asked for her hand, and each time she'd declined, he clearly could not believe he would be denied. Could he not fathom that in becoming his forever, she'd be trapped by rules that would never protect her?

Marriage would give him every control over her life. That was the last thing she would give anyone.

She glanced at his discarded clothing upon the floor and stepped over them to begin dressing to take her leave.

She glanced at the earl discreetly, watching him reclining so at ease on the bed. He seemed to see nothing wrong with what they'd done, or in lying about naked, either. Aurora had proven her unsuitability to be anyone's bride today. He'd bedded her thoroughly. Taken his pleasure with her. The lack of blood on the sheets, the lack of evidence of the loss of her innocence, should give him pause when he took a moment to consider what that meant.

She'd showed him beyond a shadow of a doubt that she was no innocent young miss meant for marriage, and a rather poor matchmaker besides. She heaved a sigh at that lost opportunity to have him as a first client. She couldn't depend on him to help her business begin anymore by writing a letter of reference, either. Aurora would have to look elsewhere for a recommendation, and return the money he'd already paid her.

He patted the space beside him. "Come back to bed."

Aurora didn't snap to do his bidding. But she turned to look at him. "Do you intend to tell anyone about what I did with you today?"

"No. Of course not." He grinned. "This will be our secret, until you're ready for it not to be."

"It must remain a secret forever, my lord," she told him curtly.

His smile slipped away. "You did not like it. Making love to me. I thought…"

"Of course, I enjoyed being with you." Clearly she would have to explain the rest, and it would spoil anything they'd ever done together, or ever *could* do. "I have something to say, and you will not like what you hear," she warned.

He jumped off the bed and pulled her into his arms before she could say more. "Listen. We can talk about whatever troubles you about my proposal another time. Come back to bed. There is so much more we might share today, because who knows what tomorrow will bring. I don't have to know your reasons not to make a match with me, but I do want to be with you now. Any way I can."

She searched his face, wondering if he truly meant that. What they'd shared so far had been much more pleasurable than she'd expected, but it couldn't last. She really ought to go.

But she also didn't want to. She had no plans. It was past the time to make morning calls to her friends. She had no one to go home to at Wharton House, and she would likely dine alone in her room tonight unless she heard from Eugenia beforehand, which seemed unlikely. If Sullivan could cease proposing, she would not have thought of going at all yet. There was really no need to stop indulging with him, though she couldn't imagine their intimacy could get better.

She put her hands on his bare chest for the first time. He was solid, well-muscled and the warmth of his skin drove the chill from her soul momentarily. "If I stay, you would have to promise to stop asking me to marry you."

"All right. I promise I will not ask you again today. But know that I am always thinking of your place in my life," he promised.

Aurora closed her eyes. Gods, he was stubborn. He'd be glad to be rid of her when he knew the truth about her. It was on the tip of her tongue to spill her secret here and now, despite his wishes…but he would look at her with pity or disgust after she was done with the telling. "My place is where *I* want it to be."

"Indeed," he said, surprising her with his easy acceptance. "But I will do my best to convince you that it's to be with me, too, someday," he vowed, and then swept her back into his arms and carried her to the bed. "Just give me a chance and the time to prove I'm not so bad," he murmured, before he settled her onto the bed.

He wasn't the problem. When Aurora looked up to tell him that, the earl loomed over her wearing that wicked grin he'd only recently begun sharing with her. Her warnings went unsaid as he leaned in to kiss her again.

He was even more desirable when he was playful like this. And for some reason, he wanted to be hers.

Aurora lay back slowly on the bed, her pulse and anticipation growing as he bowed over her stomach and started to trace around her belly button with his talented tongue. She'd be a fool to end the affair before she'd wrung every pleasure from their secret meetings. A lover like him might never come her way again.

Chapter Ten

Drew kicked the door shut softly with his foot, his arms full of the simple fare he'd purchased from a passing pie seller in the hope it might satisfy his lady's appetite.

His body hummed with satisfaction after a long afternoon of mutual lovemaking. It had been another exciting day of meeting in secret. For three days in a row, Aurora had come to him at this house on Conduit Street, and he'd gloried in making love to her.

He did not take Aurora's involvement in this amorous encounter lightly. She was skittish in ways he couldn't quite put a finger on. Accepting of intimacy but fearful of voicing any sort of emotional commitment.

He set out their fare on a small table by the fire and went to her. She'd been standing at the heavily curtained window when he'd left the room and was still there now, naked, and oblivious to her state, it seemed. She wasn't standing around naked to be provocative for his benefit. She didn't seem to possess any modesty at all.

Drew placed his fingertips to the small of her back and with gentle pressure, guided her away from the window. The sun would not set for another hour, and there was still so much he wanted to do with Aurora before she was gone.

"Feeding me changes nothing either," she whispered. "I will not marry you because you won't let me hunger."

How odd of her to suggest that was his motive for

offering a common courtesy. Drew was certainly not so deluded as to think an apple pie would improve his standing in her eyes. She was still resistant to being with him openly, but here in the bedchamber she was as generous as he could hope for.

However, this, their secret meetings, changed everything in his mind. Their continued affair cemented his decision that only she would do for him, but he kept that opinion to himself. He'd promised Aurora not to talk about marriage, and he wouldn't propose only to be refused yet again.

When they reached the low chairs, he dropped his head so his lips grazed the tip of her shoulder, and kissed her skin. He was quite in love with the curves of her body. He would like to spend years worshiping them. "I'd love to see you bathe," he whispered.

She looked at him, seemingly alarmed by that suggestion. "Why? Do I smell?"

"I love your skin," he assured her. She smelled divine. So good, so soft, he'd love nothing more than to spend an eternity in close proximity, touching her. He did not say that out loud though. Voicing any sort of commitment seemed to be another taboo. All he'd managed was to arrange for them to meet one day at a time. "I'd watch you bathe because you'd be naked and wet. My fingers could slide over your skin, delve between your legs. I could bring you to climax that way."

He saw her gulp, then pant. Excited by his plans for her pleasure. "I don't believe the wash basin over there is large enough for even one of us to try that."

"I happen to know of one elsewhere that we could both fit in together." He chuckled softly and nipped at her ear. "It can get a bit messy. Bathing together. Soap and water get everywhere. My hands, too. The fun, of course, is in the cleaning up. I'd use my tongue to lap all the water droplets from your body. I might easily get distracted by your curves though. They are so very appealing to me."

Aurora's eyelashes fluttered as she leaned into him. Her skin was cold against his bare chest. Drew wrapped her in his arms to warm her, and she sighed, content it seemed to be held against his body for a while. He glanced down at her face, curious about the creature he craved more and more each day. "Have you ever made love in water?"

"No. I cannot swim."

"I must remember to take you to the hot springs as soon as we get—"

He stopped abruptly. He'd been about to say as soon as they were married and went home to Kent. However, now was not the time to discuss their future living arrangements. The present moment with her was much too compelling.

Drew had hoped to find a like-minded woman in London, someone with an open mind and adventurous nature toward intimacy. Aurora seemed quite naturally inclined toward pleasurable activities at least, if not the wedded state. He detected no hesitation or doubts in the bedroom.

That was a refreshing change from his experience with his late wife, especially in the last months of their marriage. Clare had become irrationally prudish as the birth of their child had drawn near. Toward the end, he'd looked to his hand for satisfying his own hungers.

He shook away the bad memories. "We'll find the time one day to do it, I'm sure," he promised.

He couldn't get too far ahead of the present moment. Aurora was still resisting his requests to even think about marrying him, but had not denied his need for passion or her own. He wouldn't give that up for anything.

He feathered his hand down her body, pausing just above the nest of dark curls between her thighs.

She squirmed, brushing against his groin.

It wasn't an innocent brush.

Aurora knew desire.

Had experienced it before with someone else.

He had so many questions about that. But they could wait until a less delicate time in their budding relationship. He brushed his fingertips in slow passes across her abdomen, teasing, heartened by her reactions.

Aurora seemed a lady quite content to be worshipped and take all he could give. She slowly lifted her arms to encircle his head. "You really have been living a lie, my lord. You're not good at all. I think you're positively wicked."

He kissed her hair. "I was only hiding my amorous side until I found my proper bride."

He cursed under his breath, hoping he'd not just spoiled the start of another bout of lovemaking with his slip. But how could he not think of her future with him? He'd not had a better day in a very long time.

"Yes. Virgins are often frightened by desires they don't understand."

Aurora was not a virgin, and to him that was not a mark against her. "And sometimes experienced women are, too."

He kissed her brow and then scooped her up into his arms. He'd done enough standing around Aurora to last a lifetime. It was time for action, and he wanted them both comfortable for the remainder of their time together. He dropped her gently into a seat and when he covered her up with a blanket for warmth, Aurora drew up her knees between them.

The pose also suggested she needed some separation from him. He could give her that. He sat beside her and winked and passed her the first pie. "You are exquisite, you know. In any setting, but especially this bedchamber."

A soft smile lifted the corners of her mouth, and her feet lowered to the floor as she sat up straighter, pulling the blanket tighter around her breasts before she took the pie from his hand. "You've a hidden talent for flattery, my lord. I never would have expected that of you."

"I am only speaking the truth," he promised, watching her nibble an opening in the crust and suck out the pie filling from within with delicate precision.

Drew wolfed one pie down, and when it seemed clear Aurora wasn't as hungry as himself, he took the third. Love-making made a man hungry. He'd forgotten that in the years since Clare. He didn't count how long it had been, but he was glad to know he'd not lost his touch. Aurora had liked what he'd done with her so much, she'd climaxed twice in short order that day. The third had been much longer in coming, but perhaps the most rewarding, judging by her desperate cries.

"Thank you for the pie. I needed that," she whispered, casting him a shy glance beneath her lashes.

After all that they'd done so far in bed, he was astonished by how that look stiffened him even now. It seemed utterly out of character for the woman he'd known for so long. But perhaps she'd never really tried to flirt with him before.

"My pleasure," he promised. "I only wish I'd thought to bring better for us to share. Next time I will."

"This is enough," she assured him. "I'm not the sort who expects to dine as lavishly as other women might."

Other women. Why did Aurora always speak of herself as different from others? "You do deserve the best, and you shall have it…next time."

Her brow furrowed. "Next time?"

"Yes, next time. Tomorrow?" He stole a kiss, and then another, letting instinct override caution to go slow with her. "I'll be here, every day this week, waiting for you in that bed over there. Naked."

Aurora threw him a saucy smiled, clearly pleased by the image he'd described.

There were definitely advantages to Aurora's prior experience with a lover. She was not timid, and he didn't have to be either. And he didn't want to talk right now and say the wrong thing that might drive her away.

Instead, he turned Aurora sideways on the settee, inhaling the irresistible scent of her skin. Kissing her body, and nipping, too, on occasion.

To his playful nips, Aurora moaned.

And then she started to nip him back, and he laughed. "Now that is what I want," he cried. "You're still hungry."

He flipped them over so Aurora lay atop him and pushed her long dark hair back from her face. The press of her sex upon his cock was wondrous after so long an abstinence from bedroom pleasures. Drew had nearly forgotten how much he'd enjoyed lovemaking in the afternoon until Aurora had become his lover.

He put his hand on her hip and squeezed tightly, pressing her down on his erection, which had never truly subsided completely since their first kiss of the day.

"Make love to me," he whispered.

Her brows drew together in confusion.

"Take me in hand, woman," he suggested playfully, putting his hands behind his head. "I'm all yours."

So far, he'd been the one taking charge of their amorous activities. The one who determined how they made love. But he wanted to see Aurora's face above him, taking her pleasure, using him as she rode to her own completion without thought for his.

But she didn't move. In fact, she'd become so still, he thought he might have shocked her with his request.

Had Aurora never been on top of a man before? She didn't have to unless she wanted to, of course. There was no rule saying she must.

But just as he was about to turn Aurora under him, she wriggled back to sit over his thighs. Her slender fingers fell upon his skin, and then wrapped around the base of his cock. She stroked him, and his hips bucked up from the settee of their own accord.

Her grip was firm, her strokes slow to begin but increased in speed the longer she held him within her power. She had done this before, too.

She bent her head, unbound hair falling forward over her face. She stared down at his cock, skillfully toying with him to the exclusion of all else—even him.

Drew wanted to see her expression, and he reached out to move her hair back from her face. Aurora evaded his hand, and he saw determination in her face…and something that alarmed him, too.

Distaste.

He quickly brushed her hands from him and reached out to catch her chin in his fingers. He lifted her gaze to his immediately, and a panicked expression crossed her features.

"Did you not like it?" she asked quickly, and reached for his cock again.

"I did, of course." Drew gripped her wrist to stop her stroking him. "But you don't have to continue if you don't like doing it."

"I do," she whispered, but Drew knew a lie when he heard one.

He sat up but kept her over his thighs. She wouldn't meet his eye anymore. He leaned in. "You were not enjoying making love to me. So, we stop. Now."

She nodded quickly and expelled a long shaky breath. "I had been."

Had? As in the past?

He swung them around so his feet were flat on the floor, and Aurora immediately cuddled into him, holding him tight but he was sure he felt her tremble. They remained enveloped in an awkward silence for a long while. Drew pressed a kiss to her brow, worried about what had just happened. Something had spooked her.

"When I suggested you take me in hand, I did not mean literally. I meant for you to do whatever you wanted with me. To be on top, rather than under, if that interested you at all. To determine how we make love to each other."

"Oh. I thought you expected me to…to…"

She did not continue her comment, and Drew wondered why she held back. A cock in hand was one way of climaxing for a man. But was she revolted by the idea he might expect more, like having her take his cock into her mouth, too? While *he* had enjoyed that in the past, he was aware some ladies didn't find the idea appealing at all, especially if they'd been forced to do it before by another man. The idea of her being in such a situation had him drawing her tighter against him.

Aurora did not seem to mind and relaxed into him slowly. After a few minutes she sighed heavily. Her fingertips danced lightly over his bicep. "You're more muscled than I imagined you to be."

He nuzzled her hair and allowed the topic to change. "You thought me idle and weak, too?"

"No. Of course not. I've seen statues, of course, but the reality of you is quite different from my imagination."

"I'm warmer, for one, and made of flesh and blood." He caught her eye. "When did you first imagine me naked?"

"When we first met," she admitted shyly, ducking her head again.

He hugged her tight and kissed her brow. "I'm flattered. I really should have paid you more attention before."

She glanced down between them at his erection. It had softened completely in the face of her distaste. "I never expected you too."

He sighed, thinking of the lost time when he might have been with this woman, getting to know her better. Wooing her into his arms and later, his bed. "You should have. Give me a kiss, lovely. It's been too long since our last."

Aurora leaned toward him but stopped inches from claiming his lips, her expressive green eyes fixed upon his. There was still wariness reflected in them, but at last she settled her lips against his. It was a hesitant kiss, so unlike their earlier passion that he paid more attention to making the moment better.

But he was worried. Aurora's mood could change in the blink of an eye if she didn't like what she heard.

No, that wasn't it. He'd asked her to do something sexual

to him, and she'd reacted as if he'd given her no choice in the matter.

He would have to remember not to order Aurora about in the bedroom and choose his words with more care. Some women forgave men some bossiness in the bedroom, others didn't. Clearly, Aurora was one of the latter.

She moved her hips slightly closer, teasing his cock with the brush of her curls, and a shudder shook his whole body. Just one touch from her and he was helplessly aroused. He caught her eye as he broke the kiss. "Does it please you to know I'm becoming hard for you?"

"Yes," she said in a whisper. "I like knowing that."

"I was hard the moment you appeared at the door," he confessed. "You're everything I want, and if it doesn't always come out right, I'll ask your forgiveness. Lust makes me blunt and perhaps a little bossy about what I want."

"Men are all the same, be they a lord or a poor farmer," she said, turning her face aside suddenly. Her breath rushed out of her lungs loudly as she rose up against him, and then settled with the definite intention of placing the tip of his cock at her entrance.

But Drew was stuck on what she'd just said. Farmer? What farmer? He closed his eyes and wondered where Aurora had met someone like that, to know how they acted around the women they made love to, too.

He shook aside his questions for and concentrated on the woman willing to make love to him again. "That's it. Use me any way you like."

Without expecting further discussion, he settled back, leaving Aurora to decide what happened next between them.

Aurora rose up and sank down with a sigh.

She settled him deep, and he twitched inside her. Dampness surrounded his cock as she slowly slid and twisted against him. Seeking her pleasure. Hunting for that elusive thrill of satisfaction only good lovemaking could provide.

She put his hands on her breasts, and he caressed, then kissed them. Became even more excited to hear her moans. He helped her come that way, delighting in her unguarded responses. Her face elated and free of doubt at the end.

That was how he hoped to always make her feel. Not ashamed or feeling any obligation to do his bidding. He wanted her to put on no act around him.

Aurora came back to earth slowly, her gaze lowering to his.

"Oh," she said quickly, gulping. "I'm sorry."

"I'm not. You were meant to come, and I did nothing to hinder you," he said, casting a wry smile at where she sat nestled against his hard cock.

He hoped she'd stay there awhile.

He wanted to come, too, now.

But only if she let him.

He reached up and brushed her hair back from her damp face, and then caught her under her arms.

He twisted to lie down again, settling her over him.

"Catch your breath here against me," he suggested, wrapping her in his arms. Holding her fast against his chest.

Aurora was more complicated than he expected but that in no way diminished his interest in marrying her eventually. She allowed his embrace for only a few minutes before she started to squirm. The friction against his cock, wedged still inside her, made him moan out loud.

She rose up, frowning down at him.

He bucked his hips against her, smiling cheekily. "Do you know what a flying fuck entails?"

She looked about them, studying their position. "Somewhat like this, I imagine. A woman astride a man."

"Not quite. It's sex like this but actually riding a horse."

She looked shocked. "Isn't that dangerous?"

"Oh, yes."

"You've done it?"

"No. But I'm willing to try it at least once with you. Carefully though. I should hate for either one of us to fall off and be found with our hindquarters exposed to the elements or the view of others."

He hoped she might laugh at the picture he'd painted of an embarrassing tumble. But her eyes narrowed. "I'm not a great rider."

"No matter." He would be happy to teach her one day, after they married. "There are so many more positions to make love in that it hardly signifies to lose that particular one."

She wriggled a little more, sliding up and down his length again. "Do you want…"

"Want?"

"To come?"

"I do, but there is no rush, is there?" He didn't want them to part, though they had to eventually.

But later. Drew placed his hand on her hips, steadying her movements even as he bucked under her until her mouth formed a o from renewed pleasure. Drew could devote many more hours to their mutual satisfaction if she'd grant him more time today. There was much more to pleasure than racing to come first.

Her brow scrunched up as she twisted against his cock, trying to drive him deeper, faster, as she always did. Drew kept her at bay, and she looked upon him with lust-filled eyes. The sight took his breath away.

She panted, shifting and twisting. "So, you don't need to come next?"

"My dear lady, I will never keep score when it comes to the pleasures we share." He smiled quickly. "I want you to be well satisfied before we part company."

"Oh," she whispered, eyes fluttering shut. "Yes."

He lifted his head to whisper in her ear, "Being with a woman who takes what she wants excites me more than you will ever know."

That made her moan. She sat up abruptly, took his free hand, and pressed it between them, low against her sex. "I don't know why it's different with you, but I seem to need to come all the time," she whispered, before she devoted all her attention to seeking her next climax.

Drew watched, encouraged, and had the very great pleasure of being very well used by his insatiable lover.

Chapter Eleven

Engaging in an affair this season hadn't been Aurora's plan, but it was harder to forget about Sullivan's passion when they were apart than she'd ever imagined it could be.

It had been almost two weeks of secret meetings with Drew, of sly touches, stolen kisses and those glorious afternoons making love as if they were the only two people in the world. Never in a hundred years had Aurora imagined such a perfect arrangement could be hers with a gentleman of the *ton*. Drew had even stopped asking her to marry him, too. That made their time together utterly perfect in her opinion.

When they were alone, Sullivan barely resembled the man she'd once thought him to be. Gone was the proper, serious lord concerned with keeping up the appearance of a respectable man of society. In private he was playful, affectionate, and usually naked…or at least half dressed. He made her crave his hands on her body every moment of every day they were together, which was why it was so hard to say no to him every time he asked to see her again.

But they only planned so far as their next meeting, the next day, which suited her purpose. She could not give him more than one day at a time.

She carefully fluffed out the skirts of her new sky-blue silk gown she'd chosen specially to wear for the night's amusements. She was looking forward to showing it off to

Drew without anyone ever realizing she wore it because he liked the color on her. Every time she wore blue, Drew became particularly amorous. She wanted to see if she could tempt him to misbehave, or at least think about doing so.

She had not spotted him yet, but he had mentioned he would be attending Lady Rothwell's ball tonight. Aurora's attendance would be a surprise for him, having been a last-minute decision by Eugenia to attend, and take Aurora along, too. If Aurora had known she would be here tonight, she would have arranged a rendezvous to meet Drew in some secluded, out-of-the-way place. There were certainly enough dark corners in the poorly lit home, to her eye.

Aurora tripped along behind the Duke and Duchess of Exeter, nearly bouncing on the balls of her feet in her excitement to see Drew's face again. She had to suppress a groan each time the duke or his wife stopped to speak with someone they knew. The pair were quite tall, and blocked her view farther into the ballroom.

She glanced sideways at Eugenia as her cousin was introduced, and then waited impatiently for it to be her turn to meet another society stalwart.

At the mention of her name, she offered her best smile, but it faltered when she heard the man introduced as the Duke of Northport.

Drew's father.

She dipped a curtsy, her mind in a whirl. This man had harassed his oldest son to marry again before he was truly ready. She knew a great deal about him, and not much she considered good. If not for familial pressure, Drew might have been a lot happier, and might never have needed to meet her and her cousins, either.

The older man nodded. "Well, Exeter, I see you're still a draw for beauty despite your recent marriage to this remarkable woman," Northport said as he gestured to the duchess. "Young women still flock to your side."

"They hardly ever flocked," the duke replied with a dismissive laugh. "But the younger lady is not here for me, but is a guest of her cousin, who you might recall married my heir this past year. Miss Hillcrest has beauty to match her older cousin, Mrs. Berringer, and is possessed of a great wit and intelligence to go with it," the duke murmured with a fond nod in her direction.

Northport was shorter than his son, and rather stern. He had the most amazingly wild eyebrows though. They dominated his face, and made Aurora want to laugh and tease him about them. But she knew from Drew that Northport wasn't the sort of man who would tolerate any sort of playfulness.

His brows drew together in a frown as he looked upon her smiling face. "Miss Hillcrest, did you say?"

"Yes, Your Grace," she answered, but her skin began to crawl as he continued to stare. She began to worry that he might know something about her, and she feared Drew had mentioned her by name as a potential bride. But she lifted her chin, determined not to reveal any distress over that possibility. "Miss Aurora Hillcrest."

His gaze flickered from her to Eugenia and back again. When he looked at Aurora, she saw utter disapproval. "How do you do?" But he said it dismissively. Coldly. As if he'd stumbled upon someone unpleasant he was forced to acknowledge anyway.

She kept a smile fixed on her face. "Very well, thank you."

Northport turned back to Exeter immediately, and the two arranged to speak later, though about what he didn't say. Then with one last glance her way, he stalked off into the ballroom.

Exeter stared after him. "That was odd."

"How so, my love," the duchess murmured, running her hand up her husband's arm affectionately, as she so often did.

"I don't know. Something is certainly on his mind tonight," the duke said quietly, and then patted his wife's hand with a smile. "But this is neither the time nor the place to question him about it. I'm sure to find out later, never fear, and then I'll tell you all about it. It's probably nothing of any importance."

"Yes, most likely nothing important at all," the duchess agreed.

Aurora gulped again, and prayed it wasn't about her and Drew meeting in secret. She had not told Eugenia yet, and Sylvia was still away from Town, so she didn't know either. She had not meant to keep her affair with Drew a secret from them, but how could she say anything at all without getting their hopes up? Her cousins wanted her to marry, and they liked Drew very much, knew too well that he was looking for a bride. Arguing with them about why she refused Drew's repeated proposals was something she'd like to avoid.

Aurora sought to recover her excitement in the evening, but it wasn't quick in coming. Though finally, she could see beyond the Exeters to the milling crowd.

The dancing had already started, couples farther in twirled together elegantly, and Aurora still hoped to join them. She owed Drew a dance. She hadn't forgotten her promise to dance with him at the next ball they both were attending. This was meant to be *the* night to put him first on her dance card for once.

But with his father here tonight, and the way he looked at her, she was anxious about giving her interest in Drew away now. If they danced together, would anyone notice that perhaps they might look at each other with *too much* interest?

Tonight, her empty dance card burned in her hand, and she lowered her eyes so as not to encourage anyone to approach her. She had assumed to see Drew first and quickly, so he might claim any spot on her dance card the following sets. Unfortunately, they had arrived so late, and the ball was well underway.

It seemed to take an eternity to reach the ballroom perimeter at the slow pace the Exeters moved.

Eugenia nudged her with her elbow. "I think I see an attachment forming."

Aurora could care less about other romances and didn't pay her cousin any attention at first. She was too excited by her own secret affair. Once Sullivan had given up trying to make her his bride, they had certainly gotten along better.

He was a lot more interesting than she'd originally given him credit for. They talked about everything now, including his asking her opinion on plans for improvements to his new investment property where they met. No longer were their conversations plagued with mentions of his late wife and child, or his quest for a bride but the rest of his life he talked freely about.

He'd traveled, taken an extensive grand tour in his youth, and one afternoon he'd brought a book of maps to their tryst and shown her all the places he'd gone. She'd been in awe of his knowledge of the world ever since.

She craned her neck in search of him.

"Definitely wedding bells," Eugenia murmured. "What do you think, Aurora? Is our most troublesome client about to finally put the past behind him and announce he's to tie the knot with a deserving lady soon?"

She finally turned her glance toward a distant corner her cousin pointed her to—and froze. She'd found Drew. *He* was the former client her cousin was speaking of with so much barely concealed excitement.

Drew stood not too far away with the beautiful Miss Lavinia Hayes hanging on his arm, and his every word it seemed, as well. The young woman was sister-in-law to Drew's best friend, Lord Wade. The viscount and his wife watched on with an indulgent smile beside them.

Eugenia fluttered her fan before her face as she spoke. "They make a handsome couple, don't they?"

Aurora pressed her lips together tightly. They did. She'd thought that already. They were laughing together, and Miss Hayes crooked her dainty finger and urged Drew down to hear whatever confidence she wanted to share. Drew smiled, clearly besotted.

That smile was the one she'd started to think was reserved for just her. Usually, Drew was much more sober-faced at tonnish events.

The Duke of Northport joined them, and he kissed Miss Lavinia's outstretched hand, gazing at her fondly. Not the way he had done with Aurora. The duke liked the young woman being presented to him.

Aurora gulped as she reached a conclusion that turned her stomach into unwelcome knots. Given such obvious happiness of all those gathered around Miss Lavinia Hayes, she could imagine they appeared a couple to so many others in the room, too.

Expectations had been raised. Drew likely needed no help from a matchmaker now, if he ever had. She tore her eyes away from his smiling face, cheeks becoming hot with a flush of embarrassment. "You think he's chosen her?"

Eugenia nodded. "I've seen them together quite a lot of late," Eugenia whispered. "You know Sullivan and Wade are close. They've dined together almost every week this season, I hear."

Aurora looked at her cousin, stomach knotting further. "How do you know who Lord Sullivan dines with?"

Eugenia smiled. "I still have an interest in our former clients. Sullivan, of course, more than most."

Aurora had not heard anything about Drew spending so much time with Lord Wade, or with Miss Lavinia Hayes, either. In the weeks of their affair, she felt Drew ought to have said something about the close connection. Especially if he was considering another lady. One who just might say yes to becoming his countess and eventually his duchess.

Lavinia Hayes was popular and lovely. Aurora liked her and believed she'd make a good wife for Drew. Clearly Northport approved of the potential match, given his continued smiles for the young lady. For the *couple*.

"It's only a matter of time before a match is announced, I suspect," Eugenia confided. "She's the right age and possesses a good fortune to bring to the marriage. He's known her for quite some time, too. I think it's a match made in heaven."

Aurora slowly lifted her eyes to look at Drew again, and at Miss Hayes. The young woman was regarding Aurora's secret lover with unabashed affection.

They were good friends.

Fond of each other.

Could they be more? Was she looking at the woman who would take Drew away from her?

She winced at the possessive thoughts filling her with dread. As Drew and Miss Hayes laughed together again and turned in unison to speak with someone else, those thoughts turned into a wail of despair. He was having a wonderful night, and he wasn't with *her*. Aurora shrank a little inside.

She was always the last to know when she was no longer needed, but this was the moment.

She shouldn't have come tonight to see this, but she had. And now Aurora would do the right thing. Now she could again do something good for him.

Eugenia moved off and, instead of joining her, Aurora turned on her heel and headed directly for the front door.

She would not stay. She didn't need to. It was never meant to be her who had caught Drew's eye, after all.

She fled outside and asked a footman to hail her a hack to take her home immediately. Unfortunately, the fellow was too slow to prevent anyone seeing her leaving the ball alone. Scarsdale's carriage deposited him right at her very feet.

His grin was wide as he noticed her. "What are you doing milling about out here, Miss Hillcrest? The party is inside."

"Yes," she said shortly, eager to avoid any prolonged conversation with him and looking for an approaching carriage to take her away as fast as possible.

The footman returned, apologizing for the delay. As a carriage drew up in front of her, Aurora realized she carried no coin to pay for the journey home. She winced and turned to Scarsdale. "I need money."

He immediately dug in his pocket and held out a careless handful of notes, far in excess of her needs. Aurora snatched up what she required, promised to repay him tomorrow, and shouted out directions as she dived inside. She barely noticed the odor of stale beer and cheap gin permeating the carriage until they were well underway, and Scarsdale was left behind gaping after her on the pavement outside Lord and Lady Rothwell's town house.

The she put her head in her hands, feeling sick to her stomach.

Aurora was completely unsettled by the idea that she was soon to be replaced in Sullivan's life, and troubled by her own reaction to the news. Of course, she'd anticipated being replaced. Planned for it, too. Meant for it to happen. One day soon. But she had been so caught up in the excitement of their secret affair that it had slipped her mind for a short while. Obviously she couldn't go on meeting Sullivan forever and he knew that, too.

He wanted marriage, and he should have it.

But with someone else. Someone who wanted to be a wife to him.

That was not Aurora.

The trip flew by, and when she was deposited at Wharton House, she was more or less ready to face the servants.

On her arrival, Aurora dutifully followed the night footman from the carriage and inside without her customary chatter to him about their respective evenings. She was glad when he left her side, after ascertaining she wanted nothing. To be somewhere as much home as anywhere she'd ever lived. She should have a message sent to her cousins at the ball she'd just escaped though, explaining why she'd gone in such an abrupt manner. A vile headache, or sudden stomach upset was a useful excuse to come home early, and might be easily believed by the duke and duchess. She had no great faith Eugenia would believe that tall tale, but at least she would know where she'd gone and that she was safe.

Tomorrow, Aurora would have some explaining to do.

She went to a desk where she'd find writing paper in the library and scratched out a note for her cousin. Once she'd summoned a servant to deliver it, she'd go up to bed.

However, she was not at all tired. She was too cross with herself to imagine sleep would come easily tonight.

She remained in the library, and Aurora even filled a glass from one of Wharton's hidden bottles in a bookshelf and sank herself down in a comfortable chair to ponder her foolish reaction to the news that Drew would wed.

Drew owed her no explanations. She'd always known best what he needed.

And it wasn't ever her in his life.

She looked about her and grimaced. Wharton House and those who lived here didn't need her, either. Even without the master and mistress of the house, the servants went about their duties with silent precision. None needed Aurora to lift a finger to direct them, which was why she'd decided she needed a profession that could occupy her days, and her nights too.

Her affair with Drew, while thrilling, had distracted her from her purpose—to make herself a career that gave her days some greater meaning. But that distraction had to end tonight. She could not possibly go to him tomorrow as arranged. She couldn't even tell him why which might reveal how the news of his upcoming marriage had affected her.

Aurora thought about it for only a moment and then sat down at the writing desk again. Sullivan didn't really need her to make a match, but someone else could.

Even though her stomach still churned with misplaced

jealousy, Aurora made plans for pursuing her own interests that would mean she was too busy to see him for a while. She could not give up on her dream to run a thriving, financially sound business and support herself at last.

It was time to think of her future and what she needed most out of her life. For one, a new first client. Someone she didn't find the least bit appealing.

Chapter Twelve

Drew was beyond upset as he left his mount behind with an urchin to hold in Hyde Park. He was angry, more than he had been in some time. He stomped through Hyde Park, eager to reach the woman who'd apparently decided to spurn him this past week without offering an explanation.

Aurora Hillcrest had disappeared from society without telling him she was otherwise occupied, and by doing so, effectively putting an end to their mutually satisfying affair. With no appearance of consideration for his feelings, she had abandoned him completely.

He'd no idea what had caused her abrupt decision, but he intended to find out. Today. If not for his oft-stated intentions to marry her, and the time they'd spent alone together, he might think she didn't care about him at all. But she surely must.

They had become so close in those stolen moments of shared intimacy. He would not believe he'd done anything wrong this time.

Seeing her on the arm of some strange man now, smiling up at him, made him see red.

Anger was a rare condition for him when it came to ladies he loved. He'd only been this angry once before, in fact. He'd been furious the day his wife had died, and taken their son with her. Not that it had been Clare's decision to die, of course. He'd railed at the sky, at anyone who had tried to comfort him. He'd fumed, impotent to change fate that had left him alone and lonely for his family.

Today, he could at least vent his spleen at the one person responsible for causing his heartache in person. She was almost in arm's reach.

Three strides.

Two.

One.

He reached out and spun Aurora about to face him by the shoulder, ignoring the squark of alarm from the ridiculous young gentleman at her side.

Aurora seemed so genuinely startled to see him towering over her in a rage that he worked to rein in his temper.

"What are you doing here?" she managed to say—before he threw away the rule book and kissed her soundly, right there in Hyde Park where anyone might see.

He did not hurry the kiss, releasing a week and more of pent-up frustration over her unannounced departure from his life.

As had happened on every encounter before, Aurora's response was immediate and just as passionate as his own. She wrapped her arms about his neck and seemed keen to climb into his arms. But as much as he wanted to hold her, he couldn't, and let her go.

But when they parted, they were both panting and trembling with lust for each other.

She pushed at his chest weakly, but Drew held his ground. "What the devil are *you* doing here?"

"Excuse me," she replied haughtily, before turning away to smile contritely at her other suitor and apologized. "I am sorry you had to see that. Lord Sullivan is an old friend, albeit misguided about propriety. Let's move away from him so we might continue our discussion."

"The hell you will," he bit out.

He was her suitor whether she liked it or not.

The other fellow took a step back, eyeing him with alarm. "I don't want any trouble, my lord."

"Then I strongly suggest you be on your way," he said in the deadliest tone he could manage. "Miss Hillcrest and I have unfinished business."

The fellow wisely fled.

Drew turned Aurora back around to face him, glaring.

"How dare you interfere—"

"You cannot think to replace me with that...*boy*," he complained, waving at the retreating figure. He was not leaving her side again until the matter between them had been settled to his satisfaction.

"Of course, I have to replace you," she said firmly, planting her hands on her hips.

Hips that had been his to hold as they made love. "Surely not. You and I—"

She cut him off, her stare angry and defiant. "You are not my client anymore, and so I must find someone else."

"No? I will not be replaced," he said, and then her words sank in slowly. "Client?"

She arched her brow, her lips twisting into a smile. "You hardly need my services anymore do you, my lord?"

"I need you," he insisted, lowering his voice a little. "Why did you not come to see me, or arrange to on another day?"

She folded her arms across her chest. "I had other business to attend to. So do you. I was not needed at Conduit Street."

He gaped. He was trying to create a life for them. Fashion a home. He could not do it without her there to give her opinion. "Why would you imagine that? I've been waiting for you there every day. Naked in bed, where I told you I would be!"

She blushed and started to turn away. "I'm sure you were amply entertained in my absence."

He grabbed her arm and held her still. "I heard you went home ill from the Rothwell ball. I sent flowers anonymously the next day, and called at Wharton House a few days after that, but you were never at home to me. It wasn't until yesterday that I threw caution to the wind and asked Eugenia for your whereabouts. She did not tell me very much, but I learned you were well though busy. I've looked everywhere for you."

She winced. "I made you no promises."

"Well, I made them to you," he countered. "We had an arrangement. I've been courting you."

She scowled. "That's not what you've been doing with me."

"I've been trying to get close to you the only way you will allow me to!" He threw up his hands. "I want you. You know that. I will not pretend to be indifferent. You want me, too, the same way. If I had started to court you properly, everyone would have seen my preference for you clear as day. You beautiful, contrary woman. You have my happiness wrapped around your littlest finger. I made a promise not to compromise you, and I am trying to honor it and be patient. But you didn't bother to keep yours and meet me as arranged."

She looked down at her feet. "I'm surprised you found the time with your other woman vying for your attention."

"What other woman?"

Aurora lifted her head but looked out across the neatly clipped lawns and wrinkled her nose. "It is well known you are courting Miss Lavinia Hayes, on the verge of proposing to her."

He reared back, stunned that Aurora of all people would believe such utter nonsense about him. "Good God, no."

She looked up. "Why not marry her? She'd be perfect for you, and you like her."

"Are you mad? Not that way. She's an infant compared to you." He moved her to stand in front of him, so she had to see his face. "Do I understand clearly that a *rumor* I am to wed Lavinia Hayes has caused this rift between us? Were you jealous?"

She looked away, shrugged again, and wouldn't meet his gaze. "Why would I be jealous?"

"That is the question that most needs answering right now. Why? You won't marry me or let me speak of it." But her breathing had sped up and a telling blush had reddened her cheeks now. "Your kiss tells me nothing has changed between us in the time we've been apart, Aurora."

"My lips lied," she whispered. "They don't want you."

Oh yes, they lied now, and he didn't know why she should make the attempt. "We could kiss again just so you can prove you feel nothing for me once and for all, but I'm afraid we might be seen."

"That didn't stop you the first time," she complained.

"I was jealous of that other fellow, but now that I understand I have not been replaced, I will behave." He grinned slowly. "Unless you prefer I not bother."

Aurora settled her bare fingers over her lips briefly. A gesture surely meant to protect them from him kissing her again. "The discussion is over. You shouldn't have interrupted my meeting."

"Yes, your meeting." He looked away in the direction the young man had gone and found the fellow lurking nearby. "Is that a potential client I almost scared off?"

"He might not have been so timid had you not been so rude," she complained, and then saw the fellow too. "Oh, dear."

"I will make amends in a moment. But first let me dispel an erroneous assumption you seem to have made about me. I am not the sort of man who would ever carry on with two women at once. If I had doubts, I wouldn't be intimate with you. Period. Making love to you is all I want to do. In the whole time I've been in London, not one woman has ever aroused me the way you have done so effortlessly."

"You stopped asking me to marry you," she whispered quietly.

"Yes!" Had Aurora been offended that he'd stopped? Drew might not have considered her as a potential spouse from the very beginning, and perhaps she'd refused him out of pride ever since. It was clear to him now that she was attracted to him, as much as he was to her. Mutual desire was high on his list of needs for a second marriage. He had not told her that outright in the beginning of their acquaintance, judging the matter much too personal to mention to a spinster.

But what had convinced him that he was at last on the right path was his own reaction to her. Drew could have gone on seducing her in secret forever. But he had never felt this way about anyone he'd met in the last two years. "My question was getting in the way of us being happy when we were together. I still want to marry you. Nothing at all has changed my mind. Will you be my wife, Aurora?"

He stared at her, and noticed she had taken her lower lip between her teeth, worried about his response to her answer perhaps. He knew then it would be another *no*.

A sudden movement caught his eye, and he turned his head to find the young man had returned. He looked to be about to interrupt, too. Drew held up one hand. "One moment more, sir. The lady has an answer to give."

Drew gritted his teeth as the fellow stepped back but stayed within hearing range.

It was too late to hide that he had just asked Aurora to marry him. The man was close enough to have heard and seen the whole of their exchange. Hopefully he was not the type to spread slander about women who were being ardently pursued for marriage. It was far too late to pretend he and Aurora were anything less than lovers, as well.

"We need to discuss us," he urged.

"What more is there to say?" Aurora said quietly. "Attraction makes no difference to my answer. It will always be no. If you cannot accept that then go home, my lord, and tonight, settle upon a more suitable bride, one keen to be your lady in every sense of the word. The season is in full swing. If not Miss Hayes, pick a bride from one of the great families and forget me. It's not too late."

"How poorly you think of me to be so capricious. We have come too far for me to turn back now," he warned.

Aurora threw up her hands. "Damn you, Sullivan! I gave you my answer, and it has not changed. What more do you want from me?"

The truth. The reason she kept saying no when they could be so good together. "A chance."

He foresaw no issue with marrying Aurora but her own doubts. One cousin of Aurora's had married a man destined to assume the Exeter duchy, the other had married the Marquess of Wharton. Both were love matches and widely accepted by society. Theirs would be no different. Given her connections, his father could be easily persuaded to support the match for the sake of family harmony, too. Northport believed in love like he did. He'd loved his duchess, Drew's mother, and the mistress he'd taken up with soon after mother's death was dear to his heart too.

There was not even a need for Aurora to bring any money to the marriage. All he wanted was someone that he liked to talk to, and who excited his passions. Aurora did both quite easily.

Aurora shook her head. "I said *no* more than once, and I'll say it again now. I will not marry you no matter what you say next."

He put his hands on his hips, exasperated. "Why the hell not?"

"Must I spell it out?"

"Yes!" he threw out, frustrated beyond words. "We could be so perfectly happy together if you just gave us a chance."

"You're a fool if you think I'm in any way perfect. And a true gentleman would not ask for a reason. He would accept my refusal and withdraw his suit for his own good." She glanced at the fellow who might become her client, squared her shoulders, and then beckoned him close. "Now, Mr. Lambert. You've heard us enact how it might go if your lady is violently opposed to marriage," she said to her potential client. "The trick is knowing when the moment to depart has arrived and make a gracious exit before it is too late to remain friends."

She threw a warning look Drew's way and he bit his tongue over a retort that they were far more than friends.

The fellow nodded quickly. "Yes, I do see that now, Miss Hillcrest. Thank you for explaining to me how awful a refusal might feel to hear, too. She's popular with all the lads. Thank you as well, sir," the fellow said to Drew.

He gaped at Aurora as she asked the fellow to give her another moment to talk to her *spurned* suitor before they resumed their discussion.

Aurora then turned to Drew with an apologetic look. "I had to pretend it was a bit of theater, so he wouldn't feel badly of you for being refused."

"I hardly care for my disappointment, but I do care about you." Drew moved closer to Aurora and whispered, "I'm not looking for absolute perfection, Aurora. Neither should you be, or your dimwitted client over there."

"Of course, you are." She snorted inelegantly, and then winced. "You are the most proper gentleman I've ever met. Mr. Lambert could not have had a more perfect lesson if you were anyone else."

"Then you should accept your fate and marry me. I've compromised you. The young man probably heard every-thing. I am your fate."

"Are *you* dimwitted?" Aurora hissed. "Mr. Lambert will say nothing about our meeting today if he wants me to put in a good word for him with the woman he's enamored of. I am to arrange an introduction as soon as possible, so that they might meet discreetly far from her other suitors. Now excuse me," she said, before she walked toward the fellow to resume their conversation, leaving Drew behind.

The farther away Aurora went, though, the lower Drew's heart sank. He was losing her...and if he'd not earned her trust by now, there was little more he could do to win it tomorrow.

As she spoke with the young man, Drew waited patiently. He heard some of their plans, and Drew remembered Aurora giving him some of the same advice. Patience and the hint not to appear too eager all at once. Was he guilty of that?

Drew probably had been too eager in every respect when it came to Aurora. But damn it all, he finally knew what he wanted. He couldn't waste any more time or feared he might lose her to someone else.

Their hands shook and the exchange ended. Drew walked out to meet her. "Allow me to see you to your carriage."

Aurora looked up at him slowly, wincing. "I came on foot."

He glanced about, realizing belatedly there was no maid or footman waiting to go with her, either. "I'll walk with you then," he decided, giving her no choice in the matter.

He retrieved his horse quickly and led the beast to her side. Aurora offered his horse a wary glance. "What's his name?"

"Horse," he told her with a shrug. "Unimaginative, I know."

"It suits him," she told him with a straight face, but then a smile played upon her lips. "He suits you, too. A noble and distinguished beast and his handsome rider."

Her almost smile lit him up from the inside. He felt a small ray of hope return. She had been busy starting her business. She'd simply had no time for him. She could have written him with to explain that, though.

Perhaps he would have a chance with her still, and he *had* been helpful to her today. But he needed time, patience, and more privacy to persuade her that he wasn't so easily set aside.

He'd never met a more vexing creature in his entire life than this woman though. She was well and truly under his skin. And it was clear she liked him.

They set off at an easy pace, and Drew quickly adjusted his stride to match hers, catching up on the events of their lives from the past few days. It was comforting to be with her again but arguing with Aurora earlier had certainly heated his whole body. He loosened his cravat a little as they walked along. "Where did you meet Mr. Lambert?"

"On Bond Street," she confessed, glancing at his throat, and then shyly looking away her cheeks turning pink with a becoming blush. "He was staring quite forlornly at a distant lady, and I struck up a conversation with him then and there."

"That was quite brave of you, and inspired too. Meeting people at the right time will be a great challenge in the beginning." When he saw her rub her arms, he looked at her in concern. "Are you cold?"

"No. I just don't like to argue with you…or anyone, really. I'm sorry if I worried you. I didn't mean. I just thought it would be easier if…"

"You went away. Apology accepted. Let's not speak of the misunderstanding again. But let's make a rule here and now to never believe any rumors about each other. To ask each other anything at all, no matter how bold or intimate a subject. I'm keen to help you with your new venture if I can, too."

"I'd like that, but there are some matters that I won't talk to you about. I will try to be more forthcoming, though," she whispered. "And I will try to send word when I am otherwise engaged again."

"That is all I ask," he promised, guiding her across a street and safely through traffic. "Have you found any other clients yet other than the young man back there?"

"Just the one so far." Aurora related the details of the plans she'd made to bring about the match, which were not at all momentous but interesting to him all the same.

"Serendipity, indeed, meeting Mr. Lambert the way you did," Drew praised. She was as keen to get started as she'd been when she first spoke to him about the venture. "However, I do hope you will not tutor him in the same intimate manner as you've helped me of late."

She inhaled deeply and her eyes flicked to his. And there it was again.

That look.

Desire, flashing in her vibrant green eyes.

If they were anywhere else, who knew where that look might have taken them.

Or perhaps that was useful, being in the outdoors.

He could not become distracted from what he came to do. They exited the area around Hyde Park with him leading his horse, but he kept his chin low in a belated effort to hide his identity from members of the *ton* who might be passing by. It was important to conduct himself as a gentleman from now on in public, especially near one of her clients.

Aurora kept pace with him, but then stopped abruptly when he would have turned toward Wharton House. "Where are you going?"

He pointed toward the square they were approaching, which could just be seen ahead. "I was taking you home."

"But I had another destination in mind for the afternoon," she protested.

"Where?"

She lifted her chin. "Guess?"

He sighed, and then realized this was a test. "I'm not willing to voice any assumptions that might cause another argument between us today."

"Oh, you could have wagered on this decision of mine and won handily," she said, with a shy smile. "Now my interview with my client has ended I am at liberty to spend the rest of my day doing as I please. As you said, we have unfinished business, my lord. Could you hail a hack for me. It's a long walk to Conduit Street, and your horse cannot take the two of us together. You can ride, or tie your horse to the carriage and join me inside if you like. I had some thoughts to share for the house's improvement, too, if you'd like to hear them. Unless you have somewhere else to be this afternoon?"

"I have no other plans," Drew said quickly before she changed her mind, but he studied her a long moment, utterly stunned that Aurora was coming back to him so easily. He had honestly expected her to put up more opposition to seeing him in private again after her week of silence.

They were far enough from Hyde Park now that few would recognize them, so he hailed a hack, and bundled Aurora into it before he tied his mount to the back.

He joined Aurora inside and took a place beside her.

She smiled at him. "There, that is better, isn't it?"

"Yes. Quite cozy indeed," he agreed, reaching to take hold of her hand, which she allowed.

Aurora looked out the window as they traveled together in silence, and Drew watched her, trying to figure her out. He'd known few women with an active dislike of marriage. But almost all he *did* know had suffered an indignity somewhere in their past. A scandal hushed up. A love lost.

Aurora had not been an innocent the first time they'd

made love. He'd never brought it up before, and she had not explained it, either. Did Aurora cling to some memory of a lost love, like he had done for his late wife? Is that why she never wanted to marry herself? It would certainly explain a great deal about her interest in seeing other people happily matched.

She knew his every doubt, every regret over his first wife's short life. Perhaps she might still feel the same about a similar situation she'd been in.

Regardless of what her past might have entailed, he would not let her push him away. He would stay until she explained herself, and perhaps even if she *wouldn't* tell him anything of her past. He could be as patient with her as she had been with him in the beginning of their acquaintance, and he would prove his constancy should never be questioned…and perhaps then she might take a chance on love again as he already had.

Chapter Thirteen

Drew continued to hold Aurora's hand as they rolled along, sitting side by side in the close confines of the carriage.

Aurora was silent but occasionally looked at him with a soft smile playing on her lips. He still could not fathom that she had so little faith in a man's word. He would not look elsewhere for a bride, or a lover either. Not now.

But Aurora must have a good reason for not putting her future and happiness in his hands.

He did not believe it was anything he had done or not done to give her those doubts.

At his new home, Aurora allowed him to assist her out. He knew none of the neighbors yet, which was fortunate. They would not recognize Aurora or know she shouldn't be here with him without a chaperone or maid's protection.

Aurora removed her bonnet and set her reticule on a hallway table and looked around.

The house was still as quiet as the first time he'd come here with her. He'd yet to engage servants for the place, having only settled the purchase just yesterday. But all the dust cloths were folded away, and the fires were ready to be lit.

Aurora nodded, looking around again. "Have you found a tenant yet?"

"I have someone in mind." Himself. He'd decided to move here, with or without a wife. It would make meeting

Aurora in secret easier, since none of their friends would know of his change of address for a while yet.

"That is good news. When will it be occupied?"

"Oh, any day now, I should think," he promised. His servants were packing his trunks at this very moment.

"We will have to find somewhere else to meet then, I suppose," she remarked, dragging her fingers over the wood paneling as if she adored the place.

"Not as soon as all that," he promised quickly, lest she put him off again. He took off his hat and gloves and left them beside her bonnet on the hall table. He would move in and surprise her with his new address the next time they met here. Today was for easing her into his arms again. Willingly. He hoped she might stay a while longer than she had the last time they were together. It had been days since they'd been alone. "Have the Whartons returned yet?"

"No. But I expect them on Friday," Aurora promised. "I had a long letter from Sylvia explaining that they had all decided to stay in Bath a little longer than originally planned."

"Good." Wharton's return, and particularly Sylvia's, would complicate matters and make it harder to see each other. "Would you care for a drink or a light repast?"

"Do you have food here now? I thought you said this was an investment."

"Oh, you are not wrong. But I've been spending so much time here the past week, waiting for you, that I brought some things along in case I miss the pie seller passing by. Were you hungry?"

"I'm only hungry for you."

"That is exactly what a man hopes to hear." He walked to her, took her face in his hands, and kissed her gently. He'd been much too angry with her earlier to have enjoyed their first kiss of the day. Seeing her with a young man had made him insanely jealous. Until he'd realized the man was a potential client, he'd felt threatened. He ought to apologize now and clear up the misunderstanding. "I must apologize for my earlier behavior. I have no excuse."

"I made you angry. People say and do a lot of things in such a condition," she replied in an offhand manner that again gave him pause.

"That is not the behavior of a gentleman," he admitted, embarrassed even now by the way he'd carried on.

"That's the behavior of every man I've ever known," she informed him with a shrug. "You are all bossy creatures. You want what you want. When you want it, and heaven help anyone who gets in your way."

"I will try not to be as bad as all that in the future," he promised, but Aurora only patted his chest and walked around him toward the staircase.

She stopped, reached back, and fluttered her fingers in his direction, inviting him to go with her up the treads. Drew did not hesitate to follow.

The bedchambers were also ready for occupation, and she led him to the chamber they'd made use of the last time.

She glanced at the large bed, the one they'd lain in together, and cast him a wicked smile. "You made the bed again?"

"It's one of my newly acquired skills," he answered. "You should see me chop wood."

"That must be where you acquired all those muscles I admire so much," she suggested, turning with an arched smile.

"The muscles you were so surprised I had?"

"The very ones." She perched on the edge of the bed, teasing the hem of her gown above her ankles.

Drew watched, enjoying her flirting with him. "I had some free time before the season started. Could we talk first before anything else happens between us."

She let her gown fall and her smile vanished as Drew moved to sit beside her on the bed.

Aurora owed him some sort of proper explanation for trying to end their affair. Abandoning him on the assumption he was about to be married hadn't produced the result she'd hoped for. He wished to continue their affair, even if she would not marry him. If he proposed today a second time, he could expect her to refuse again. They would argue, and around and around they would go forever. Drew was ready for the refusal, but the latter, arguments about her lack of reason, would likely not please him.

"I wish you could be satisfied with pleasures and forget this foolish desire to marry me," she began. "I would make you a very poor wife indeed. I would make anyone a bad wife, actually. All I hoped for between us was a little affection, lust satisfied, and the hope we could remain on friendly terms once the affair had run its course."

Aurora always talked of endings, which was the furthest thing on his mind.

Today as on any other, he was living a life with her. An hour and more had passed since their meeting in the park and every moment they'd spend together since felt right and good. How could she not want more of that?

She'd expected him to shrug off her absence and return to his search for a proper bride. But he had not done as she'd assumed. He never seemed to do what she expected of him. She was exactly the same from his perspective.

She nibbled on a lock of her hair, watching for his response.

"I feared you'd never come back to me," he whispered.

"I knew I couldn't stay away the minute I saw you in the park today," she answered softly.

He reached out, and Aurora immediately put her hand in his. He squeezed her fingers and pulled her toward him, Aurora rising up the closer she got. With a single tug more, she was standing between his thighs.

He fell back, dragging her into bed with him. "Promise me you won't ever do that again. I felt such a fool, tiptoeing around your cousin asking about your whereabouts."

"I'm sorry. I thought…"

"You thought I'd be busy bedding other women by now." He kissed her fingers. "There's no need to feel jealous of Miss Hayes, or any other woman I speak to. I cannot dine with Wade without his sister-in-law likely being there. I like my friend and want to spend time with him. When I married, we hardly saw each other."

She met his gaze. "Because you moved to Kent with your wife?"

His hand rubbed along her side and stopped on her hip. "Yes…and with the uncomfortable realization that he might have been in love with her, too. Yet I won her favor with his help."

"Oh," she said, wincing. "That must have been awkward."

"It was. When I came back to London, I wasn't sure we could be friends still. He hadn't known about Clare's passing, and he was understandably upset when I told him. But as time passed, we are back on a familiar footing. He's happy now, so all irritations have been removed between us. I am well aware of what everyone suspects will happen between myself and Lavinia Hayes. Even her own family thinks I will propose. But I have asked *you*, and I am committed to you. Nothing has changed that. Not even your doubts about marriage will drive me away."

"I will not change my mind," she whispered to him. "You will have to marry someone else eventually for your heir."

Drew turned her onto her back.

He sought her mouth, and his kiss was soft and tender. Aurora tightened her fingers in his hair, determined to explode their passion yet again. But Drew would not cooperate. There were many things yet to say.

Aurora broke the kiss and stared at him. "I want you."

"You have me," he promised, smoothing back her hair from her face.

"No, I don't," she said, loosening her grip on him. "Your thoughts are elsewhere. I've displeased you."

"No. Not really. You haven't told me anything you've not always said. But now I am thinking of a future I never envisioned for myself, or for you," he said slowly. "It's been on my mind for a while now."

She wriggled away from him. "What is the thought?"

"Something unpalatable." He felt so sad. They could have lived a far different life together. A life lived openly, loving each other, and with no reason to hide their attachment. "Before I mention it, I ask you to marry me again…and for the last time, I beg you to say yes finally."

Aurora froze. "No," she whispered.

He raked a hand through his hair. "Will you at least tell me what your reason *isn't?*"

She frowned. "I don't understand."

"Are you a thief, a murderess?"

"No."

"Were you married as a young woman, like Eugenia was, and have an assumed-dead husband who might suddenly put in an appearance one day?"

Aurora raised her chin. "I have never been married."

"Are you in love?"

"No. Never."

"Very well then," he said, and then glanced at a nearby drawer. He sighed, thinking of its only contents. "Is that your final decision? You will not marry me?"

Defiance flashed in her eyes. "I am unsuitable for so lofty a position."

He frowned at her mention of being unsuitable. Hadn't she alluded to that before too. "Tell me why, please?"

"I cannot."

He peered at her face. But she'd closed him off again, and he did not believe she would ever give him a satisfactory answer unless she *wanted* him to know. He'd given her every chance. There would be no marriage between them. No vows spoken, no wedding breakfast with family and friends. No legitimate children that might inherit his title. "You leave me no choice."

He caught a flash of various emotions crossing her features.

Sadness. Regret. Acceptance.

"That should have been obvious from the start of our affair," she whispered.

He smiled wryly and stared at the ceiling a moment.

Aurora likely thought she'd won. Convinced him. Pushed him away at last.

How wrong she was. She had only deepened his commitment to her in a way she'd obviously never imagined.

He retrieved a small, heavy box from a drawer. He sat on the edge of the bed next to her, weighing the wisdom of such a gift as he held. He turned it around and around in his hands. It was not a gift he could give to just anyone. It was a gift for a beloved lover, or a wife. Once seen wearing it, people would know something was between them.

Aurora was slow to stir to curiosity. Like a frightened animal afraid to trust that they'll be well treated, she reached out to calm his fidgets. Her fingers felt cold, and he raised them to his lips and kissed each one. He held her fingers to his cheek and caught her gaze. "You leave me no choice but to extend an offer that you become my mistress."

Her eyes widened in shocked surprise, and she gaped at him for a long while.

He had her attention now. He meant to keep it forever. "Aurora Hillcrest, my dear lady, I offer you this town house to live in, a generous allowance, as many servants as you need to do your bidding and more. A town carriage and the finest clothes money can buy."

"Drew!"

"And me, of course." He counted her use of his given name a vast improvement of their intimacy. "If you will not be my wife, I have no choice but to suggest the only alternative that is left to me. I will not give you up. No matter how often you run from us. What we have begun is far from over."

Her eyes were huge, and her pale hand fluttered at her throat. Although a blush brightened her cheeks, she was at last fully engaged with his intentions to have a serious conversation about the future of their association.

Aurora could not be rushed, and he was done fighting the inevitable. Respectability was optional. If the only way

Aurora could be his was outside of matrimony, he'd gladly create a scandal to be with her. The days spent apart had been aimless, waiting for the moment they'd be together again. He needed her.

She remained silent, staring at him as if she'd never seen a man so desperately hoping for love before. He went willingly anywhere she led him. Living a scandalous life together was much better than an empty one alone.

"You cannot tell me you're suddenly adverse to my company and adoration? I know you well, and you know me. If marriage is to be denied us, I will have whatever is left of your life to claim. I want you and no other."

She stared, wonder in her eyes. "I would never say I didn't want you. I just never imagined you would be satisfied with anything less than a bride. All the times you spoke of the future it was about finding a wife, from the right family, with the right connections, and it seemed that was all you would accept. I thought you too proper to keep a mistress."

He shrugged. "I never wanted to before. I will do whatever it takes to be with you, Aurora," he promised, kissing her fingers. "You are my dream come true."

He'd prefer to marry her, of course, buy his woman pretty clothes and jewels. But if a lesser connection was all he could hope for, he'd take it and be thankful for that small commitment. He could still spoil her. Take care of her. Protect her.

And since he intended to live with his mistress, talk to her any time of day or night, there was endless joy ahead for them both.

Aurora would have his attention and complete fidelity—not that she realized it yet.

The needs of the family succession were at complete odds with his desire for happiness with Aurora Hillcrest. He'd never marry. Never have a legitimate heir to inherit his title or that of his father, the Duke of Northport. But he was an earl possessed of a fortune and two younger brothers who already had healthy infant sons. Either brother could manage just as well as Drew might have, or their sons would.

He brushed his fingers against her jaw. "What answer will you give me now, hmm? Will I finally hear a yes from you?"

"To become your mistress only."

"Yes. I will not ask you for more than that ever again."

Her brows drew together in a frown as she studied his face. Whatever she saw in his expression seemed to reassure her because she sagged. "Good."

"Well, say it. I need to hear the words."

"Yes, my lord. I would be honored to become your mistress."

He hugged her to him and rocked her in his arms, relieved and excited. This was what he wanted. To know Aurora was his. That she would accept his love and understood his commitment would endure anything.

Her breath against his ear was warm and comforting.

He released her slowly and pressed his lips to her cheek. He opened the box and presented her with a heavy diamond bracelet set in yellow gold. It was no mere token gift. It was meant for the woman he loved. It represented a substantial investment in Aurora's happiness and future. There would be more gems later, when he knew her preference for stones. But for now, this was as close as he could get to giving her a betrothal ring.

"I'll prepare the agreements and send them to you within a week. We'll begin when you're ready to leave Wharton House. Take as long as you need. I'll wait," he promised.

"I won't make you wait for long."

He held no strong hope that she'd ever change her mind and wish for marriage instead, but he was satisfied with the bargain they'd made. For however long she'd have him, he would be her devoted beau. Hadn't his father loved his mistress for over a decade, and remained perfectly happy with their arrangement?

Drew could do no better, and this was all Aurora would allow him anyway.

He kissed her, trying not to think of what her family would say about their arrangement. Her cousins might have a *lot* to say about his offer, and berate him, too, for ruining Aurora's reputation. However, if they knew anything about Aurora, he hoped they could find a way to understand why their romance had taken this drastic turn. Many in society would condemn them, surely, for living in sin together.

He rolled Aurora under him again. Her fingers were tight on his arms and then her own rose to encircle his neck. The bracelet was cold where it brushed against the back of his neck and he shivered, hoping that wasn't a portent of any ill to come.

Aurora hugged him tightly though, and whispered, "I give you leave to use my given name now, Drew."

He laughed softly at that, because he always had. "Aurora, my dear. Thank you. Thank you for trusting me with your passion and happiness. I promise to be the best protector you could ever want."

"You already are," she promised. Aurora kissed him, teased her tongue into his mouth again, and this time Drew did not temper his reactions. He indulged them fully until dawn.

Chapter Fourteen

Change was always difficult. Aurora knew that better than most. She looked up and winced as her cousin swept into the room.

"Your message said there was an emergency," Eugenia said as she tossed her shawl aside carelessly and rushing to reach Aurora.

She hugged her cousin and prayed the news she was about to impart didn't send her into a swoon. "Thank you for coming so quickly."

"I'm just glad to know you're well," Eugenia said, settling into a chair. "I've been so worried. Your message didn't explain very much at all, and you've been so quiet of late. Much more so than usual."

"I do apologize for that," Aurora murmured. She had started three letters in the past week, explaining her decision to become Drew's mistress and leave them today, but she had eventually thought better of putting something so personal in a letter that anyone might read later.

"What is amiss?"

"If you could wait until Sylvia joins us, I'll explain every-thing to both of you then," Aurora promised. "But it's to do with what we've been talking about on and off since we all met and came to London."

Eugenia's brows rose. "Have you finally reconsidered your aversion to matrimony?"

"No," she said quickly, lest they begin yet another long-winded debate about the value of her seeking a husband. "It's not about making a marriage at all."

Eugenia grasped her hands. "I don't understand why you don't want someone to adore you and cherish the wonder that you are."

Aurora had that now with Drew, without a ring about her finger.

She had received three letters from Drew in the last week. The first was a legal document, setting out the terms of her arrangement with him. She'd signed it and returned it and remained astonished by his generous terms. She would be quite wealthy when their affair had run its course.

The second letter provided her details of the improvements he'd made to her new home, along with several sketches of the rooms, drawn by him, with questions about some other changes she had suggested the last time they'd been together at Conduit Street.

His third missive had delivered a key for the front door to Conduit Street, and contained a letter of such warm affection and longing to see her that she'd slept with it under her pillow each night since receiving. Drew wrote that he missed her, and she had to admit she was impatient to see him as well. However, she had been hesitant to leave Wharton House before Sylvia's return today. She owed her cousins an explanation, and it would give her the opportunity to take her leave of them all.

She did not expect a warm reception of her news. Not when she was about to become an earl's scandalous mistress.

Finally, Sylvia slipped into the room, whispering apologies for her tardiness. "The housekeeper had a problem to discuss. We shouldn't be interrupted for quite a while."

Aurora nodded. "That's probably for the best. What I have to tell you is a delicate matter."

Sylvia sank into a facing chair, her expression grave. "What has happened?"

"I know you both had the best of intentions when you suggested we all come to London. You wanted for us all to have the best in life, and you have both succeeded far beyond your dreams. I couldn't be happier for both of you that you've found love with men who suit your natures. You were both meant to be married."

"So are you," they promised as one.

Aurora shook her head, clutching her cold hands together in her lap. "I am so proud of all you have accomplished in such a short time. And I know you will tell me I should have a life much like yours. But you know my past. I never expected to have a husband. I never will."

"What about your suitors?" Eugenia asked. "There's been a keen interest in you this season and the last. I'm sure you'll find you are much in demand, now Sylvia has returned to escort you about Town."

"Indeed, more than one gentleman had sought us out to have a private word about the size of your dowry before we left," Sylvia promised. "Wharton's committed to seeing you happily matched as well. He's asked more than once who you favor. I never gave him a name. I promised never to interfere. But I swear there is a look in your eye now and then. A wistful look of longing around the newly married. I don't understand why you cannot admit to wanting more than a little flirtation."

"I like men. But I'm not willing to keep one amused for long." She smiled softly, remembering her time with the earl with fondness and exasperation with herself. If she'd known he was so wicked at heart, she might have encouraged him sooner. "I'm not meant to be a wife, but I can have what I want now without strings attached."

Eugenia sat forward, squinting. "What do you mean *without strings?*"

"I had a suitor, and at last, he has finally accepted I will not marry him."

Eugenia's eyes lit up with excitement. "Someone proposed? When? Where?"

"Several places and times." Aurora would not say specifically the number. "But I could not encourage that."

Sylvia sighed. "Please tell me you did not hint at what was done to you?"

"No. Of course he might have wished I'd been more forthcoming when I refused. He has not looked too deeply into my past, or the family pedigree, and for that I am grateful." She wet her lips. "However, since I am adamant I will not marry him, he has offered a more agreeable arrangement. Agreeable to me, but perhaps not to society at large…or to you two, either, I suspect."

Eugenia reached for Sylvia's hand. "Tell us."

"I have been offered carte blanche, and I have accepted. I will be Lord Sullivan's mistress."

"Sullivan?!" Aurora's cousins gaped together, and then Sylvia looked away.

"He shouldn't have done that!" Eugenia growled. "He should be ashamed of himself after all the care and attention and worry we've felt over his situation. The nerve of the man to offer a lady less than you deserve! I have gravely misjudged him."

Aurora winced. "He is not to blame. The fault lies with me. He could ask me a dozen times to marry him, and I would still say no to him each and every day. My mind was made up long ago not to marry. I gave him no choice."

Aurora turned her gaze on Sylvia, who had yet to say anything. She still had her face turned away. Was she offended with her for agreeing? Embarrassed they were related by blood? Disgusted?

Eugenia poked Sylvia in the thigh when she noticed their cousin's continued silence, too. "Well, say something. Stop her!"

At last Sylvia looked back, and her expression was bleak. "I always feared it might come to this one day. That you'd accept a lesser status than you deserve because of what happened when you were younger."

"It's what I expected, Sylvia. All I want and need." Aurora lifted her hands to gesture at the riches surrounding her. The palace she currently lived in felt like a prison so often. A gilded cage where she never dared put a foot wrong for fear of displeasing the marquess, and the dowager marchioness, particularly. "I was never meant for this life."

"Neither were we. But if you married Sullivan, you would grow accustomed to it like we have," Eugenia whispered. "Sullivan is set to inherit Northport, after all."

"And he will. And he'll marry eventually, too. Once he's over his obsession with me, he'll be able to move on with someone else," she promised them, even as she secretly wondered if he could. He was so stubborn. He was just like her in that respect.

Eugenia and Sylvia exchanged a long look and then turned to face her, each with one brow raised. "Obsession?" Eugenia asked.

Aurora shrugged. "How could it be anything else? He

refuses to turn aside, and he doesn't really know me. Only you two know my darkest days and don't judge me."

"It's not as if you had much say in the matter," Sylvia whispered.

"Neither of us has ever blamed you."

"*I* do. It's only right that I return to my level. I choose to be a mistress and am content with that. Sullivan has provided me with a town house, a generous allowance, jewels, servants, whatever I want. All the usual riches a courtesan could expect from her protector will be mine."

Sylvia slid to her knees and crawled across the room to kneel at Aurora's feet. She did not touch her, but her eyes were swimming with tears. "Don't do this. It's not too late to change your mind."

"It's done. I gave my word," Aurora whispered. "It is the only thing I have of any value."

"I'm sure if he's proposed a dozen times, he's still hoping you'll change your mind," Eugenia suggested, joining Sylvia to kneel before her.

She shook her head. "He promised never to ask me again. He gave his word, and you know him almost as well as I do. He wouldn't break a promise to a lady."

Eugenia stood. "You know what this means, don't you? You'll be excluded, whispered about most horridly."

"I'm sorry if what you hear in the future will upset you. But they are speaking the truth. I was a whore once, and I'm still one."

Sylvia scowled. "Don't you ever call yourself that again!"

"It's the truth." Aurora smiled sadly. "I traded my virtue for my survival when I was young, and this time, I have no doubts. I leave tonight. Sullivan has sent the key to my new home already. He's expecting me to be there this evening to receive him."

"You cannot go," Sylvia said, grabbing her arm tightly.

But Aurora shook her head and removed her cousins fingers from her arm gently. "I'm sorry but this is where we part company. I have loved living with you both. I've never cared about any women more than I have the two of you. You are the older sisters I always wished for when my spirits were low. I cannot allow you to call on me at my new residence. It wouldn't be proper for either of you. You must think of your reputations."

"To hell with that!" Eugenia cried. "You are family."

"Yes, by blood until the end of time." Aurora stood. The lump in her throat grew harder to swallow around and her vision blurred with unshed tears. "I love you both, so very much," she managed to say in a whisper.

The pair embraced her, begging her to stay, which of course she could not agree to. After a while, Aurora was not sure they would ever release her, their grip was so tight. But she had to pull away, extract herself from the pair. Partings were painful but at least she had a chance to say a proper goodbye, unlike everyone else Aurora had ever loved.

She glanced at her cousins' faces, noticed both were wiping their eyes.

"Be happy for me, please."

Eugenia clucked her tongue. "How can we be? You were the one we both wanted to marry the most, because you deserved it after all the pain."

Sylvia caught her arm again. "You'll take a footman with you. If you will not allow us to visit, Mr. Bloom can be trusted to carry messages between us. I'd feel better knowing someone we trust was there with you. He can protect you, too, if needed, or fetch one of us to do so."

Aurora shook her head. Bloom was her favorite footman at Wharton House, but she knew he had ambitions. "I couldn't take Bloom. He belongs here in this grand house, where he can take care of you. Sullivan is sure to have already arranged all the household staff I could ever need."

"No. Bloom is devoted to you, and I'm sure he'll prefer going." Sylvia hurried from the room, calling for the butler to find Mr. Bloom immediately before Aurora could stop her.

Left alone with her oldest cousin in the Wharton House drawing room, the silence was near deafening. Aurora looked up slowly at her cousin, tongue-tied. She wasn't sure what was left to say, and it was too hard to smile right now.

Eugenia was silent, too, for several minutes. "We will not become strangers. I absolutely forbid it."

Aurora laughed softly at her tone. "When has any of your threats ever changed my mind?"

"One can hope, still." Eugenia took up Aurora's hands. "Promise me you'll write and keep us informed of how you fare. I've no concerns that Sullivan will treat you poorly, but it's a vastly different life you've chosen for yourself than we planned together. If you need anything, anything at all, you may always depend on both of us to arrive at your side to support you in any way we can."

Aurora was relieved to hear her cousin still wished her well. She would have hated to lose this precious connection with her only family she had left. They'd been through so much together this last year. She was glad to know this wasn't really the end.

Mr. Bloom arrived, wide-eyed and panting, as if he'd

come running. "I'll have a carriage outside in a moment, Miss Hillcrest."

She turned to him. "No, my good sir. I can't ask you to follow where I go tonight," she told him, full of regret. "You have a good position here and are certain to advance."

But he shook his head stubbornly. "I'd follow you to the ends of the earth, Miss Hillcrest."

Aurora's eyes filled with tears again. The footman was prone to exaggeration but had been fiercely loyal to her and her cousins. She had depended on him, more than any other servant living at Wharton House. He could be discreet. "All right, but should you change your mind, I'm sure my cousin will reinstate you to her household in your current position."

"I won't change my mind," he insisted. "Have you much luggage to go with you?"

"Yes, it's all packed, upstairs in my bedchamber."

Bloom disappeared immediately.

Aurora wasn't taking very much with her, really. A few gowns and trinkets, gifts from her cousins, since they'd started to have some money to spend. She had kept nothing at all from her childhood. Nothing to remind her of her parents. That was for the best, too.

Sullivan had promised her a new wardrobe, and she'd have plenty of gowns befitting her new status in short order, when she found a new modiste to patronize. Someone who wouldn't spread tales to society gossips. She wanted to separate herself from her cousins' proper lives as much as possible to spare them any awkwardness.

She retrieved her reticule from where she'd hidden it under a frilly pillow earlier, before her cousins had arrived.

Sylvia was shaking her head when Aurora looked her way.

Her eyes were sad as she said, "No matter what we said to try to stop you going, you were always running away today."

"I thought it best to be prepared before too many knew of my decision."

"Wharton will not accept this."

She knew that. The marquess would be furious, no doubt. "I'll leave you to explain it was my choice, should he seek to blame Lord Sullivan." She fiddled with her reticule, lingering a moment longer, and heard the approach of a man's steps. Hopefully Mr. Bloom with her trunk so she could go. "Well then…"

"Don't go," Eugenia asked one last time. "Stay and let's talk about this further."

"My mind is made up," Aurora whispered. She curtsied deeply to her cousins, and finally turned away. "Goodbye."

Chin high, she headed for the front door and heard no response from either cousin.

They did not call her back, but as she closed the door she heard the unmistakable sound of Eugenia, the most reserved of the pair, begin to sob. The sound tore at her heart.

She forced herself to keep going, past Mr. Bloom and out the front door of Wharton House, and into the waiting carriage.

She tugged down the carriage curtains as soon as she was inside, and she shivered as Mr. Bloom arranged for her trunks to be loaded and then joined her inside.

Her eyes stung again as the carriage lurched forward, taking her away from her family.

Tears spilled by the time she left the square behind.

Bloom changed seats to sit beside her. "If I may be so bold, Miss Hillcrest?" He took up her hand and squeezed it tightly.

Aurora had no idea what he thought of her, but Bloom was familiar, and when a sob tore from her throat, she turned her face into his bony shoulder and wept as she had as a young girl, stumbling after her old neighbor into the dark, all because he'd promised to take her in.

But protecting her had been the last thing on his mind.

Chapter Fifteen

"I think that is everything," Drew said as he added a pair of gloves to his smallest travel case and then glanced around his bedchamber in the house he'd leased in Upper Brook Street for two seasons, to make sure he hadn't forgotten anything important.

"Yes, my lord," his valet of ten years, Potts, said as he also took stock of what possessions remained. The man picked up a woman's silver hairbrush and hand mirror from the dressing table. "What of these?"

They had been Clare's brush and mirror set. Drew had kept them with him since she'd died. Mementoes of their time together had always littered his room. But they had to go, along with anything else from that short time in his life that he'd been married. "Pack them into the boxes bound for Kent's attics."

"Of course, my lord," Potts replied, adding the items to a growing pile of objects spread out on his bed. Keepsakes from his marriage had been a comfort once. But in moving to live with Aurora, Drew had decided to start afresh. There would be nothing of Clare's coming with him. No reminders of Pip, either, though of those there were precious few. There was only the blanket he'd been wrapped in for so brief a time while Drew had held him.

That memory had to be packed like all the rest, but his son would never be forgotten.

It was time to move on with his life.

He'd gathered enough clothing for tonight and for the first few days of living in his new property with Aurora as his mistress. The rest of his clothes and property would be sent over the day after tomorrow. He wanted to be sure Aurora actually came to him before he made it known he was moving to live there, too. There was a small chance still that she'd change her mind and continue living with her cousins, where her reputation would remain intact. He still hoped, but that hope was quite small at this stage. She'd hardly hesitated to accept his scandalous proposition.

So, on the presumption that she really would throw her reputation to the wind to enjoy an intimate and prolonged affair with him, he was meeting her halfway and moving away from the heart of Mayfair. It hadn't been his first choice to have a mistress, but Aurora was the only lady he would do it for. He was eager to see her again. It felt an eternity since he'd asked her to become his.

Drew had spent the days they'd been apart concluding some pressing business. He had also visited friends one last time without warning them of what he was about to do. He and Aurora were both about to scandalize society, likely offend many people in their lives, as well.

He glanced around and decided that he'd forgotten nothing he couldn't live without, and let out a heavy sigh. The vast majority of the furnishings here belonged to the owner of the leased premises he'd been occupying anyway. There was actually very little furniture to his taste. The rooms were too dark and the furniture too heavy. That had not bothered him when he'd first arrived, since his spirits had been so low. Now though, he hoped for light and bright surroundings and laughter. He would not even return one last time to sweep the premises before he returned the key to the landlord.

He was done with being a grieving widow.

Drew had sent his regrets to Lord Wade and family about next week's customary dinner, apologizing for not being available again without explaining what would keep him away yet another night. Wade knew nothing of his interest in Aurora yet, and Drew wasn't sure how to explain it in a way his old friend could understand.

The viscount was a little cutting of gentlemen who engaged in prolonged romantic affairs outside of marriage, and lately had become fastidious about the proprieties. Likely on account of his young and impressionable sister-in-law. Lord Wade would certainly disapprove of Drew taking a mistress rather than the wife he'd come to London to find.

Drew wondered if he could ever expect to sit down to dinner with Lord Wade and his family again. He would miss their companionship, and wished they might know Aurora one day. Unfortunately, he could never invite them to Conduit Street to see his new home, or her. They would refuse to dine with a mistress and he understood why they would.

Yet Drew couldn't live without Aurora in his life. A respectable life, a wife, and a need for an heir paled in comparison to the fierce longing he had for her. And it was not just passion alone that made him feel he needed to protect her, too.

She was hiding something from him. He was certain of that now, given her quick acceptance of his offer to become his mistress. Why would an otherwise sensible lady commit to a scandalous liaison instead of a respectable marriage like her cousins enjoyed?

He'd been asking himself that question all week.

Aurora was so set against marriage. Both to him and to anyone at all. If he could uncover why, and what had made her feel ill-suited for marriage, he would sleep better at night. Aurora had promised him she'd never been in love, married or committed a serious crime. She had laughed at the idea, but still had not given him another option that made more sense. But knowing even that much did not really give him any comfort. If possible, he still hoped to overcome her every objection in time.

No matter what happened after today, he still hoped they'd marry.

But he *had* given his promise not to propose again, and he would keep to his word until she was ready to discuss the matter honestly and openly.

"Is there anything else you need me to do, my lord?" Potts asked.

"No, thank you." He smiled at the man he depended upon most to make his life run smoothly. "I believe that is everything packed away. I trust you will install the new servants in the house in good time."

"Yes, my lord. The essentials—butler, cook, housekeeper, footman, and maid—are already going about their duties at the house now. I will arrive tomorrow no later than a quarter to two o'clock with the rest, after seeing your possessions sent off to the country, and will make ready to shave you as soon as I arrive."

"Thank you."

Potts inclined his head and disappeared into the adjoining room to continue packing Drew's clothes into his trunks.

Drew tucked another present he'd bought Aurora

yesterday into his coat pocket, picked up a traveling trunk by one handle and walked out, finally ready to close the door on his bedchamber and his past.

It was time to start over.

He couldn't wait to see Aurora at the house he'd purchased for them. It wasn't an overly large dwelling, but he thought that would be perfect for a couple who might rarely entertain in the foreseeable future. He imagined his name, and hers too, being struck from any number of guest lists once word of their arrangement spread. Drew had already sent his regrets for every invitation he'd received since Aurora had decided to become his.

Mingling wasn't at all important to him anymore, especially when he'd no purpose in showing his face in public now. For these last two season, he had been invited for the sole intention of meeting unmarried daughters in search of a good match. He regretted very much that Aurora must suffer the cold shoulder from society. She liked people and parties much more than he had.

She liked to dance with handsome men.

He headed down the stairs—but stopped on the landing in shock to see his father, once again standing in his home, eyeing him with obvious anger. "Where have you been?"

"Father," he said, settling his trunk just out of sight before finishing his descent to the entrance hall. "What a pleasure to see you again."

Father glared at him still. "I expected to see you at the Sorenson dinner last night."

Drew shook his head. "Unfortunately, I sent my regrets last week."

"And failed to inform me yet again," Father snapped. "I have looked the fool for the last time, young man, chasing you all about Town. I expected to see you on the dance floor with a pretty lady on your arm. What do you think you are about, eschewing society for no good reason?"

"I have been busy."

"Too busy to do your duty to your own father for weeks now, too. Young man, you cannot win unless you join the hunt! Well, I will have an explanation, Sullivan. What have you to say for yourself?"

Drew gritted his teeth and gestured to the adjoining room. "Brandy?"

"No." But the duke strode into the room anyway and stopped only when he reached the fire. Northport turned and set his feet wide apart before the only remaining source of heat in the house, glowering and puffing out his chest. "I am waiting."

Drew sighed and shut the doors to the room. "It's not at all complicated."

"I will be the judge of that."

Drew thought it too early to share, but Northport would not leave until Drew accounted for his activities these past weeks. At least some of them. "You are aware that I have been wishing to invest in a London property for some time now."

"Yes, I remember you saying something about it last year. I trust you've settled on a place by now. There's a shortage of suitable investments in Mayfair. You should expect to pay a steep price for something worth your time and distinction."

"That is true." He settled on the arm of a sturdy chair, relaxing in the hope his father might do the same. "I have looked about and have had to conclude this part of Mayfair is far too expensive for my pocket."

"You would have been better served spending your time in ladies drawing rooms. Choosing a bride is where you should have focused your attention, my son," Father advised. "You already have a home here, and a thriving estate in Kent."

"Both belong to someone else," he said quietly. Kent was Father's secondary country estate and part of the duchy's entail. Drew could never buy it from him. Given its distance from his primary seat, Father had lent it to Drew to make something more of it. He'd done well, learned all he could about land and livestock. Taken Clare there upon their marriage and had the run of the place for years. But he'd not had the final say in anything, really. He'd always had to account for every penny he'd spent. "I want something that belongs to me."

"Have I not given you a free hand at Kent? The profits you made there were exceptional in recent years, though you were never one to boast, were you?" Father looked about him and grimaced. "Have you spoken to the leaseholder about taking over this place permanently?"

"No. It does not suit," Drew murmured.

Father's eyes narrowed on him. "You are too particular, but that is what sets you apart from other young men. You will make a fine duke one day, and when you inherit after me, you will have more money than you can ever spend. I am confident the Northport estate will be in good hands with you. You are usually sensible and frugal to a fault."

"Usually?"

"In other matters, we disagree. I think it is foolishness indeed to save yourself for a second marriage as if you were some simpering virgin. Go out there and demand the best bride. Chastity is ill-suited to a man of my lineage."

Drew nearly laughed at that suggestion. Lineage had little to do with acting on desire. He was no longer saving himself for marriage, if he ever had. But he'd found the right woman for himself at last. It was the way Aurora made him feel. Comfortable in his own skin once again. "It was not an intentional abstinence. I simply never found someone I liked enough," he promised.

Northport inhaled deeply and then let it out slowly, seemingly thinking about what he might say. Drew hoped he wouldn't ask which tonnish event he would be attending next. He wouldn't be happy with the answer, when it would be none.

"Well, I'm glad to find you in better spirits than last season. I always hoped eventually you'd see sense and throw yourself back into the fray of life again," Father said, nodding. "A gentleman always requires female companionship no matter his age."

Drew inclined his head. "Indeed, he does."

Father narrowed his eyes on Drew, looking him up and down. Drew almost squirmed under such close inspection. "Well, well, well. Is it an investment or a woman who has diverted you from society? I shall forgive you any absence from the ballrooms if that is the case and cause for your ease today." He pointed at Drew's upper coat pocket. "Is that a gift for her? Let's take a look then."

Drew glanced down and saw the jewel box sticking out of his coat. Reluctantly, he dug in his pocket for the gift and revealed the gems to his father.

Northport nodded approvingly. "Not too miserly. Not too gauche. An excellent choice for a first lover."

"First and only," Drew said under his breath, but his father heard him anyway.

Northport shook his head. "Never say never, young man. There are plenty of women out there for you to enjoy."

Drew hastily put the gems away and brought up a subject that always improved the duke's mood. "How is Juliette?"

Unfortunately, the duke scowled at the mention of her name. "How the devil should I know or care?"

Drew gaped. "Did you not see her this morning?"

"No." Father waved his hand in dismissal. "She was weeping the last we spoke, and I have not bothered with her since."

"I'm sorry to hear that," Drew murmured, but he closed his eyes, appalled at how callously the duke ignored his long-term mistress' emotional distress.

If Northport thought Juliette might have ceased crying because he was avoiding her, he was in for a rude shock indeed. Likely the woman had taken to her bed in an even worse state. Drew might call on her in a few days and see if there was anything he could do to patch up the rift. Something must be behind her tears. Juliette had given up a respectable life and a chance to marry to be mistress to a duke. She had probably always hoped for more from Drew's father. Like a proposal, and even children, too. Neither had happened that Drew had ever heard about.

Drew would never treat Aurora that way. He was proud that he was not made in his father's image. He would marry Aurora when she judged the time was right. "I'll see you out, Father."

"Yes, yes. Going to White's now, and then on to that scandalous place, Mrs. Bradshaw's, tonight. I hear it's all the rage with the younger set. The ladies, I hear, are simply scandalous."

Drew had been a member of Bradshaw's since last season, and until now. He'd never had much use for low places, not that he'd ever indulged there, but friends went frequently. He hadn't been the least bit tempted the few times he'd gone this year to do more than dine. Hearing his father was stepping out on Juliette with prostitutes did not please him to hear. "Enjoy your evening."

"I intend to. I wish the same for you," the duke said with a spring in his step as he set his hat at a jaunty angle and headed down the stairs and into his gleaming black carriage waiting before the house.

Drew stood watching until Northport was well on his way before he had the butler bring his carriage back while he fetched his small trunk from the landing. He thanked the butler and wished him well for the future as he climbed aboard. He gladly gave directions to his new abode, and imagined the woman he loved, waiting for him to arrive.

Chapter Sixteen

Aurora heard the front door open and the rumble of masculine voices floating up the stairs as the butler spoke to someone. She jumped to her feet, hoping Drew had finally come to her. She had been expecting him every moment since she'd first arrived at Conduit Street.

Her stomach fluttered with excitement. It had been some time since he'd been within reach. And when she did reach him at last, there were any number of things she wanted to do with him, starting, of course, with kisses. She was going to enjoy every moment she had with her handsome lord.

She stood, collected herself, and headed for the door of her boudoir wearing her prettiest blue dress and smile just for him. She was a mistress now and had unique responsibilities, few of them proper. She glanced down the staircase to see Drew was still in the entrance hall, handing off his hat and gloves to Jenson, her new butler, a small trunk resting at his feet.

Drew looked up suddenly and smiled to seeing her watching him. "Now there's a sight for sore eyes. Good afternoon, my dear."

Aurora rushed the rest of the way down the stairs to him, raising her face for a kiss despite the servant lingering nearby, and jumped into his opening arms. The servant slowly backed away from them and disappeared, taking Drew's trunk with him.

Sullivan kissed her soundly and then sighed as he pressed his forehead against hers. "I wasn't sure you'd be here."

"We have an arrangement. I'm yours until dawn," she answered with pride and excitement in her heart. During the day, when he was gone, she intended to pursue her idea of a matchmaking career far from the society Drew moved in. She no longer needed money, but a hobby would help her pass the time until he returned. And when he made a proper match of his own, she would pursue the enterprise with more vigor.

But his marriage was none of her business anymore. She truly hoped they never discussed that again. She wanted to be happy, not argue with him constantly.

She embraced him tightly and then let him go. Being with him like this was all she needed. He was a man who kept his word. All the comforts of a home were now hers, as he'd promised.

Sullivan hooked her arm through his and held her at his side for a moment as he smiled down at her. "Have you eaten yet?"

She shook her head. "No, I was waiting for you to arrive. Would you care to join me for dinner tonight?"

"Indeed, I would, but later." Sullivan's arm snaked about her waist as soon as the servant was gone. "What do you think of the house now? Comfortable enough? Has every-thing been done to your satisfaction?"

She turned in his arms and inhaled his familiar scent as she looked up at him. She might never tire of it, or him. "I love it. Perfectly decorated to my taste. I cannot thank you enough."

His smile was everything she'd hoped for. He'd moved mountains in the days they'd been apart just to please her.

Everything she'd suggested when she was here last had been carried out. Furniture moved; drapes replaced in certain rooms. She was impressed and very grateful. She'd doubted he could do it all in one week and been proved quite wrong. But it couldn't have been easy to rearrange the entire house in so few days.

"Might I tempt you with a drink, my lord," she asked.

"There should be sherry in the library, too." He grinned. "I remember you preferred that."

She gaped at him, startled that he'd noticed her preference when he was supposed to be watching other ladies, and then a smile grew on her face. Drew surprised her at every turn. He was so thoughtful. "I believe I will have a small glass."

He led her to the library, a small room without any books yet but lots of empty shelves. She'd have to do something about that soon. Not that she was a great reader, but the earl would expect her to have any number of dust collectors lying about for him to peruse when he was here. "I'll pour," he offered.

"No. No. It is my responsibility to wait on you while you are here, my lord."

He frowned at her. "You may do whatever you care to for me, but I do not expect you to wait on me like a servant might."

"It will be my pleasure to spoil you any way I can," she assured him, smiling for his reluctance to make any demands. "What shall I pour for you, my lord?"

"There should be brandy somewhere about."

"I know. I found it earlier. I came in here soon after I arrived and sampled all the bottles to know which was which." Aurora went directly to the sideboard, and he followed, watching her pour for them both. "How long have you known? About my fondness for sherry, that is?"

He looked thoughtful for a moment. "I actually thought you preferred tea until late one night at Wharton's. The special blend you all drank certainly stirred my curiosity, since it was never shared. Imagine my surprise when I helped myself to a cup of cold tea before the servants could clear it all away one night when you were done and gone off to bed."

She winced. "My cousins and I enjoy the novelty and the pretty design on the tea set."

His brow rose. "And fooling everyone else, I imagine, too."

She raised a haughty brow in return. "Not you, apparently. Wharton doesn't know half of what we got up to under his roof." She sighed. "I will miss my cousins."

He straightened. "Have they disowned you because of me?"

"No. They know my mind is made up and cannot be change, though they did try their best. All I meant was that I shall not see them nearly every day as I've become accustomed to. I'll miss being able to stroll into their room when I cannot sleep just to talk to them late at night."

"You'll have to wake *me* to do that now. No matter the hour."

"You won't always be here," she said with a laugh, assailed by a feeling of acute loneliness at the thought of being alone here when he went back home to Upper Brook Street. "I'll get used to being on my own soon enough, I'm sure."

"You'll not get rid of me so easily. I will be here more often than you imagined," Drew promised with an easy smile. "I thought I might stay the week."

"I do not mind at all," she promised.

But he had a town house miles away and responsibilities to his title and his family he would go back to eventually. He would split his hours between them all, and it was highly likely that she'd see him the least of everyone. She understood that. She accepted that. Whatever time he could spare would be enough.

And he still had to spend some part of his days in the courtship of a proper lady.

She handed him his drink and led him away to take a seat on a burgundy brocade settee large enough for two by the fire. "Do you want to tell me about your day, or should I strip you where you sit and ravish you before dinner is served?"

He laughed and quickly set his drink aside before he patted his lap. "I don't think I'm in the mood for bed sport yet. I'd rather talk to you. It's been so long since we saw each other."

"It has." She slid onto his knees primly. Drew would have none of that, though; he pulled her back into his arms and sighed. She glanced up at his face. His eyes had already closed, and he seemed weary. "Are you going to dine with Lord Wade and his family next Thursday?"

His eyes opened slowly. "How do you know about that?"

"A mistress hears things."

"More gossip?" He snorted. "I sent Wade my apologies again. I cannot dine with him while his family thinks there is a chance to make a match with me and Lavinia." He dug in his pocket. "I was going to do this later, but perhaps you'd like to wear these for our first proper meal here together." He pulled a square velvet box from his coat pocket and placed it in her hands. "If you don't like them, I'll find something more to your taste."

Aurora let out a small squeal and hastened to view her second gift from Sullivan.

Inside the box, upon red velvet, was a tasteful pair of diamond ear bobs. Not too large but obviously on par with the bracelet he'd given her already as far as quality was concerned. Both gifts must have cost him a great deal, and she adored them on sight.

Drew helped her to thread the wires through her pierced ears. When it was done, he flicked a gem with the tip of his finger and then sat back, grinning. To have Sullivan dress her in diamonds made her breath catch. He'd promised her jewels, but she'd not really believed she'd see so many, so soon. She jumped up and went to the nearest mirror to admire their sparkle. "They're lovely. Thank you."

But it was such a shame she had no ball to wear them to and show them off.

Drew's eyes were bright and flashed with pleasure as she returned to sit on his lap again. And then his lips were on her neck, his breath a hot rush against her throat. Her toes curled in her slippers and her quim tightened in anticipation. It had been a week of unsatisfying fantasies about him, about them together upstairs, making love. Today she would wear her diamonds to bed with him. "Drew?"

"Hmm."

She walked her fingers up his chest, stopping at the knot in his cravat. She tugged on it a little, hoping to loosen it a lot more than she seemed able to do one-handed. "Are you sure you're not hungry?"

He chuckled and sat back. "Just practicing for when we go to bed later tonight," he promised. "How else did you spend your day?"

Drew settled her against his chest, ignoring her pout of

disappointment that she was to be denied what her body craved—more of him. "After I spoke with both my cousins, I came here. I spent the hours exploring my new home of course. The housekeeper and cook are experienced and kind. I wasn't sure I could expect such a warm welcome as I've found so far. I am scandalous now, you know."

Scandalous. Fallen. Impure. Those were some of the names she'd be called soon enough by society.

"The servants had best be discreet if they wish to keep the extravagant wages I'm paying them. I will not tolerate any disrespect toward you from anyone."

She toyed with his cravat again. "There will be some who will speak meanly of me and our arrangement. I know that."

"Yes. I will do my best to shield you from the worst of it. If you have a problem with anyone, be sure to let me know," he demanded.

"I will," she told him, but secretly planned to fight her own battles. Or she would ignore any disrespect. It would depend on who was being rude to her, or Drew. He might want to protect her, but she doubted he could from everything and everyone. In time, the notoriety of their arrangement would die down.

When Jenson appeared to interrupt them, he announced he'd taken the liberty of arranging for dinner to be served early. They rose together to go into the dining room immediately.

Drew put his arm around her back on the way, and she briefly snuggled into his warmth. She was happy, more than she'd been in a long time.

He held a chair for her and seated her himself, waving off Mr. Bloom, who'd been waiting to do so. Drew stared at the servant she'd brought with her from Wharton House, clearly trying to place where he'd seen him before. But eventually he shrugged and ignored Mr. Bloom's presence.

Aurora glanced out over the table and smiled at the variety offered. "I hope everything is to your liking, my lord."

"You are, so I'm sure everything else will be." Drew dismissed all the servants then with the flick of his hand, asked them to close the door, and said he would like to serve her himself. "I don't know about you, but I've always hated being watched while I eat."

"Me too," she whispered back in case the servants were listening at the door.

He leaned close as he added ham to her plate. "It's better this way. Just the two of us," he said, offering to feed her a bite of food from his own fork.

Aurora took a dainty nibble, watching him smiling at her.

Then she loaded up her own fork and held it out to him. "What's good for one…"

"Is a pleasure for both," Drew agreed, snatching the morsel from her fork in one big bite.

She watched him chew, and then he swallowed and licked his lips. Aurora felt that lick as if it had been placed between her legs instead. She gulped at how easily her lover could arouse her, and in so many ways. "More?"

"Definitely more." He moved his chair closer, right beside hers, and they fed each other every bite until she could eat no more.

Drew wasn't satisfied yet and continued eating, cleaning off every serving dish spread before him.

She winked at him. "You really were hungry."

He smiled slowly. "Yes, and I still am, too, because of

you." Drew suddenly pulled her out of her chair and onto his lap. "Wherever you are, is where I want to be."

"Oh, Drew!"

He met her gaze slowly. "You must know that when I am with you, I feel I am home," he whispered, cupping her skull tenderly and pulling her face close to his. "There's nowhere else I want to be but here. Let me show you how well we fit together."

Aurora nodded, imagining a long night of lovemaking ahead. She hoped when it was his time to leave, he would not propose again. She would only say no, and he'd go away with a sour parting.

She grabbed his hands. "Yes, let's go upstairs."

"That's not what I meant?"

"But we've been apart for days and days."

He raised a brow. "You missed me?"

"I missed a lot of things about you, but this is a special occasion. My first day here as your mistress should be a memorable event. I want to please you."

He tucked a lock of hair behind her ear. "Already done, my dear."

"No, I mean the other way."

"And what would that be?" he asked and then chuckled to himself. "I think it safe now to make a wager on your likely answer."

"I'm sure you might be right." She stood and caught hold of his hand. She tugged. "I won't make you chase me anymore."

"But I might enjoy that," he answered, rising to stand. He towered over her a moment and then grinned. "Run."

It took her a moment to realize he was in earnest. He meant to chase her through the house and to her bed. She took a few steps back, and he advanced, one seemingly threatening step at a time. Aurora stopped when the door was at her back. She fumbled with the handle and eased it open. He winked, and Aurora caught up her skirts, raised them above her ankles, and dashed out the door. She bolted for the staircase, laughing because she hadn't run anywhere since coming to live with her cousins.

She had stopped doing a great many things that had made her happy in a good long while. Everything except Drew. He was her only true indulgence.

Drew had longer legs than hers, and he'd reached the bottom before she was halfway up the flight of stairs. He waited a moment then took them two at a time, bounding after her in great leaps and laughing as he came.

Aurora's heart did a little flip of joy. She loved it when he was playful. She let him catch her at the door of her new bedchamber, and nearly swooned into his arms. She kissed him, threading her arms around his neck and holding him tight. Drew lifted her feet from the floor, so she only had him to moor herself to, and deepened the kiss.

Aurora was vaguely aware of the doorknob being fumbled with behind her back before they were in her chambers, her spine pressed against the other side of the door a moment later. Drew began to hike up her skirts, while Aurora attacked his cravat and the buttons on his shirt. His big hands settled on her bare bottom, his hips wedged against hers and her knees spread wide to allow him to stand between her legs.

The press and thrust of his arousal against her sex was exquisite, and very distracting.

"Aurora, I have something to ask you," he whispered.

"Not now," she complained.

"It can't wait," he whispered. "My question is…can I take you here and now?"

She looked at him in surprise. That was not the question she'd expected from him at all. But it was one she wanted to say yes to very much. She nodded quickly. She was already aroused enough for a properly long tumble. "Anywhere. Anytime."

His hands were between them then, unbuttoning his trousers. He shoved them roughly down and then he was there, sinking into her with agonizing slowness. Aurora bucked on him, seeking the friction she craved from his cock.

He grabbed each of her hands and lifted them up above her head, pinning them to the hard door she rested against. When he began to move inside her, it was unexpectedly frenzied from the very beginning. He kissed her and took her with such single-minded urgency, Aurora was soon swept along with his lust and moaning with each and every thrust.

Their kiss ended, and Drew adjusted his grip on her, letting her hands fall to his shoulders as he captured her rear again. He squeezed and kneaded her flesh, panting hard against her ear.

Aurora wrapped herself a bit tighter around the earl as he buried his face into the crook of her neck. The change of angle had increased her own passion so much, she moaned.

"Yes, yes," he whispered. "Louder. Let yourself go."

Aurora slipped her hand between them. There was little room, but she managed to finger her clitoris. The bump and grind didn't make it easy, and Drew did not stop or even draw back very much.

He suddenly roared out as he climaxed. Aurora felt the hot flood of seed and increased slipperiness between her legs. She caught some on the tips of her fingers and used the lubrication to bring about her own climax on him. She shuddered and sobbed as the pleasure rolled through her in never-ending waves, arms and legs still clinging to the wicked earl.

He held her tightly and then began to move, taking tiny steps because his trousers were somewhere down around his ankles now.

Unfortunately, he tripped, and they fell. Aurora shrieked in alarm, and the earl cursed. He landed atop her, both of them partially on the bed mattress.

"That was not supposed to happen," he complained as he kicked off his shoes and trousers. "Did I hurt you?"

"No, my lord. I survived a frantic tumble with you," she promised, looking up at his flushed face. She pushed a lock of his hair back from his brow. He was devilishly handsome when he was truly wicked. She hoped he could be this way all the time when he was here with her.

"Hold onto me again," he whispered, and when her arms were secure about his neck and her legs tightly wound around his hips, he lifted them up and placed her properly onto the bed.

Aurora sighed and released him, adjusting herself on the bed and attempting to straighten her skirts so they were not so twisted. She smiled, happy and sated for the moment, then looked at Drew.

He was next to her now, eyes closed, arm thrown over his head, trousers missing. She let her gaze roam over his half-dressed body, liking what she saw. This man was all hers. The tall man she'd wanted to climb from the moment they'd met. Not that he'd let down his guard enough then to know he could be what she'd hoped for. But he was now, and she was glad to be the one to bring out his wild side.

In truth, he was all she wanted in a man—unselfish,

generous, and even when he was in a frenzy of lust, he was surprisingly gentle and considerate. Aurora turned on her side and drew her knees up to rest against his hip.

Drew opened one eye to peek at her and then brought down his arms to pull her close against his side. "Is that better, my love?"

My love?

Aurora let out a shaky breath at hearing those words. It couldn't be possible that he thought he loved her. But she didn't want to argue with him and closed her eyes to avoid the inevitable discussion of feelings that had been abhorrent to her for so long. No one had ever really loved her as she was. They had always wanted her to be someone else.

Chapter Seventeen

Marriage might have been Drew's original goal once but having Aurora as a mistress would do. He had everything he needed right here in this cozy house on Conduit Street. He'd lived for a week in a home that was warm and comfortable, and he wanted nothing more for his life.

A sort of wedded bliss had taken hold of him since he'd risen that first morning from Aurora's bed and went downstairs to start his day. He no longer felt a driving need to be anything but himself. He was content in a way he had not been for years.

When he rose particularly early, he exercised Horse in the park and, after staying away a few hours to give Aurora time alone, he came back to the most gracious and welcoming lady that he silently called his own.

During the afternoons, he read in the library and, most important of all, kissed Aurora whenever she came near.

He almost didn't mind that Aurora would never be his legal wife. She was to him in every other way that mattered already. They had a great deal in common and laughed together a lot. She made him feel good, and he hoped he'd done the same for her.

Currently, Aurora had gone out to see her latest client, Miss Mosby, taking the servant she'd brought into the house with her as an escort. Drew had offered to go with her, but she'd not wanted to delay him from his appointments.

He hadn't the heart to tell her he had no appointments that day, no obligations to do anything for the next week or two. She did not realize he'd given up the house on Upper Brook Street, but he would have to tell her soon. So far, he'd made excuses for never leaving and she readily believed them all. But she was a bit distracted, caught up in her new enterprise. She'd become deeply involved in her new venture and spent much of her day out meeting new people in the hope of making a match for them.

She had a growing list of clients, some Drew had met or only seen from afar. He kept a distance from the women particularly, preferring they not discover he was not a husband yet.

But he was his own man now and cared little for the opinions of others in society. Or rather, he cared only that he had Aurora's good opinion. He was her gentleman to order about when she ever cared to. They'd create a good life together, even if it would be a quieter one than he'd first imagined them sharing.

Today was another new and fresh beginning. A clean slate. A life now in progress again.

Before Aurora had turned his life upside down, Drew had started to feel he was merely going through the motions of living. But one of his favorite discoveries was that he liked never knowing what would happen from one day to the next. Aurora was a bit unpredictable.

Drew set the last of his new books into the shelves in the library and turned at hearing loud footsteps coming toward him. He was astonished to see a fellow lord walking through their town house unannounced.

"Scarsdale, what an unexpected—"

Drew ducked at the last second to avoid a wild swing aimed at his head. He backed away from the man quickly.

"Scarsdale!"

"How could you?" Scarsdale shouted, seemingly enraged, and followed to take a second swing at Drew's head. Scarsdale again failed to hit him. "How could you shame her like this?"

Drew sighed. This was the first conversation he'd had about making Aurora his mistress. Scarsdale had liked her, and it was too much to expect that he wouldn't be confronted by an angry former suitor of hers. But he'd not expected violence, least of all from Scarsdale. The man had seemed to treat all women as exchangeable commodities.

Drew maintained a distance between them, but it was clear the initial burst of anger had been as much a shock to Scarsdale as it was Drew. "You're a fine one to talk. I know you pursued an affair last year with her, and she refused you."

"And I accepted her decision. I made a mistake. And I have made amends ever since." He pointed at Drew's chest. "Clearly you are not a gentleman at all. You care nothing for what she wants."

"She agreed to this," Drew said quietly. "She was never offended. Not even for a moment has she expressed a doubt."

Scarsdale shook his head violently. "But how could you? Don't you understand what you have done?"

Drew had lost sleep over his decision, both before and after his offer had been made. "I perfectly understand the sacrifice she has made for me. I gave the matter a great deal of thought."

He'd lost a lot of sleep over Aurora's resistance to marriage, as well. But she was not resistant to his advances.

She'd encouraged them. Wanted them. She wanted this life with him. Even if it was going to a scandalous one.

Scarsdale clenched his jaw and sucked in a deep breath. Drew prepared for more violence. However, Scarsdale slumped instead—all the fight draining out of him. He raked a hand through his hair. "What happens to her when you marry, eh? Will she be cast aside or hidden away while you live a proper life with your wife? I might not have asked her to marry me, but at least I wasn't hunting for a bride at the same time."

Drew had decided the path of his life when he'd first met Aurora. A wife, a family again. A son to inherit his title if he were lucky. But he'd changed his mind about all of that now. Happiness was more important to him than anything. With Aurora, whether she changed her mind about marriage or not, he would have it.

He'd prefer his decision not be widely gossiped about yet, but he would have to reassure Scarsdale for him to understand. "I will not marry."

Not unless Aurora asked him to ask her. He'd do it in an instant. Being with her, just being able to hold her hand, had been the most satisfying moment of his life since coming to London. They had talked a lot over the years, and now they always could. Aurora suited him, and for no single reason he could ever put his finger on.

He just knew she was the one.

Scarsdale glared at him. "Everyone knows you're on the hunt for a bride this season. And were the last season, too. She knows it as well."

"I am no longer on the hunt," Drew said as he took a chance to approach his friend. Or was it former friend now?

"I concede the field, the marriage mart and all the ladies, to you, Scarsdale. Good luck."

"A lot of good your bowing out does me," he complained and then shook his finger at him. "But I know *you*, like everyone else, will buckle and hope for a well-dowered wife and a healthy male heir."

Drew shrugged. "I only ever wanted a family again. A woman to come home to, companionship, and children one day. Boy or girl. It didn't matter which."

"Any children she bears for you will be bastards."

"I know." It was something he expected to regret one day, too. Any children they had would not be part of the *ton*. His own family might shun them as well. That was not something he could control, though. "What happens between Miss Hillcrest and I now is none of anyone's concern. I can promise you, I will treat her well and remain faithful to her forever."

"Then why do this to her? Wait…" Scarsdale waved his hands about then peered directly at him. His eyes widened. "You *asked* her to marry you?"

Drew nodded.

"She refused you?!"

He nodded again, and Scarsdale dropped into a chair, any remaining fight and bluster knocked out of him by Drew's admission. "She'll share your bed, live with you in shame, but she won't marry you. What's wrong with her?"

"Nothing," Drew snapped, annoyed that anyone would think so. Aurora was complicated.

Scarsdale squinted at him. "She cannot bear the thought of marrying you or anyone, it seems. I know of three men who thought they were in love with her, only to be spurned."

Drew sighed and turned for the sideboard to pour Scarsdale a drink, hoping that would help the man accept the situation. He passed the fellow the glass and he took it without thanks or looking up. Scarsdale seemed to be having some difficulty accepting their scandal was entirely of Aurora's making. It had taken Drew time to accept that she viewed intimacy and marriage as two separate situations. One was desirable, the other utterly repulsive. He still didn't know why she thought that way.

Drew took a chair and waited for Scarsdale to think things through in his own good time.

Scarsdale finally raked a hand through his hair and looked up. "Why would she refuse you? You're probably the best of us. An earl, wealthy, no obviously offensive vices."

"Why, thank you," he said dryly to accept the compliment for what it was. "She has her reasons."

Scarsdale sat forward. "I'd like to hear them."

Me first, Drew thought. He stood, noticing Scarsdale had ignored his glass of spirits. If he wasn't going to drink with him, he'd rather him go before Aurora returned home. "Was that all you wanted to say today?"

"Yes. No." Scarsdale sat back untidily in his chair. "Do you know what they are saying about her already? About you being together? It's only been a week and the knives are out."

He winced. "Yes, it was inevitable. Society frowns on such relationships. I'm sure I have displeased many."

"Her cousins are at home to no one that calls. The dowager marchioness has taken to her bed again, too. Wharton has said enough to make me wish I'd not called there this morning."

Drew tugged down his waistcoat, grimacing. "I have not laid eyes on Lord Wharton in weeks."

"I would not admit him here, if I were you. When I

heard, I knew I had to come to talk to you. Make you see sense." Scarsdale winced. "You must leave her, for *her* sake."

Drew sighed. There was nothing he could do about Aurora's fall from grace, or his own. It was done. They were in this together till the end.

He heard a noise, horse's hooves perhaps, and rushed to the front window. Aurora had returned from her meeting with her new client.

He turned to Scarsdale. "I want your word that you will make no mention of any gossip to Miss Hillcrest when she comes in. If you cannot give me that assurance, you will leave via the servants' entrance immediately. Say one word out of line, and I will not swing a fist but strangle you where you stand."

"Of course, I will say nothing. She is my friend," Scarsdale insisted. "But surely she must know what's being said about all this."

"I have no idea what she's heard others say. We have not wasted time on gossip. If she doesn't care, neither do I, but anything you say might make her unhappy. If you cannot hold your tongue, wait here or go."

"I'll say nothing. I promise."

"Good." Drew headed out to the hall. He opened the door for Aurora, beating the butler there by a hand's breadth. She laughed to see him waiting for her and kissed him soundly. "Don't say you missed me again? You'll give Jensen the idea you're going to replace him as my butler."

"I know better, madam," the butler murmured with a fond smile for Aurora, stepping aside to allow Mr. Bloom to pass into the house. Aurora had charmed the servants easily and wrapped them around her little finger with her kindness. "I bought us something while I was out," she murmured, digging into her reticule.

She produced a parcel wrapped in cloth and uncovered three pies. "Apple for our supper."

"Thank you, my dear." He kissed her cheek and dropped the parcel into the butler's outstretched hands. "For later, Jensen. I would eat them now, Aurora, but we have a visitor. Scarsdale is here."

"Oh," she said, looking past him with a worried expression.

"You don't have to speak with him if you don't want," he promised quietly.

But she smiled and nodded. "Of course, I do."

They walked together back into the library, arm in arm.

Scarsdale was waiting, a bright smile on his face. He came forward immediately and bowed to her. "My dear Miss Hillcrest, it's been too long."

Aurora curtsied. "My lord, it is an honor to have you visit my home."

"The honor is mine," Scarsdale assured her. "I'm glad to see you looking so well."

Aurora's grip tightened on Drew's arm momentarily as she looked up into his eyes. "I am very happy indeed."

A world of affection was aimed on him in that smile, and he basked in the warmth of Aurora's approval. "We both are."

Scarsdale cleared his throat repeatedly, reclaiming their attention.

"Yes, well," Aurora murmured. "I'm sure you gentlemen have much to say to each other. If you don't mind, I have some business to attend to."

"Of course," Drew murmured, sorry to have her go so soon but perhaps it was for the best. She had responsibilities as the lady of the house and likely some letters to write on behalf of her clients. He knew better than to interfere in that venture until she asked for his involvement.

"Until next time, Miss Hillcrest," Scarsdale called as she slipped from the room and turned toward the study.

Drew turned to face Scarsdale, uncertain of what to expect from him now.

The man was fighting a smile. "Now that is something I never expected to see."

"What is that?"

His grin widened. "Why, I do believe Miss Hillcrest is in love."

Drew gaped. "Love?"

"Oh, absolutely. I've known her as long as you. I've watched her around other men. I've known the fellows she thought handsome, the ones who attracted her. Those who didn't pass muster, she ignored. That would be *me*, by the way. No matter how I tried, I could never capture her attention the way you have. But never in all of our acquaintance have I ever seen her in love with anyone." Scarsdale slapped Drew's chest. "Congratulations. You are one lucky bastard."

Drew shuffled his feet and looked toward the study, where Aurora had disappeared a moment ago. She had never said a word about loving him. She cared, she lusted, but that deeper emotion had never been spoken of between them. Could it be true? Having Scarsdale, who wasn't the sharpest card in the deck, see her regard went a lot further than he'd suspected, giving him profound satisfaction. What they had together was good. But being in love was certainly better. "Do you think so?"

"Oh, yes. Definitely in love. I learned early to avoid those types of women. Too much trouble. They'll never betray their husbands for a quick thrill up against a wall with me, or if they did, there'd be weeping about their betrayal for months on end after." Scarsdale nodded. "Keep doing what you're doing, and one day I'm sure I'll sit down at your wedding breakfast."

"That is a lot to expect at this juncture."

"And yet you still hope, or why else put yourself through a scandal? You could have walked away," Scarsdale said, spreading his arms wide. "Besides, hope is never a waste of time. But it's your life and I'm not in your position. You ought to tell her you're in love with her, too. She hasn't the faintest idea how committed you are."

Scarsdale left the room abruptly, leaving Drew alone with his thoughts. He sank into a chair, troubled by an omission he'd never meant to make. He had *not* told Aurora he'd fallen for her…because he'd thought it was blindingly obvious. He wouldn't have gone so far if he'd not held her in the highest regard.

Love, absolutely. He'd lost his heart a second time and had no regrets.

But he also had no idea how to bring up their being in love with each other, or even if he needed to. Some things just happened naturally.

"Are you so beyond the pale that you've forfeited the ability to keep an employee around to answer the door," Northport barked loudly behind him. "Or even write a letter informing me of your change of address?"

Drew looked up and then shot to his feet. "Father!"

The duke thrust three envelopes at him. "You will be at these events this week."

Drew managed to only catch two, but a glance at the seals on the back of each made his heart sink. They were from important families. They had daughters to be married off this season, as well.

Drew stooped to pick up the third letter he'd failed to catch and shook his head at the seal of another great family he'd already sent his regrets to for their ball. He could only have been re-invited for one purpose. To make a match. "I have plans."

"Plans not to be seen. Plans that include abandoning Mayfair and a search for a wife? For what? To create a scandal living with a mistress who cannot give you a legitimate heir? Believe me, mistresses are for short-term pleasure and nothing more."

He squinted at his father, astonished by that remark. "Is that why you're still with Juliette? Fifteen years of loving her hasn't been for naught."

Father paused a moment. "I will not be distracted by babble of misplaced sentiment. You have a responsibility to the family and to me. You will be married again, and I expect an heir to arrive in the first years of your union. Pick your new lady from one of those invitations, woo and wed her before the week is through, and you will have my blessing on the match."

Drew stared at the duke in shock at his demand, but quickly saw there was more he was going to say. He took a steadying breath and waited.

When the silence lingered, Drew took a step forward. "Or what?"

The duke turned away, prowling the room with his hands behind his back. Drew had seen him do this before as a child, right before announcing some punishment for a misdeed, or poor attention to his studies. Then, Father's displeasure had terrified him. But now…what could Father do to him, really?

"It gives me no pleasure to say this," the duke began. "I blame myself entirely. You were always given to flights of fancy. I never should have taken my eyes off you once you were widowed. I thought you'd get on with the job, do your duty to the family without my involvement. However, it's clear that getting you to do the right thing will require an incentive."

Drew leaned back against a table and folded his arms over his chest. "Since the moment Clare and Pip died, you and everyone else expected me to remarry. Almost immediately. The earth hadn't even settled over their graves when we had our first little talk about my *duty* to the family. What about me? What about my happiness?"

"We do not get a say in how we live our lives," the duke insisted, slamming his fist into his own palm for emphasis. "The men of our family do their duty. I offered for your mother the day after I met her."

"You loved her."

"That was not a requirement of the match in the beginning."

"Well, I damn well loved Clare before I married her," Drew warned.

"Clare was different, special. Everyone understood you had no choice but to offer for her in the end," the duke said. "But our high expectations for you continue, and you've allowed yourself to become distracted from your purpose by a cunning light-skirt keen to empty your pocket by buying her a house and expensive jewels."

Drew stood slowly, fighting to keep his temper. How had Father known his business so quickly? "I'm not distracted. Aurora Hillcrest is the woman I love."

"Love?" The duke gestured around him dismissively.

"This is not love. The shame you bring upon family is beyond embarrassing. I will not have it!"

"This is my home," he announced.

"You had a proper home in Upper Brooke Street," he cried.

"A lease. I never intended to live there forever."

"You had the choice of another house in Mayfair recently shown to you, and of course your apartment at Northport House still awaits you and your future bride."

"I told you I prefer to be on my own," Drew reminded his father. Living with family, inflicting them upon a new bride, was the last thing he'd ever intended to do.

"But you are not on your own. You are shacked up with some eager hussy!"

That was enough. Drew would not humor his father's ill temper a moment longer. Aurora might hear him from the other room. "Do not *ever* call her that again. I will not forgive you a second time."

"Forgive me? *Forgive me?* Do you hear yourself? It is worse than I feared! She has her claws into you well and truly, I see." The duke planted his feet and faced Drew. "If you will not commit to doing your duty, I shall have no choice but to force you. Make an offer to one of those young women within a week and you shall inherit everything."

"And if I don't?"

"I shall disinherit you with pleasure. Cut you off from the family fortune entirely. The price of disobedience will be high indeed."

Drew gaped. He had considered many reactions from his father about living with his mistress, but not this one. A few years ago, Drew might even have been cowed by such a threat, but Drew did not need his father's money anymore.

He was wealthy in his own right. A fact father seemed to have forgotten today. The title of duke would come to Drew when his father passed whether Northport liked it or not. The only thing the duke could do was beggar the estate, drain it of all funds or leave unentailed personal property to another son. Drew could not see that happening. "I see," he said slowly.

"You understand now the degree of my displeasure," the duke said softly. "Marry in short order and we might never speak of this unfortunate affair again. We will talk again when the announcement of your choice is made public."

The duke took his leave, his words bouncing around in Drew's head.

Being threatened with disinheritance did not really change things but it was a disappointment that father would resort to blackmail. A future of duty and honor would always await Drew. The life he'd been raised for, educated for, was as much a part of him as needing love in his life.

He'd been preparing for the burden of great responsibilities to fall his way since he was a boy. Even if Northport could go through with his threat, Drew would never choose a title over following his heart. Northport was leaving him no choice but to cut him out of his life entirely, too.

Drew shuffled the letters in his hands and then opened each one.

Chapter Eighteen

Aurora closed the door to her study as fast as she could before the Duke of Northport saw her as he stormed out. She leaned upon it for support, in the grip of shock at what she'd just overheard the duke demand of his son.

That Drew had been threatened with disinheritance because he'd taken a mistress and not a wife upset her immensely.

"No, no, no, no, no," she whispered to herself. She hadn't expected Drew could have displeased his father so much with their arrangement, not when the duke had kept a mistress himself for years and years.

She *had* noticed Drew was always here, more often than she'd expected him to be. She'd believed he would eventually go back to Upper Brook Street and out into society again and see her less often. But she'd enjoyed having him around so often. She should have, however, already given him a push, a nudge, to get him to think properly about his future with someone else. But she'd been entirely too wrapped up in being with him to see that she was the worst influence he'd ever had.

There was a cost to any happiness, and he was paying high when it should have been her bill to reconcile. And it was too high for her to stomach. Their arrangement threatened Drew's future, his claim to a title and riches he deserved.

Of course, Drew's life was not utterly ruined yet. Not like hers. He still had a week to make a choice of bride.

She winced. He'd had two seasons and already chosen the wrong woman once. But could she help fix things to ensure he was never disinherited?

Aurora had refused to marry him for good reason. She wasn't a suitable bride for any man, and certainly not the duke's choice, given the way he'd just described her. But Drew had refused to give up, continuing to ask for her hand long after he should have known to walk away. And he'd chosen this life of shame, just to be with her.

It was clear he had no good sense where she was concerned.

He couldn't even see it.

But *she* certainly did now. She had to help him keep his inheritance, no matter what it cost her personally.

It would be up to Aurora to end their affair so he would have no choice but to return to society for companionship.

She looked around at her home. No, it was *his* home, according to Northport. Drew had given up his Upper Brook Street abode and moved here without ever saying so out loud. She surely would have remembered that conversation if they'd ever had it.

Aurora walked slowly to the study desk. Sitting down, she spread her hands over the desk she'd only just begun to think of as her own. She could live anywhere and be happy, couldn't she?

As much as she would like to stay, she could not if Drew was here. She would move out today and he could remain without her.

The thought of leaving hurt her heart. Leaving him would not be easy or simple. She could not go back to either

Sylvia at Wharton House or Eugenia at the Duke of Exeter's residence. She did not expect to be welcomed with open arms by their husbands. She had known there would be consequences.

Just not for him.

Not like this.

Not disinheritance, and estrangement from family and friends, and all for something she'd driven him to do by refusing to become his bride.

Her hand fluttered to her throat as heavy steps warned of Drew's approach up the hall. She wasn't ready but offered a smile as the door opened. "Are you busy?" he asked, coming into the room. "I wanted to ask how it went with your new client, Miss Mosby?"

"Very well indeed," she told him, feeling sick to her stomach. How could Drew be concerned about her matchmaking business when his future was under threat? She gulped and continued, watching his reaction to every single word she uttered. "We will meet again in a few days to work on her conversational skills."

"A little too blunt?"

"No, she babbles a tiny bit whenever she sees the man she admires."

"She needs to steady her breathing, the way you showed me to do last year," Drew mused, seating himself in front of the desk and crossing his legs at the ankles. He seemed in no way upset by his father's visit.

But she was, almost too much to think clearly. Aurora stood and moved around the desk to be nearer to Drew while she could. "Yes, I did suggest that."

She perched on the chair close to his, wondering why he'd moved here and not bothered to tell her about it.

"Scarsdale is long gone," Drew said. "I hope you were not startled to see him here in the house."

"No. Not at all," she promised, forcing a smile to her face. If Scarsdale had not come, she might never have retreated to this room and overheard the duke's arrival. She hadn't needed to eavesdrop to hear Northport's demands. He had been loud and blunt, and he had opened her eyes to what was really going on.

Poor Drew. He shouldn't ever have been put in this position.

She sat awkwardly for a moment, uncertain of how to begin the conversation she knew they had to have now. She had enjoyed…no, *loved* being Drew's for the time they'd been together. He'd become her only concern, without her realizing she'd let it happen. She should never have begun this affair and cast her shadow over a good man's life. Not with someone she'd truly cared about. Someone who had meant more to her by the day. Someone she…

She closed her eyes slowly, but her heart slammed hard behind her ribs. Drew was someone she'd let come too close to her heart, and she had to give him up. Like all the others, he must disappear from her life. But it would be her decision this time, however painful.

"I love you," Drew whispered, as he picked up her hand and brought it to his lips to kiss. He cleared his throat when she remained silent. "Did you hear me, Aurora? I love you."

Hearing him say the words that were in her heart brought only pain. Because she could never say them back to him. If she did, he would never let her go.

She made herself shrug, as if what he said was unimportant. Love was just a word. A *bad* word. An emotion she'd never trusted. "I heard you."

He sighed. "You don't seem surprised. I always assumed you must know you stole my heart without me having to say it out loud."

She wished he'd not said it now. Today. He couldn't love her, certainly not the way he'd loved his late wife. The perfectly irreplaceable woman the Duke of Northport had approved of.

Aurora stood and picked up her notebook. She had to leave him. Today. But she couldn't meet his eye. "I'm neither pleased nor displeased."

"It's not something I say often," he said, sitting back in his chair. "I've only said it once before. But I am in love."

Her smile felt strained, painful. "Yes, I know. To Clare."

"I love you the same," he promised, rising and casually perching himself on the edge of the desk closer to her.

Aurora glanced up at the ceiling, fighting against the impulse to fall into his arms one last time, tell him she felt the same and stay. But he couldn't love her the same way as he had his Clare. He'd not pine when Aurora was gone from his life. Not the way he had for his countess. He'd consulted strangers, for heaven's sake, seeking absolution from his guilt over the woman he'd lost and must replace.

Aurora didn't ever want him to love her that way, and for his sake, they had to part ways before he became more deeply confused about what they meant to each other. Aurora was not the forever love he was looking for. "That's not possible." She looked toward the door. "You should go up and prepare for the Thompson dinner tonight."

"I sent my regrets last week."

"Did you? I thought I heard somewhere you would be going," she murmured, walking away to look out the window. He was trying to keep secrets from her. Keep her in the dark, but it was too late. She knew the risk to him was something he couldn't avoid. He had to be out in society again. He had to keep his claim to the Northport fortune by marrying well enough to please his father, no matter how much it rankled. She swallowed, disliking the feeling of despair growing in the pit of her stomach.

Drew ought to have mentioned Northport had called by now.

"Now that I've said it I must say it again. I love you," he repeated, joining her at the window, rubbing her arms. "I love Aurora Hillcrest. My lady, my lover."

She gripped the fabric of her gown at her waist and then she turned to face him again. "You couldn't love me."

"I do," he promised, looking bashful for a moment. "From the very first day of our affair, I knew you were the one."

She scowled. "I do believe you said that about your first wife, at our very first interview, no less. Do you remember how you kept staring into space, thinking of her instead of talking to us? We had to remind you several times we were waiting for your next words."

He winced. "She was on my mind a lot then. At the time, I could not conceive of how my life could be good without her."

She stiffened a little as a feeling of envy and bitterness grew inside her. "Yes, you said as much. Many times over the course of our acquaintance."

"That is why I'm happy to be proved wrong, and by you no less," he promised. "You have changed my life."

For the worst. Not that he would admit it. But surely Drew must know he could never have what he wanted most with her. No marriage. No heir. And there would be endless trouble with his family if she stayed with him. "Have I made it better?"

"Most definitely. I'm a happier man for loving you."

No, he could not see it, or admit he was wrong about her place in his life. She moved away from him, rubbing the gooseflesh from her arms. "You've become embroiled in scandal because of me. A development that brings me no joy at all."

He laughed. "What makes you think I care what other people think about me?"

"You did before." She shook her head. "Even now, you pretend that everything is as it was. That nothing has changed."

"Before what."

"Before me." She clenched her hands at her sides. "Are you going to attend the dinner tonight?"

He frowned. "No. I told you, I sent my apologies."

"But you have been re-invited now, yes?" She clenched her hands together tightly. "I know your father was here, Drew. I know you quarreled and you've said nothing at all about his visit."

"What he said was not important."

She stared at him, saddened that he would lie in an attempt to spare her feelings. She was entirely to blame for today's threats. "Is that the truth? Don't bother answering me with more lies. I heard everything you didn't want me to know very clearly today. You know what you have to do, even if you don't like it."

Drew held out his hands to Aurora, but she wouldn't take them.

He let his hands fall. "All right. All right. Everything is not fine with my father. I only wanted to protect you from the unpleasantness of his call. Family pressure to remarry continues."

"You must be seen to court one of Northport's choices to keep him happy," Aurora said sadly. "And marry them quickly to keep your inheritance, too."

Chapter Nineteen

"I'll not," Drew promised, but he gulped. It was not a decision he'd made lightly, but it was the right one for him. He met Aurora's gaze and realized she had overheard everything his father said to him. "I'll not bow to blackmail and have already written letters to the hostesses, sending my regrets again. Father will calm down soon enough about my forgetting to inform him of my relocation from Mayfair, and having a mistress now, too. He's kept a mistress himself for years. No one thinks twice about it now. The family want me wed, and an heir on the way, and that is all they have *ever* cared about. They do not understand that what *I* want is to be with the woman I love."

Aurora winced. "You keep saying you love me and yet you cannot mean that."

"I love you more than anyone in the world," Drew promised, annoyed that Northport had come now and upset Aurora. "I will have my way. I love you more than the title and fortune that's been dangled before me all my life. My family can go to hell for all I care."

"Anyone living," she murmured, looking at him hard.

"What?"

Aurora closed her eyes briefly, and when they opened, they were bleak as they looked upon him. "She'll always be your first love. First choice. The one you dream of at night. The one you cannot let go. If she was alive, you'd never want me. I'm merely a temporary replacement until you marry again."

He gaped. "That is not true!"

"Of course, it is true. You've told me many times how empty your life had become without her. You were lonely, and I knew from the start your heart was already taken."

"Aurora, no."

"You've spoken so much about Clare and the wonderful life you shared together that I can see it too. It was the life you were born to live. Not this. Not with me, here of all places. You belong with your family and to be a leader in society. You talked so much about what you lost when Clare died that I came to pity anyone who might have married you before you were over her loss. It is not possible to compete with a ghost."

Drew rushed to take up her hands. "What we have is different."

"It's just a little passion, so you can forget her for a short while. I was lonely too. But I'm sure not a day goes by when you don't regret her loss still."

"I cannot deny I don't wish Clare still lived," he whispered. "I'd be a cold-hearted bastard if I did."

"And you are anything but," she promised and then her smile slipped away, and she winced. "But I know how easily men's minds can be turned to lustful interest with a female they find attractive. I saw your desire for me and instead of turning aside from it, I allowed your seduction to succeed. I thought being your lover would help you forget Clare so you could marry. But don't think that you can own me now, too, or control me."

"I would never seek to control you," he protested. "Why would you even suggest it?"

"That is what all men do to women in the end."

"Not me." He promised. "We want the same things."

"Yes, we did. Once."

He tightened his grip on her hands. "There is no reason for anything to change between us because of my father's threats."

"There is every reason," she promised. "I never imagined this. Living together. The duke said you moved from Upper Brook Street, and you never told me! I thought you would come and go."

"But it's our house," he argued, becoming annoyed that she would give up on them so easily. The calmness of her voice unnerved him, too. She had always been much more passionate when they discussed their affair.

"You offered me a house to live in."

"And me!"

"But you never said it that way in the beginning. You just assumed I'd have no objection to keeping house for you along with sleeping in your bed."

"This is our home. This is where we love each other," he protested. "No more secret meetings. No hiding our love. It was what you wanted."

She lifted her gaze to his slowly. "When did I ever say I loved you?"

Her question hit him like a punch in the gut. "You do."

She pursed her lips a moment, and then her expression set in determined lines. "I never said it, and I won't."

He could not believe that. Even Scarsdale saw it clear as day. He leaned close to her, looking deep into her eyes. "Are you trying to suggest you were pretending to enjoy being with me?"

"No." A brief, uncomfortable smile fluttered over her

lips. "You have been excellent company, my lord. A good friend. I have enjoyed the time we have spent together."

He drew back from her. With every word out of her mouth he felt as if she'd just delivered more blows to his gut that left him breathless. Friend? Friend! His instincts told him she couldn't possibly think so little of him. "You're lying to me, to yourself as well, if you think friendship is all we have. Love is not something you can brush aside so easily. I know you care for me," he told her.

"I am not brushing anything aside, my lord. I do care about you but I'm being practical, too. Now is the time to protect your life before any lasting harm is done. Let Northport claim the moral high ground this one last time, but you know the truth that he has none. Pursue one of his choices and marry them, but do not allow him to threaten your inheritance ever again."

They stared at each other for a minute, her words burrowing into his brain. How could she say any of this to him? He'd give up everything for her. To love her. "Northport cannot disinherit me."

"I know but he can ruin the estate before you inherit out of spite," she whispered. "You could need his fortune one day."

"He would never beggar the estate."

"But blackmailing his son is perfectly normal behavior to you?" she said. "Think of the worst he could do? Too many people will depend on you to make their lives better when he is gone. You must give me up and marry someone good."

He stared at her, noticing the stubborn set of her face and sagged. He'd made his choice…but she was not his still. "All this time, I thought we were making a life together. A future you wanted as much as I did."

She fiddled with the diamonds on her wrist. His first gift to her sparkled in the afternoon light, mocking him. He'd imagined it the first of many presents he could bestow, including eventually seeing her wear the family rubies upon their wedding day, in the dim far-distant future. A future that she claimed never to want, even now.

He lowered his face and gulped. She loved him. He knew it, felt it, every time she was in his arms. Every time she smiled his way, his hope had grown little by little that he could have it all. "This is love."

"I'm sure it seems that way to you right now, but that was only desire leading you astray," Aurora promised with a sigh. She fingered the bracelet on her wrist and unbuckling the clasp. "I ought to give this back."

"Keep it. I don't want it without you too."

She put her hand over the gems. "There's nothing left to say then, my lord, and I can see no good can come in prolonging the inevitable parting. I must go, and you should return to live in Upper Brook Street where you belong."

He reached for her, shocked she'd suggest abandoning everything he loved about his life. "No. You can't leave yet."

She glanced at his outstretched hand with a frown.

He pulled his hand back with difficulty. "We need to talk about this, Aurora. Wait a moment," he begged, unwilling to give up yet. "I'm sure we can figure this out."

"There is nothing left to decide but your choice of bride." She shook her head. "My answer will always be the same. I don't belong with you. I never did. I am sorry if I've led you to believe I ever could."

"And so am I, because I don't belong anywhere else now," he said, raising his voice on the last words.

She flinched at the anger in his voice, and Drew worked

to control his temper. He couldn't believe his promises counted for nothing. They were in love. He'd prove his devotion. He just needed more time to make her see Northport's threats were nothing to worry about. She had to change her mind and stay.

He looked up just as Aurora took a step back from him. "Goodbye, Drew."

She turned away to snatch up her reticule from the desk, and clutched it against her chest a long moment as they stared at each other.

When she turned away, Drew called out before she could leave the room. "Where are you going?"

She paused at the door.

Drew stared at her straight back, at the tight set of her shoulders, and hope bloomed in his gut.

"You don't know, do you? This is a spur-of-the-moment decision."

She shook her head. "I'm going where I belong. Don't follow me. I don't want to see you again."

"Damn it, Aurora. We belong together!"

She said nothing to that and hurried from the room, calling for Mr. Bloom, her faithful servant. Drew followed as far as the study doorway, watched her rush out of his life without looking back.

But he was left reeling with shock, his feet stuck to the boards beneath him, and his heart torn to pieces all over again.

The front door shut loudly behind Mr. Bloom as he rushed out, following Aurora to the street.

Drew waited a moment, then went into the hall, hoping she'd change her mind any moment and return to him. But she did not return after ten minutes of standing there waiting, and he had no choice but to go look out to the street running before the house.

The woman he loved and adored, the lady he was giving up a greater fortune for, had left him.

He closed his eyes briefly. Devastated that he'd lost everything important to him in one day. Drew had never been able to change Aurora's stubborn mind in the whole of their acquaintance. He'd never really had her…and now there was nothing left he could do. She'd taken his happiness away.

Chapter Twenty

The hotel where Aurora was staying was a bustling place of business catering to country gentry more than to members of higher society. She'd thankfully not seen anyone she'd recognized so far.

Aurora rose from her dressing table and walked to the window. Below, the street was busy, too, as new guests came and went despite the poor weather, headed inside for the areas reserved for paying guests before being shown up to their rooms.

Remaining here longer than a few days had not been expected, but Aurora lingered still, two weeks after leaving Drew. She had never stayed in a hotel before and had so much trouble sleeping at night in the strange bed.

But during the day there was plenty to see, and always someone coming and going at all hours. The servants never seemed to sleep very much at all.

Aurora had planned to be just like those other guests in the beginning. Pretend to be taking a short holiday in the great city before returning to the countryside, all the poorer for it. Upon leaving Sullivan, she'd used her own savings to secure lodgings, claiming her possessions were following some days behind.

She'd been too much of a coward to ask Mr. Bloom to return to Conduit Street to fetch her possessions at first. Bloom, however, must have taken matters into his own hands. Her possessions had simply appeared in her rented chamber one morning with no discussion of how they had gotten there. She'd dared not ask if anyone had tried to stop him, and Bloom never said anyone did. She was glad for the silence on the matter of her leaving Conduit Street. She did not want to know that Drew was no longer there.

It was hard enough living with the knowledge that he'd be going back to the life and family he'd always been meant for. Back to his hunt for a suitable bride. She'd done all she could to ensure he would not be disinherited. The rest, making a match, was up to him.

She wanted to wish him luck, but her heart was not capable of that yet. The first week had passed in loneliness for him, and then another, without her reading a notice of his engagement in any of the papers she'd scoured every day. But she was a long way from the heart of the *ton* now. Besides a few notes to and from her cousins, she'd heard no gossip about anyone she knew personally. They never spoke of Drew because she'd asked them not to.

For herself, she was indecisive and troubled by not knowing what to do next. Before taking up with Drew, Aurora had intended to become a matchmaker to support herself. She'd had no idea how difficult she'd find it to think of increasing the happiness of others after leaving him.

Especially, too, when her heart twisted painfully in her chest every time she remembered how Drew kept repeating that he loved her the last time they spoke.

She believed him. Had wanted to tell him she loved him in return.

But love had never done her any good before, and it was only harming him now.

In time, he would surely forget all about her. She was

heartened by the knowledge he wouldn't grieve for her loss like he had for his late wife. And when he was married and settled back in Kent, he would simply be too busy to recall he'd been led astray by a woman so imperfect, she couldn't dare tell him why she was.

She glanced out the window again, filled with disappointment for the dull view. It was raining, and seemed determined to continue all day.

But today, at least, Sylvia was coming to meet with her around noon, so that was a welcome distraction and something to look forward to. She had to be ready. Put on her best dress, her happy face, to convince her cousin that she was unaffected by the scandal she had created, and by her decision to put an end to it so abruptly.

Sylvia peppered her with questions when she'd discovered Aurora had left Drew. But at the end, had only insisted on an answer to one: did she know what she was doing?

Aurora had assured her older cousin that she had a plan for her life.

Truthfully, she hadn't a clue what to do with herself from one day to the next anymore. Opportunities for matchmaking were scarce, and when you lived at a hotel, had no fixed addressed, she was without an aura of respectability. It was difficult to convince anyone to trust that she could help them. During the days, she haunted the hotel's public spaces, bored, or returned to her room and slept fitfully.

But nights were the hardest, and lonely, thinking of all the balls and amusements she could no longer attend with her cousins. Thinking of Drew charming some perfect young woman into his arms there.

She hugged herself quickly. She had no reason to have regrets or doubts about her decision. She had funds left, an expensive diamond bracelet and ear bobs, but no occupation to give her purpose. Just as before.

She turned away from the view and collected her hat and reticule from the narrow bed, and then tugged at her gown. She wore the same clothes she always had but they never seemed to feel comfortable anymore. Even her diamond bracelet weighed heavily on her arm. It was always secured around her wrist, but she kept it hidden under her glove, where no one could see its worth and think to take Drew's gift from her. The ear bobs she couldn't wear in public, though, because they were too valuable and too easily seen. She'd sewn them into the stays she wore to keep them safe and close to her skin.

She had to remember she was not among the safety of family or the *ton* any longer. She had to live now like she had as a young woman—keeping what few things she held dear well-hidden but assume she would lose everything of value in the blink of an eye. It was the only way she knew to protect herself from disappointment. One day, she probably would have to sell the jewels Drew had given her, quickly, too, if she didn't find a way to support herself before she became that desperate.

But she had few skills that anyone would want…besides her on her back, under a stranger.

She shuddered, determined not to sink so low as all that, and kept her chin up.

She went down to the private dining room reserved for guests and glanced about the room, looking for someone who might want to talk to her today while she awaited her cousin's arrival.

There was a married couple by the front window, peering out, and an older woman on a chaise, alone by the fire.

Aurora had seen this solitary matron before, but they'd not spoken to each other yet. The woman was as well dressed as any Mayfair marchioness, with jewels on her fingers and feathers in her hair. She never smiled, and she had a lost look about her eyes, as if she was in the wrong place and didn't know how she'd gotten there.

There was an empty chair opposite her, and Aurora bravely decided upon sitting in the seat. "Forgive me for intruding, but might I join you?"

"Of course." The woman looked up, peering at her. "Do you know you are the first person to speak to me besides the hotel servants and manager in two whole weeks?"

"I'm sorry. If you'd rather be left alone…"

"No, it's a pleasure talking to someone for a change. I have been a little lost here, to be honest."

Aurora knew that feeling well and sat forward a little more to extend her hand. "I'm Aurora."

"Juliette," she said, giving Aurora's fingers a squeeze. "Lovely name, isn't it?"

"Yes, indeed," Aurora agreed.

The woman sighed heavily. "I was told when I was younger that it was the name of a woman destined to make men fall at her feet."

Aurora laughed softly. "And did they?"

"One did, I thought…but I was mistaken." The woman winced. "I dared asked for too much, and he ran off in the other direction."

Aurora didn't need more details to know she was facing a woman with a broken heart. Men could be so cruel.

She winced. So could women, too…but it had been for a truly good cause in her case.

She spotted Mr. Bloom at the doorway, seeking to interrupt. Sylvia must have arrived at last in her carriage. "I'm afraid I must leave you, but perhaps we could speak together another day if you are still here like me?"

"I'd like that. I have nowhere else to be," Juliette murmured, looking down at her fingers. "It could have been so different if he hadn't let me love him."

"Who?"

"It doesn't matter," Juliette said with a sniff. "He suddenly decided I wasn't good enough for a man of his position. He said he had set a poor example for his family, and I had to go. After all the years I devoted to him, I still don't understand why he waited till now, when I'm old and no one else would want me. I gave him my best years."

Aurora settled in her seat again. "When did he say that?"

"Two weeks ago, now, it must be. On a Tuesday afternoon. A lovely, sunny day. He came home in a terrible temper, complaining about his son."

"You lived together?"

"No, it was a little place he bought for me where we could meet. He called it our love nest...and so it was for many years. But then suddenly love didn't mean anything to him. I was unprepared for the end. That's the reason I find myself here, not knowing where to go next."

The woman reached into her reticule and dabbed at her eyes with a scrap of delicate lace handkerchief.

Her grief was understandable. She'd thought she had it all, until she didn't have anything.

Aurora felt a pang of guilt. Drew had felt the same for Clare. Both Drew and Juliette had had their lives turned upside down by fate.

She got up, moved to sit beside the weeping woman instead of leaving to meet her cousin. Sylvia would understand the necessity of the delay. Aurora took hold of the older woman's hand and squeezed her fingers. "You're going to be all right. I know it."

If nothing else, Aurora could appeal to her cousins to help the woman decide where to go. Sylvia would certainly assist, and she had limitless funds at her command.

She brightened slightly at the realization. There were still people who might be in need of Aurora's help.

She looked around and spotted Sylvia at the doorway, giving her a look of obvious impatience. She gestured the marchioness over and introduced her to Juliette, without revealing Sylvia's title.

Her cousin didn't seem to mind making a new acquaintance and breezed past the omission of her title with only the slightest questioning look in Aurora's direction. She even asked if Aurora wanted to stay for tea, instead of going off in her carriage immediately.

Juliette seemed pleased as punch to have more company, having spent so much time sitting alone at this hotel. But she excused herself for a moment, leaving them waiting by the fire together for a few minutes.

Sylvia glanced her way. "What are you doing with Northport's mistress?"

"Northport's?"

"Oh, did you not know? Mama pointed her out at the start of the season as the only mistress she had any time for. When did you meet her?"

"We met here, just now." But then she winced, recalling what Juliette had said. "She said Northport ended their arrangement and it must have been on the same day he threatened Drew with disinheritance. It's *my* fault she's alone now. Oh, I have to help her!"

Sylvia squeezed her hand. "You always try to take the blame for every evil done around you. But what Northport does is not your fault. Men can be cruel and show a selfish streak a mile wide."

"I could not agree more about Northport's selfishness. She loved him."

"Much like Sullivan loves you," Sylvia said quickly, before Juliette returned, wearing a smile. They sat down to tea and found many subjects in common.

The guilt, however, built inside Aurora until she knew something had to be done about the duke. He could not continue treating his son and mistress so poorly. When she thought of everything she had done to keep Drew in possession of his fine future, and for a man so cold as the duke, her blood boiled.

Drew would make a wonderful duke one day, no matter who he married, or even if he did not. He would always be kind and fair to all who depended on him to make their lives better. And he deserved to be loved, by someone who made him happy.

Aurora sat silent for the most part but listened hard to every word the former mistress uttered about her situation. That might have been her in a few years. If she had stayed longer, she might be just as heartbroken when Drew finally married the society bride he'd been meant for all along.

They would never have met but for Northport's harassment of his son, either.

Sylvia claimed she wasn't to blame, but it was impossible not to see how her decisions and the duke's, had wreaked havoc on the lives of others, and she had to do something about that.

It was time to stop feeling so sorry for herself, sitting here doing nothing with her days. She could not wallow inside a hotel forever, waiting to hear that Drew had chosen a bride at last before she moved on with her life.

Sylvia had already asked her to come home to Wharton House. The first week, she had asked every day. She said the dowager wanted her there. At the time, Aurora had refused, believing the offer was not in anyone's best interests. But she was lonely for her family, and she could not live apart from them forever. She'd needed time to get her bearings before she could be of help to others, too.

She wanted more for her life still, more than just returning to Wharton House and sitting about in drawing rooms, waiting for the next bit of excitement to come her way.

She had been part of a scandal, however briefly. She wanted no more of that in her life. But she was still not sure Wharton House was the best place for her to go. Neither was Grafton House with Eugenia, either.

She sucked in a breath. What to do? She still wanted to help people. She looked across at her cousin and Juliette, speaking with such animation, and cleared her throat. They both looked at her immediately.

She cleared her throat again and addressed Juliette first. "Tell me what you most want in the world at this very moment?"

The woman blushed. "My life back."

Aurora could understand that but surely that wouldn't be enough now, "Your life, or a better one?"

"The same but better," Juliette confessed haltingly. "I want him to realize his mistake and want me back."

Aurora nodded. "Would you take him back?"

"Yes," Juliette whispered. "In a heartbeat I would."

Sylvia winked at Aurora. "He probably should suffer first, before he was so richly rewarded."

The thought might never have occurred to the older woman before Sylvia mentioned it, but a slow smile spread over Juliette's face as the idea took hold. "How?"

Sylvia patted the woman's hand. "Perhaps we can help you with that. The first thing, though, is that we should introduce ourselves properly. I am the Marchioness of Wharton, and this is my cousin, Miss Aurora Hillcrest."

"Wharton?" The older woman blinked rapidly at Sylvia and then swiveled around to stare at Aurora. "Aurora Hillcrest. *The* Aurora Hillcrest? The one…"

"Yes, that one," Aurora admitted, refusing to feel guilty that she'd been Drew's mistress for a time.

The other woman grew very excited. "I so wanted to meet the woman who finally captured Sullivan's heart! His father was in such a rage about you. He said the only way to separate you both was to threaten Drew with the loss of his inheritance, so you would turn elsewhere for another wealthy protector and leave him alone. Then Sullivan would have no choice but to marry someone *he* picked out."

Aurora gaped. "He did all that just to get rid of me?"

"Indeed, he did. There is nothing he won't try to control his son. Drew thwarted him before by marrying Clare without his blessing. He wasn't about to risk it happening again."

Aurora sat forward. "I thought Northport liked Clare? Drew told me his father wept over her grave."

"Tears of joy, most likely. Clare was a thorn in his side from day one. There was some scandal about her, hushed up after the marriage had taken place in something of a rush."

Aurora laughed incredulously, stunned by the news. "All this time, I thought Clare the perfect woman."

"But she *was* perfect. Perfect for Sullivan while the marriage lasted, anyway. Once she was gone, all the joy in Drew died with her. I had not seen him happy in a very long time."

But Aurora had. He'd been happy with *her*.

And then she'd gone and spoiled it all by leaving him, giving in to his father's blackmail, as well.

She exchanged a long glance with her cousin, who looked at her with a wry smile. Sylvia nodded slowly.

Yes, she could still help people be happy again. She'd help Juliette make Northport see the error of his ways if she could…and then start mending other broken hearts one at a time, including her own.

Chapter Twenty-One

Drew woke with a start as someone called his name, and then again.

"Aurora?"

A man answered "no," and Drew sagged back down.

Of course, it couldn't be Aurora.

She'd gone weeks ago.

"Time to pull yourself together, my friend," someone said very loudly.

Drew blinked rapidly, briefly wondering what had become of the sun, before he hauled himself upright and looked around the room he was sitting in. Windows were dark now. Night must have fallen outside, but the servants hadn't lit any candles. Drew didn't want the light, so he had told them not to. He was glad he had slept for a while, but it was only to face another night without Aurora in his life, or in his arms.

Drew looked down and reached for the bottle of gin wedged between his thighs, lifting it to his lips. He'd started with brandy, gone through all the whiskey. There was still Aurora's sherry to go through after the gin was gone. He was leaving the best for last.

Drew drained the bottle, gulping it down. There was nothing he needed to be awake for anyway. The spirits wouldn't make him forget that Aurora had left him, but it was something to do while he waited for the pain to lessen.

He could still hear her final words ringing in his ears.

Don't follow me.

So, he hadn't.

He'd let her go, knowing any further pursuit was pointless. She couldn't love him. She expected him to move on, marry some supposedly perfect woman his father had picked out instead of her. Did she not know him at all? He was committed to her. To *them*.

But it had been weeks without her, and he had lost all hope.

He rubbed his eyes as a tall shape loomed over him in the dark library, and then light flared. He squinted as he recognized Scarsdale, in dark evening dress, as he lit a brace of candles on the mantle and brought it closer to Drew's face. Drew held up his hands between them to protect his eyes from the unwelcome glare.

"I must say, I'm not entirely surprised to see you like this," Scarsdale said, dropping into a chair opposite without so much as a by-your-leave. "Your father is also looking a little under the weather, too. It's been weeks since the falling out."

"Falling out? I think you mean attempted blackmail." Drew scowled and looked past Scarsdale for a servant but saw none hovering in the shadows that Drew could order to throw Scarsdale out of his house. "I'm not in the mood to have you of all people lecture me on my failures. Go away," Drew demanded before he slumped back into his chair.

Remembering the empty gin bottle in his lap, he tossed it over his shoulder carelessly and heard it break upon the others he'd discarded into the cold hearth hours ago. Then he hunted for a new one tucked under him on the floor, but with some difficulty.

Once retrieved, he removed the cork with his teeth but glared at his unwanted guest for a moment before he could sample it. He would probably have to offer the man a glass. He *had* gone out of his way to come and see him.

He waved the open bottle toward the younger man. "You want some?"

"I don't drink," Scarsdale confessed, crossing his legs.

"You will," Drew vowed. "If you intend to stay, you will have a glass with me. Or you can run off to whatever amusement you're dressed for. A dinner perhaps."

"Actually, I was on my way home from one. It's four in the morning, Sullivan."

Drew blinked in surprise to hear that was the hour. The clock on the mantle had fallen silent weeks ago, but he wouldn't let anyone wind it. The passing of the hours was just another unwelcome reminder that he was alone again.

Drew's drinking had steadily increased the longer he was by himself. He knew he should stop soon, but why bother? Aurora's departure from his life was final. She'd taken away everything she owned from the house. It had all disappeared by the second night. He hoped Sylvia and Eugenia had welcomed her back with open arms. He hoped they'd been kind to her, and blamed him for everything that had gone wrong.

If she was welcomed back into the family fold, he expected never to see her again. He wouldn't even try.

She wouldn't want to see him, anyway.

He took another drink directly from the bottle, willing the pain around his heart to subside. He'd once thought losing someone you loved through death was the worst. Knowing you could never be with the one you loved, or be loved by her in return, was infinitely harder to bear. But there was nothing more he could do. Aurora had not loved him even a little.

Scarsdale's hand was suddenly in front of him, reaching for the bottle. Drew clutched it to his chest, but Scarsdale proved a persistent bastard and managed to remove it from his fingers. He took the bottle from him, corked it, and put it down on a side table far across the room. "Have you been drinking every day since she left?"

Drew shrugged and put his hands under him, intending to rise and go fetch it back, and grab the sherry decanter, too. "Not the first week. After that, it seemed an appropriate way to pass the time."

"Oh, no you don't," Scarsdale said as he pushed Drew back into his chair, and then sat down across from him once more, glaring. "Why are you here?"

"I am home," he promised, looking about the place. He stayed here because the scent of Aurora's perfume lingered on the air in her chambers. He also had good memories here with her, and he wasn't constantly hounded by his father anymore. Although, any day now, he expected one of Northport's underlings to appear and confirm his disinheritance.

"I don't mean *here* here," Scarsdale clarified. "I mean, you've stopped going out entirely."

"What good would going out do?"

Drew had not bothered to meet with any of Northport's choices, either. He'd turned his back on society and had chosen to remain faithful to Aurora and himself. He accepted his disinheritance as the price of wishing for a second chance at love.

"We're all worried about you, you know," Scarsdale murmured.

"We? I'm sure that's an exaggeration," he muttered. None

but Scarsdale had bothered to call to check on him. Console him. Taunt him that he couldn't keep his mistress. "There's no reason to worry."

"I had expected to see you at the Jamison ball last night."

"Why? There's nothing for me in society anymore. Nothing I want or need at a ball." But Jamison's unmarried daughter would have attended that event, no doubt. Another of Father's choices. But not Drew's.

Never Drew's.

"I saw Miss Hillcrest there, looking breathtakingly beautiful, as usual," Scarsdale told him, sitting back with a smug smile on his face that made Drew's heart leap with anxiety.

Drew shook his head, fighting the surge of envy. It seemed Scarsdale's admiration of Aurora continued, despite the scandal. She had probably danced with him, too. She often did. "Accepted back without a qualm? Good. I had hoped for that."

"Not quite. There are some who looked at her without any pleasure in their gazes. But what could they say when the dowager Marchioness of Wharton had clearly forgiven her and was glued to her side all night? But there *was* one lady I was disappointed to see make something of a scene. Your friend's sister-in-law, Miss Lavinia Hayes, particularly glared at Miss Hillcrest half the night, until Lady Wade took her sister home."

"Foolishness. I'll speak with Lavinia," he promised. "Make her understand."

"When? Today? Tomorrow? Three weeks from now? When are you going to set foot outside this house?"

Drew sucked in a breath. "You don't understand."

"Oh, I understand you perfectly," Scarsdale promised.

"You think you can't live without love, so you won't even try."

Drew didn't deny it.

"I do applaud you for your commitment to love and to her. You really were made for each other. Just as stubborn, just as foolish," Scarsdale noted. "Intent on punishing yourselves. She wasn't alone last night."

Drew shut his eyes to hide the pain that pierced his soul to hear that news. He'd feared this news. That once Aurora was back into society, he'd lose her to some other swain. He hoped Aurora could be happy. He hoped her next lover was kind and the type of man who would treat her well.

"Yes, I saw her in the company of Northport's former mistress, actually, and she seemed to be having a marvelous time."

Drew looked up sharply. "With Juliette?"

"Indeed. I've no idea when and how they met, but the pair seemed inseparable last night," Scarsdale promised. "They were side by side the whole of the evening, left together, too. The pair were surrounded almost all of the night by every rue under the sun. Young or old, it did not seem to matter. The pair flirted with anyone and everyone, and then went back to that little hotel they've both fled to, leaving many men disappointed. You *do* know Northport dismissed his mistress, don't you?"

Drew blinked rapidly, hoping he'd misheard. But Scarsdale was nodding emphatically. "I hadn't heard. I haven't spoken to him in weeks."

"From what I understand, Northport ended their arrangement on the very same day Aurora left you," he said.

"The day he threatened to disinherit me. I suppose you know about that, too?" Drew grimaced when Scarsdale nodded. "He dangled his fortune as a means to bring me back into line, so I would marry someone of his choosing. He failed at that, and so I am his son no longer, I suppose."

Scarsdale pursed his lips a moment. "From what I hear, he's made no progress on that front."

Drew shrugged, hardly caring anymore. It was the last straw in their relationship as father and son. "But my father must have told everyone his intentions by now."

"It was only Aurora who shared that news with me."

He nodded and looked away, puzzled by his father's actions—and inaction, too. "Poor Juliette," Drew murmured, wiping his face in an effort to sober himself. "She doted on the old man. I cannot believe he could be so cruel to her."

"The way Juliette tells it, he decided it was past time to set a good example for his son."

"Hardly." Drew scoffed. "I always hoped he would marry the woman. She was so good for him. I will have to find out where she's staying. Make sure she's all right. Offer any help she needs."

Scarsdale smiled. "That is what we hoped you might say."

"We?"

"Miss Hillcrest and I are of the same mind. Dear Juliette cannot decide what to do with her life, now she's no longer a wealthy man's mistress, and she needs some guidance from someone she can trust with her money, too. Aurora wondered if you might have a suggestion for her future, or at least offer her a place to live for a while."

"She can count on me, of course," Drew promised, standing, but not well. He grabbed the back of his chair to hold himself up until he got his balance. "I care about Juliette."

"You'll need a clearer head before you see her or anyone," Scarsdale suggested.

"I was just on my way to throw my head in a basin of very cold water," Drew promised, weaving his way toward the door at a lurching pace. Juliette was a good woman. He could have sent her to Kent to be his guest for the rest of her life, if he wasn't about to be disinherited. She'd always enjoyed the countryside. Some time away from London might just be what she needed to get over the duke's defection.

He could not understand Northport, giving up a situation that made him so undeniably happy. What was he thinking, sabotaging his life just to make Drew's supposedly better?

In that, Northport and Aurora were two of a kind.

Drew made his way upstairs, called for his valet to help him change and shave, and then, dressed in fresh clothing, he dug into the enormous early breakfast cook had sent up, and felt better from the first bite.

Scarsdale sidled into the room and up to the table, helping himself to Drew's meal and drinking Drew's coffee, once an extra setting had been brought up for him.

Drew looked at the fellow likely hoping to seduce Aurora now, and winced. "Thank you for coming to tell me about Juliette."

"My pleasure. I hate to see my closest friends in pain."

"One of us is, at least," Drew murmured.

Scarsdale patted a napkin to his lips. "Is that what you really think? That it was easy for her to leave you?"

"It's what I know. She doesn't give a damn."

"Well, what *I know* is that Miss Hillcrest hid at a hotel for weeks and refused to see anyone. I *know* she had a disappointed look in her eyes last night as she surveyed the ballroom and did not see you standing anywhere among the guests. And I *know* that when she thinks no one is looking at her, she caresses a diamond bracelet she hides under her glove. She misses you, and she's too stubborn to say anything to make things right."

"She doesn't love me. You were mistaken about that," he assured the younger man, shaking his head. "She was emphatic about it, believe me."

"Tell me, what's her favorite color?"

"I've no idea. She never said."

"All right then, what color gown do you think she most often wears of late? I'll give you a hint. It's not green, red, brown or lemon. It is always the same color."

His bruised heart beat a little faster to hear that, but he dared not ask what the color was. He would only get his hopes up unnecessarily over a rumor.

Scarsdale smiled softly. "You ought to keep yourself in order from now on. The Hillcrest ladies look poorly upon a slovenly gentleman."

"I'm hardly that," Drew assured him.

"No? Really then, who was it that put drool on your lapel last night?" Scarsdale teased. "And why are there at least three empty bottles smashed in your fireplace downstairs? Should the servants not be allowed to clear the mess away?"

"She broke my heart!" Drew protested, raking a hand through his freshly combed hair. "Perhaps I got a little carried away feeling sorry for myself. You would, too, if you'd ever loved someone so deeply."

Scarsdale grinned. "How fortunate am I, then, never to have loved and lost? But I really don't think you've lost her yet."

"I have."

"What would you do if she came to see you?"

"She wouldn't. Not now," he promised, and then looked at Scarsdale, unable not to enquire. "What color gown does she wear?"

Scarsdale chuckled and stood. "I'll give you one guess. It is a match for your eyes."

Drew's eyes were blue, and he'd told Aurora he liked the way she looked in that color.

Perhaps Aurora *did* love him a little after all…but if she did, why the hell had she not come back to him?

Chapter Twenty-Two

Aurora hugged Juliette tightly outside the hotel. "Write to me when you arrive safely."

"I will. Will you still be here then, lovey?"

Aurora glanced around, grimacing as a pair of strutting gentlemen rudely brushed past them without the courtesy of a by-your-leave. It was time to move on. "Perhaps not."

Juliette released her, her smile wide. The older woman's optimism had returned almost immediately when they'd hatched their plan to make the duke regret setting his mistress aside. Last night, and for the past week, with the help of a number of friendly gentlemen in on the scheme, the duke had come to believe that Juliette was more popular than ever.

And she really was.

Juliette had received dozens of flowers every morning after a ball or dinner they'd attended, all with notes expressing a hope to see her again soon. But having had her week of triumph, she was now on her way to the country, as arranged by Drew. "Where shall I send the letter, then?"

Where indeed? Aurora had remained at the hotel for five weeks now, but she was as uncertain of her place in the world now as she'd always been. She had visited Wharton House many times, and been forgiven as if her affair with Drew had never occurred. But *she* remembered.

Aurora had not seen Drew since the day she'd taken her

leave of him, and no one else had seen him, either. He had completely turned his back on society—and by all accounts, on his father and family, too.

But he had not been disinherited. The duke had not gone through with his threat, as Juliette had assured Aurora he wouldn't.

Yet, Drew was all alone. That upset her more than she'd imagined possible.

She smiled quickly. "If I am not here, I will leave the hotel manager my address and have him forward any mail," she promised.

"That is a good idea. Who knows how long it might take for a letter to make its way from me to London?"

"That is true." Juliette was to stay at the Wharton's estate until she was certain of her situation. Wharton had been rallied to help Northport's former mistress almost immediately by Sylvia, and also by his own mother. Together, they had put together a list that offered Juliette any number of choices for accommodation. Leaving London and the duke behind was to be a first step toward embracing her independence, and she would be protected. She had money, a fortune in jewels, but had relied on the duke so much that she lacked financial skills and trusted too easily. Drew had offered his advice, and left her to make her own choices, though.

He was a good man for helping Juliette the way he was, and she would have told him so had she ever seen him.

But she hadn't. Not once.

He had not attended any of the regular dinners at Lord Wade's, or soirées at Exeter's, or even gone to Bradshaw's with his friends.

Aurora herself seemed to be invited everywhere. For a few weeks, she had been the subject of a number of rumors and speculation. Who she would pick for her next protector seemed a subject that fascinated society, and there were wagers apparently placed on how long those liaisons might last, too.

Juliette boarded the traveling carriage—Sullivan's carriage—and Aurora waved her off from the hotel. She would miss the woman, and waited on the pavement until the carriage had disappeared from sight.

She turned and found Scarsdale standing a few feet away, a smug smile on his face. He was constantly around now. Ever since her first dinner at Wharton House, when he'd been placed beside her for the meal.

She scowled at him. "How long have you been standing there, watching me?"

"Not long. I must say, you always look beautiful in blue," he replied, smiling too much for her comfort. "Are you *still* here?"

"Where else would I be?"

"Where else, indeed?" Scarsdale asked. He seemed to find her continuing to live at the hotel most amusing.

Aurora returned indoors and into the guest parlor. The room was empty today, and she took her usual place by the fire. But without Juliette sitting with her now, her surroundings seemed rather dull. It was certainly not homey.

Scarsdale looked around and arranged himself on the opposite seat. "I wanted to speak to you before I go."

"Go?"

"Yes, I am overdue to return home. I have some matters to attend to in the country that unfortunately cannot wait."

Scarsdale always did leave things till the very last minute. "You should attend them, then. Your family will be happy to see you again, I'm sure."

"All they will do is complain that I'm not married yet," he grumbled.

"Oh, you poor man," she said with a heartless laugh for his grumbling. His attitude had changed very slightly in the past weeks. He was at least ready to talk seriously about the sort of woman who might suit him, and what else he needed in a match. "At least you can tell them you did look."

"Yes, I looked, and will continue my search for a suitable bride later in the year with your help. I must say, I feel hopeful that perhaps there *is* someone I can love."

Aurora sat forward. "Why do you say that now, when you've dismissed the idea of love out of hand so often?"

He sat forward, too. "One word. Sullivan."

Aurora sat back at the mention of her lover. "Why?"

"There's never been a man more heartbroken, and yet he remains so optimistic you'll come back to him."

"I'm sure he's hardly…"

Her words trailed off as Scarsdale sat back with an amused expression on his face. "He waits for you. Yes, indeed he does. Most faithfully. He hasn't left home in more than a month."

"Surely—"

"He gave up everything for you. Without regret. It's still possible Northport will disinherit him. And yet, rather than buckle to pressure, he sits at home, waiting for you to realize your mistake."

Aurora squirmed, fidgeted with the folds of her gown, and then clutched the diamond bracelet hidden under her glove. "What mistake would that be?"

"That you thought you could live without love forever. You walked away from the only man who wanted to take the time to understand you, who accepts that you will never tell him why you won't marry. As for himself, Sullivan is not ever going to marry some mythical *perfect* creature approved by his family. He is utterly committed to you. He loves you."

"I told him I didn't love him," she whispered.

"Deep down, he knew that was a lie," Scarsdale told her. "It's not too late, you know. You can go back to him. I know you're not happy."

"I'm sure he wouldn't open the door to me after what I said to him," she fretted, scrambling to think of reasons why she didn't want to do as Scarsdale suggested. Walking away from Drew was the hardest thing she'd ever done. Going back and being rejected would be worse.

"You have a key, and I have a carriage that can take you back to him right now," Scarsdale offered, giving her a hopeful look. "I cannot bear to see two hearts once so in-tune remain broken without trying to bring them together again. I mean, who would you have instead? Me? Brande-stock? Or some stranger who might just have a dangerous temper and hurt you. You were happy with him. I saw it. You *felt* it. You belong together, and you foolishly sacrificed happiness for an empty life just to save a fortune he doesn't want half as much as he wants you."

She blushed. Hearing Scarsdale offer her advice about her romantic life seemed odd to her ears, however…he was not wrong. She was in the wrong place still. With the wrong people. The only place she'd ever felt truly herself, and believed she might have a chance to belong, was with Drew.

He was still there.

At the home he'd bought for them.

Could he really be waiting *for* her return, as Scarsdale claimed?

She gulped, imagining him waiting for her all this time.

She shook her head. She wasn't worthy of his patience and devotion. Aurora had taken her love away from him, and she was ashamed and humbled by her lover's continued hope. She had not expected that. But he didn't know her deepest, darkest secrets yet. Could he still love her once she shared her history with him?

Yet, he was the only man she wanted to tell. The only person she wanted to hope could understand. He should hear her reasons for not marrying him from her own lips, and only then could he decide if she was worth all the trouble and the sacrifices he continued to make.

She looked up at Scarsdale quickly.

"Ah, I see you finally agree with me." Scarsdale clapped his hands together. "Excellent. I'll call up my carriage and have it wait outside for half an hour. I trust that will be long enough for you to collect a few essentials and we can be on our way."

"I didn't say I agreed with you," she warned.

"You didn't have to. Fear is why you are still living here. And perhaps guilt, too. You owe him an explanation. You've been trying to decide how to apologize to him all these weeks, and wondering if he'd ever accept it. He will."

She shook her head and covered her eyes with her hand. "I was wrong to leave him the way I did."

"No, you were wrong to *leave him*. Period. But lucky for you, I'm here to point out your flaws and send you back in the right direction again."

She squinted at Scarsdale through her fingers. "I thought you'd be glad I'd left him and were hoping to seduce me in his place."

"Wherever did you get that idea?" He looked shocked, theatrically so for a moment, and then he laughed. "I've been hovering around you to protect my friend's interest, and even kept some unscrupulous scoundrels away. I know better than to interfere in young love."

Her heart sped up. Love… A word that had terrified her since she was a child.

"Go on," Scarsdale urged. "Don't think. Go. Fetch a valise or something pretty to wear to bed tonight and hurry back. I really am on my way out of Town today."

Aurora was on her feet and running for her rented room before she realized the only thing on her mind was seeing Drew again.

Once in her room, she looked around her, snatched up a few things she couldn't do without and decided that if Drew wouldn't forgive her, she could always come back.

That thought was even more terrifying than losing his good opinion.

Once downstairs again, she was hurried into Scarsdale's traveling carriage without another word. He gave the coachman the directions that would take her home.

She bit her lip as they traveled along in silence, determined to see Drew and terribly nervous. She was happy to be going home, but terrified of her reception.

Her hands were shaking when Scarsdale deposited her before the house and waved goodbye, stranding her there. She climbed the stairs slowly and put the key in the front door lock with hands that shook. It opened easily with one twist, and she crossed the threshold.

She breathed deep, and her eyes filled with tears. Home. This was where her heart longed to stay.

But was she welcome here?

Only Drew could answer that after she'd told him everything.

The butler, alerted by the sound of the door, was suddenly in the hall right in front of her. His smile of welcome heartened her. He took her bonnet, quickly pointed to the library and then backed away, vanishing into the servants' doorway, silent as always.

She took a deep breath and turned for the library, knees nearly buckling with each step toward him.

A cheerful fire was burning in the hearth, as it had on the last night she'd sat in this room, listening to Drew talk about work he wanted completed on his estate in Kent. They had been sitting together comfortably, Aurora wrapped up in his arms. It was the last time she'd ever felt sure of herself.

She took several steps into the room and looked about. Drew was not to be seen. Had he left to avoid her?

The sound of the door shutting behind her spun Aurora about.

It was Drew who had closed the door to the library. He was leaning on it. He was almost exactly how she'd left him. Wearing a coat of muted green, fawn breeches, and black boots on his feet.

But he looked to have aged. There were more lines on his face than he should've had. More lines about his eyes that were not from laughter. He reminded her of when they'd first met. He'd come to the academy, a man barely held together. Too serious to be healthy for him.

They stared at each other. "Aurora."

"Drew."

He straightened at the sound of his given name tumbling from her lips. He took a step forward. "What are you doing here?"

She winced. So, he hadn't been expecting her. She shook

off the disappointment and smiled as best she could. "I wanted to tell you Juliette is on her way to the country."

"That is good to know," he answered, his voice devoid of any joy in the news.

"You were very kind to help your father's mistress," she whispered, knowing she should never have come. A note would have sufficed to tell him that.

"Juliette has been almost a mother to me over recent years. She held my hand many times after Clare died. I owed her, and loved her for her limitless compassion," he whispered, taking a step more in her direction. "I'm glad you met her and wanted to help her, too. I had been unaware of the duke's actions until Scarsdale informed me of what he'd done."

"Scarsdale has become such a meddlesome, bossy creature of late," she murmured, taking a step in his direction.

A flicker of pain crossed Drew's face. "You are with him now, then?"

Aurora frowned. "No. Why would you say such a thing?"

"I saw you arrive in his carriage." Drew rocked back onto his rear foot. "He's always been keen on you. I understand."

"Scarsdale brought me in his carriage only so that I might see you."

He frowned. "What for?"

"About Juliette, of course."

He moved back another step. "Well…I am very glad to see you for any reason. Thank you for coming."

He crossed his arms over his chest and stepped out of the path of the door, allowing her the chance to leave if she wanted to. Aurora shuffled her feet nervously, knowing she couldn't yet. "How have you been?"

"I am as you see," he said. "Essentially the same as the day you gave up on us."

She bit her lip. "There's something you should know. Juliette told me your father never intended to disinherit you. All he wanted was for me to believe you could not afford to keep a mistress. He thought me so grasping and ambitious that I would attach myself to some other wealthy protector."

"Well, he got his wish. You left me."

She gulped. "I regret…" she whispered.

Drew's eyes narrowed on her—and his arms unfolded to spread out to his sides.

It took Aurora a single moment to decide what that might mean.

She ran to Drew, jumped up, and wrapped her arms about his neck. "I'm so sorry!"

He uttered an oath and quickly wrapped her in his arms, holding her tight against him. "I know you can't love me, but I still love you. So very much."

"Oh, Drew. I lied!" she cried, and buried her face in his shoulder and held him as tight as she could. "I do love you. I always have. Since the moment we kissed, I knew you were dangerous to my heart. That I might want you too much."

He cursed again and pressed his head to hers. "Then come back to me, Aurora, my love, my heart. We can make this work, can't we? It doesn't have to be a battle between us anymore if we can be honest about how we feel for each other."

He was so earnest, but he didn't know the sort of woman she really was underneath her fine clothes, her flimsy suit of armor.

She took his head in her hands, stared into his eyes looking for the love he professed to feel for her. His eyes shone with tears, but she hadn't broken his heart entirely. He could be hers again…but only if she was brave enough to trust in him and tell him the truth. "I want you. I want *us*," she whispered.

She drew him close for a kiss, knowing exactly where it would lead them if she let it happen. To their bed. To his hands on her body, driving her worst memories and fears to the darkest corners of her mind. Only in his arms had she dared imagine she could be loved, despite her past. But when dawn came, her secret would still be between them, coloring everything they shared.

She had to tell him so much that would likely horrify him, to explain why she'd lost her faith in love so long ago. She couldn't hide her shame from him another moment. He had to understand everything and then she would see if his love would remain hers to cherish forever.

Chapter Twenty-Three

Drew was happy again. Aurora had come back to him, albeit with a little help from a mutual friend.

His patience *had* borne fruit. He had a second chance to be with her. To love her, now she finally had admitted to loving him in return.

Drew slid his hands down Aurora's back slowly. But soon he realized there was a stiffness in the way she held herself to him.

Concern gripped him and he slowly let her go, trying to catch a glimpse of her face. Aurora quickly stepped back and turned away walking toward the fire. She perched on the edge of the settee, but wrapped her arms about her chest as if she was chilled through. She seemed so small and frail sitting there all alone when her presence had always been larger than life before.

He went to her quickly. "What's wrong, my love? Are you unwell?"

"No."

Despite her claim, he pressed a hand to her brow to check for fever. He found her comfortably warm but no sign of illness. Her hands, when he grasped them, were ice cold though. "Let me fetch a blanket to warm you."

"I'm not unwell. But I have something difficult to say."

Drew sank into the space by her side, his heart sinking with a certainty that something was terribly wrong still. Had she come back to stay or was this only a casual affair? "Are you going to leave me again?"

"No," she sighed. "But you might want me to go."

"I never would wish for that. These last weeks have been miserable for me, and for you too, I suspect. I missed you so very much," he promised, smiling despite her tears as he kissed her brow. Her return had been so emotional for him. He'd experienced such profound joy at seeing Aurora once more standing in their home. Her return had given him renewed hope that whatever doubts she had about him could be resolved to her satisfaction in time.

He wouldn't ever push for a marriage. Not unless she wanted that as well. He didn't care who they offended if they never married. His father could go to hell, too, for making demands that had convinced her to leave him. He would never let that happen again.

"How about we stay here all day and all night then and watch the sun rise over the city together tomorrow from the attic windows?"

"Sunrise is a long time away," she whispered.

"I suppose it must be?" Drew checked his pocket watch to look at the time. "It's a quarter to one o'clock," he told her, turning back.

"I've been thinking," she whispered.

He settled back at her side. "About me and our future together?" he murmured, offering up a smile that he didn't quite feel.

"Yes, about you, and a lot of other things I don't like to think about."

"Such as?" he asked gently.

He didn't want to pry, scare her, and he'd been reluctant until now about asking too many questions. She kept a great deal bottled up. Especially about her life before coming to London with her cousins. That period in her past remained a complete mystery to him. He wanted to know what had caused her sudden sadness today, and if he could help her overcome whatever had caused it.

She stared at her fingers for a long time, and he shook his head. She would only tell him what he needed to know, when she wanted him to know it, and he would have to accept that if he wanted to be with her at all.

He was on the point of rising to leave her to her private thoughts, when she whispered, "My father disappeared from my life when I was very young."

Drew held very still. Aurora had never once mentioned anything about her father. He'd assumed she had no living parents, given how close she was to her older cousins.

"We were poor, and he left us behind when he traveled to find work. We were without him a great deal. His work involved stables and horses, but also tricks with coins and gambling for money in low places, I think. My mother came from a wealthy family, though. Better than his, I know now. But I never remember meeting anyone from her family. Sylvia said that we met once, but I cannot remember. We lived a quiet life in a small village. One day, my father kissed me goodbye as he always did before leaving, and he never came back."

Drew exhaled the breath he'd held while she'd been speaking. "He died?"

"I don't know, but my mother wished he had."

Drew winced. "Your parents were not happy together?"

"They used to fight. Terrible squabbles that sent me to hide behind doors, under my cot, so I couldn't see their angry faces. Mother once threw a dish at his back, and when it fell it shattered upon the floor in so many pieces, it couldn't be saved. It is the worst rows I remember most. About money. There never was enough to please my mother."

"Money tends to make even the best families fight if it is in short supply. Even more when there is an excess, too." He reached for her hand and found her fingers even colder now, and clammy. "That must have been terrible for a child to see. Frightening."

"Yes. My mother said she had sacrificed everything, her family and a better marriage, to be with him."

"She must have loved him in the beginning then," he suggested. A marriage of unequal status was often plagued by strife.

Aurora wrapped her arms about herself again. "I waited by the door every-night for months for my father's return, but it became clear he wasn't ever coming back. Mother was a beautiful woman, always complimented. She started going out without me long before I ever gave up waiting for my father to come back, making calls, and writing letters in a fever of excitement she'd never explain. She would always say to others that my father was traveling for work, not that he'd left us to fend for ourselves."

"I can understand why she'd do that. To say your father was gone would be to admit that you were both vulnerable and without protection."

"It didn't work." Aurora sniffed. "One night, I heard a man's voice in our home, and I imagined my father had finally returned. I rushed from my room to find a neighbor entering my mother's bedchamber, taking off his coat and cravat. My mother agreeing to something he said to her before they kissed."

So her mother had taken a lover behind her husband's

back. But the child Aurora had been should never have known about that sort of thing. "What did you do?"

"Nothing. I went back to bed, and when I asked my mother about the visitor the next morning, she slapped me across the face and told me I should be grateful for the sacrifices she made to keep a roof over my undeserving head."

Drew reared back, shocked to hear of a mother speak that way to their child. It was not Aurora's fault that her father had left.

"I did not understand until much later what she meant by that…but I learned the hard way. I was a pretty child, an early bloomer, as some call it. That man was our neighbor and landlord, a widow with a grown son. The neighbor came and went as he pleased from our cottage often. Always at night. Others came, too, I think, and I stayed in my room, covering my ears to block out the sounds. Sometimes my mother cried at night, but during the day she carried on as if nothing had changed, and I started to forget the way things should be.

"When I was thirteen, my mother disappeared. She had become restless and critical of everything around her, especially me in the weeks before I found her gone. I went out and looked everywhere for her, but soon realized her best gowns had gone away with her. The widowed neighbor called a few nights later, expecting to share Mother's bed again, and he found me alone."

Aurora inhaled, sniffing back tears. "He cursed when he realized Mother had abandoned me. She owed him money, he said. Mother owed a lot of people. She'd not paid any bills in some time. I was young, and had nothing to live on and no one to take care of me. I didn't know what to do about the debts. The neighbor told me I would live with him. I was so hungry, I was grateful to go with him."

"It was good of him to take you in."

She inhaled sharply. "I shared his bed from the first night, taking Mother's place. Settling a debt that was never spelled out in any terms of value."

All the air rushed from Drew's lungs. He couldn't help but draw back from her in his shock.

"He never forced me." Aurora winced. "The widow was gentle with me, really. But it was made clear I had to earn my keep, to keep a roof over my head and Mother's debtors at bay. I was so young, I didn't quite understand what I was doing with the farmer was even shameful for a long time. You have to understand, I had nothing and no one but him I could turn to. No money, no education. I did what he wanted, every time he asked. But I had no say in anything to do with my life. I kept house for him, managed the few outdoor servants he employed, slept in his bed, and endured my midnight duties without complaint. I never had any friends. I never left the farm. I depended on my neighbor completely and lived in fear of disappointing him."

Drew was revolted—but not by her. He captured Aurora's cold hands again, enveloped them in his warmth, trying to instill some of his love and support through their joined palms. "I can't imagine what that must have been like. You must have always been terrified."

She nodded. "But I was warm, fed. He protected me from others."

Nausea rose up in Drew's throat at the way she'd accepted all that had happened in her young life. "He took advantage and robbed you of your innocence before you even knew its value."

"I know that he should have left me be…now. But I wasn't knowledgeable then. I was treated no worse than any servant, but I was never paid for my work in or out of bed. Living there wasn't all bad. I had farm animals to tend—chickens, ducks and geese that made each day worth getting up for. They were my world. My responsibility." She licked her lips, swallowed, and kept her eyes lowered. "I was with him for nearly six years before a letter from Sylvia found its way to my hand. A letter years too late to save me from the shame of being a farmer's whore."

"You are not—"

"I am a whore even now, though you don't want to admit it. But being with you was always *my* choice," Aurora whispered.

Drew gulped. Had he known of Aurora's past, he would have never made his scandalous offer. He would have waited forever for a marriage instead, no matter how long it took.

She shrugged her shoulders again, straightening. "You have no idea what it felt like to know you had not been utterly forgotten by your family, even ones you cannot remember meeting. My mother was dead by that time. Mr. Hillcrest, her father, had helped her annul her first marriage, the marriage I had been born into. She had remarried quickly after that, and her years away from the family were hushed up.

"I was not mentioned for a long interval. Not until a spinster aunt's will was read and my name revealed as a beneficiary. Sylvia remembered meeting me, and she set out to find me. She told me I had some money to inherit, if I would only answer her letter and prove my existence. It was a small amount, but I thought I could give it in marriage to a husband. I even foolishly thought the farmer might marry me."

"But he didn't, and you came to London instead."

She shivered. "Not straight away. I had a home already, and a man I'd become fond of, in my own way. He was all I had known for so long. I hid the letter and went on as if it had never arrived. Waiting for the right moment to speak with him about my future, and the money. I remained with him for another six months, and he said nothing about the future.

"I was nineteen when he started leaving the farm. There was another close by that had caught his eye. He said he was in negotiations to buy the place, but they wouldn't sell at a reasonable price at first.

"One morning, as he was getting out of bed and dressing, I saw scratches up his back. Marks I'd not seen the night before as he made love to me. When I asked him about them, he merely shrugged and turned away. But before he could leave the room, I found the courage to ask if he would marry me…and he started to laugh. It was on the tip of my tongue to tell him of my inheritance, but then he called me a slut and told me to change the sheets on the bed and move to the servants' quarters. He then informed me he was marrying that very day. He would have the property he wanted—at the high price of putting a ring on the finger of the widow who owned it. The banns had already been read, but I never knew that because I was so cut off from the world.

"So, I found myself in the servants' quarters in short order and watching the cook slave over the wedding feast. Cast aside. No one thought it important to soften the blow when all of my pets were slaughtered for the event. They didn't deserve such a fate."

Drew closed his eyes, utterly shocked by a past he'd never imagined she'd suffered through, and that her greatest sadness was reserved for the farm animals she'd loved.

There was no greater betrayal than having your family, or those you thought were some approximation of one, treat you with utter cruelty. There was nothing he could do about her family—her mother was dead, and perhaps her father, too. Everyone but Sylvia and Eugenia had treated her shabbily.

He couldn't help but notice Aurora had not said a single name to identify the farmer, or where she'd lived with him. He was furious about that. She ought to be angry, too; instead, she was protecting the devil who had taken her innocence so young.

"I'm so sorry."

"Why should you say you are sorry? You didn't do anything wrong," she whispered. "I wasn't wanted or loved enough by my mother because she made me a bastard when she annulled her first marriage. With the widow married, I had nothing to stay for. I stole money from him and left with just the clothes on my back while the married couple were celebrating. I doubt I was missed by anyone until well into the next day. I arrived at Sylvia's door without any notice, bedraggled, and so frightened that she'd see my ruin in my eyes."

He inched a little closer. "Does she know?"

"Yes. I told Sylvia everything, but only after I had my inheritance in my hands. Just in case she cast me out. I remember being surprised at how hard she cried when I told her my story. What happened to me after Mother abandoned me…it changed me. I have never been able to believe anyone could love me, especially men.

"Sylvia demanded the right to look after me. To live with her and with Eugenia when they moved to London. I'm not really a Hillcrest, you see. I'm not really anyone at all. Sometimes it's as if it happened to someone else, but at other times, I cannot escape the shame and memories of what I willingly did with him."

"It is not *your* shame to bear, and you are not alone. You never will be, if I have any say in it," Drew promised, sliding the remaining distance so they touched from hip to shoulder. "I'm here."

He wanted to pull her into his arms, but he didn't dare make the attempt yet. He knew better than to force his affection onto Aurora now. She would come to him when she was in need, when she couldn't deny it existed.

"What was your father's name?"

She shook her head. "I won't say it. It hurts too much. I've lost everyone and everything I've ever loved. I swore I'd never let anyone get close to me again. Sylvia and Eugenia managed to worm their way into my heart. But they have never understood how much of an imposter I've always felt here, pretending to be a proper lady when I'm anything but."

She sighed. "So, you see now why I could never agree to be your wife. I was ruined a long time ago, and I'm not even the product of a real marriage anymore. An earl with so grand a future as yours cannot marry a bastard daughter of a nobody."

Drew shivered at the bleakness of her pronouncement. She had suffered loss after loss, but the worst was abandonment. She must have always expected him to be disgusted with her past. But he wasn't. He was proud of her for making the best of her life. For leaving the farmer and daring to imagine a better future.

He was painfully aware that his next words were the most important of their entire relationship. He'd believed the Hillcrests had been a respectable country family, of which all the older members were dead. He'd not heard a word of Aurora's mother having any marriage annulled. But he was sure it had been hushed up, even by Aurora's own cousins—and for good reason, too. Aurora would have been looked down upon by society and would be shunned if word of this ever came to light.

He worked with great difficulty to cool his anger toward the people who'd used and discarded Aurora as if she were dirt under their feet. Everyone Aurora had counted on had abandoned her. Forgotten their duty was to protect her and love her.

Drew would not.

He turned his head and caught her eye. "If I had known all that had happened to you, it would have made more sense why you refused to accept my proposals. You don't trust people will stay. You expect nothing, so you're not disappointed. I understand why you couldn't believe in my love after all you've suffered. But if I hadn't given my word not to already, I would sink down on my knees right now to ask for your hand in marriage again.

"I love you, exactly as you are tonight, Aurora. I'm honored you would share with me something so personal and painful. All I want is to be your friend, your companion, and your lover. Someone I hope you might one day feel you can trust to build a brighter future with. You are so strong, and I'm in awe of your bravery in the face of such terrible treatment. Please don't let the disappointments of your past shape your future, my love. Trust that I will always be here for you because I want to be. After what you told me, I don't love you less…I love you more than ever."

A shuddering breath left her lips, and she suddenly curled sideways, into his arms. She cried great gulping tears of pain and heartache that tore out his own heart.

Drew held her tight and cried along with her. It was impossible not to grieve for the happy childhood she should have had. For the pain she'd been hiding from him in fear that he'd turn her away.

Nothing that had happened to her changed a damn thing. Aurora was a good person despite it all. She'd refused him to protect him from the scandal her past might have caused. He wanted to nurture her tender heart until she forgot to fear what had come before they'd ever met. He vowed to hold onto her, reassure her, whenever her doubts clouded her vision of happiness.

He held her tight and let her weep until her emotions settled, then Drew picked her up, carried her up to the bedchamber they shared, and climbed into bed with her, boots and all. He held her in his arms until she finally slept and even beyond that moment until the sun rose.

Chapter Twenty-Four

At eleven in the morning, Aurora slowly descended the stairs of the too-quiet house. She felt raw, uncertain of herself. Terrified she'd revealed too much yesterday. Far more than she'd ever intended to.

She'd woken in their bed alone, and her first thought was that she'd been abandoned. She had rubbed her arms briskly, trying to quiet her fears. Drew had made so many promises to her last night. Ones she desperately wanted to believe in. But no one ever kept their promises. Not to her, at least.

His side of their bed had been cold, and he'd left none of his clothes on the floor, as he so often did. Had he gone, vanishing without a trace just like her mother had done? If he'd reconsidered their arrangement, she didn't know how she'd go on, but she was sure it would hurt. Hurt like nothing else ever had in her life.

She lifted her chin, determined to face whatever came with the same dignity she'd tried to feel ever since she'd come to London and put one foot in front of the other.

Drew was not in the morning room. He was not in the library or adjoining study.

In fact, there seemed to be no servants lurking anywhere she went in the house.

Disturbed by the quietness, Aurora walked trembling toward the back of the house, and headed for the stables. If Drew had left to go riding, he'd have taken Horse with him.

There were a series of corridors and stairways to traverse before the outside courtyard was reached. Long before she reached for the locks on the rear door, she heard voices, unexpected laughter.

Aurora quickly pushed the doors open…and found every single servant they possessed busy in the once-empty courtyard.

A lamb bleated. A chicken crowed, half a dozen geese were honking up a storm and darting through the legs of the male servants as they sought freedom.

There were pots in corners with flowers in them now, where once had been only barren and cold cobblestones. Straw that might have once been piled up in a neat heap was spread out in all directions. The scene reminded her of the home of her childhood, before everything bad had happened in her life.

She clenched her hands together tightly, so astonished that the one happy moment in her story was suddenly recreated the very next day here in London.

"What is going on?"

From the midst of the chaos, Drew rose. His face red and damp with sweat and grinning. His coat missing, and his sleeves rolled up to his elbows. He also had a fully grown chicken tucked under his arm.

She sobbed out loud, relieved to see him. Dear God, she loved when he was this way. Smiling and happy, his grief for his first wife a distant memory.

He waved her toward him urgently. "At last. Where have you been, woman?"

She hurried to his side and whispered, "It's your own fault. You always let me sleep too long."

"I thought you could do with a rest after our talk yesterday." He gestured around him, grinning widely. "What do you think of your new responsibilities?"

She put her hands over her mouth, fighting back tears. "You bought me farm animals?"

"I'll buy you a farm, too, soon." He bent to kiss her cheek. "This motley collection is the best I could scrounge at short notice. It's a start."

She looked around then quickly went to make friends with the animals, hands trembling from the happiness gripping her at each touch. She hadn't been around animals since she'd moved to London. Drew was so good to her. He'd listened to her closely, shared her pain…and bought her the most perfect gift of all.

Aurora had never met an animal she didn't want to make friends with. They were always kinder than people.

All except Drew and her cousins.

She let each animal sniff her hand, learn the sound of her voice so they'd come to trust her. The servants drifted away, leaving them alone in the cobbled square together within a few minutes. She looked around and winced. "I'm not sure this space is big enough for all you've bought."

"I'll begin to make enquiries for somewhere close by to keep them until we find somewhere we like," he promised. "North, south, east, west. What direction shall we go?"

Drew had lived on an estate in Kent, to the southeast of London, during the short years of his marriage. But she suspected he might be reluctant to return on account of his disagreement with his father over his failure to marry the duke's choice. The Kent estate was a place she never wanted to visit before, but she had heard so much about it that Aurora yearned for at least one glimpse now. Drew's country estate sounded exactly like a place she'd always wanted to spend her days. Quiet. No one to complain if there was mud on her hem or if her hair had fallen from their pins, or if she lingered outside in the evening hoping for a glimpse of her namesake in the heavens above them. She had done that with her father so many times.

She frowned, and pushed the unwanted memory away. She had to let go of her disappointments. Her past had no place in her life anymore.

As Drew's mistress, she'd likely never be able to visit Drew's old home. Certainly not if Drew was disinherited. There was still a chance that might happen if he did not marry. He would forever be set apart from his life and family. That wasn't fair to him. She wet her lips, uncertain of what to do to change that, or if she should try to help heal the rift between father and son. Northport wanted Drew to marry one of his choices.

"You've had a busy morning," she said, hedging.

"I had a lot of time to think last night while I was holding you." He caressed her cheek. "We don't need to speak of the past again if you don't want to, but if you ever *do* want to, I'll listen. I'm here…and here to stay forever."

"Thank you." She believed he meant it, too. "You're so very good to me."

"And you to me. Oh, and Bloom should return shortly with your possessions from the hotel you were staying at."

"You didn't have to trouble yourself," she told him. "I would have gone back and…"

He put his fingertip softly over her lips. "It will always be my pleasure to look after you, Aurora." He gave her a hard kiss, then went off to chase a rabbit headed for a gap under the gate.

She laughed as he captured it and bundled it into a

cage with some others. Watched him arranging and checking their animals had feed and water, heart warmed by his gentleness toward all creatures—including Aurora herself.

With a start, she understood Drew truly meant everything he'd ever said to her.

This was just the beginning of their life together, and soon he'd buy her a farm because he thought she needed one. He'd promised to take care of her, that he was hers, and hadn't he proven his commitment at every turn? He'd turned his back on anyone who didn't approve of their affair. That must have been difficult, especially when Northport had so much power.

She'd never known *anyone* as committed to her as Drew proved to be. It made her ashamed that she'd not made the same commitment to him.

He'd wanted forever with her.

A marriage, companionship, and a family.

A full life, filled with love and tenderness.

Everything she'd believed could be too easily taken away if she dared expect those very same things. But there was nothing left in her past that might drive him away. She'd told him the worst, and he was still hers.

She wanted to be his in the same way.

"Aurora?" Drew called.

She threw him a smile, coming to a sudden decision she'd never imagined wanting to make. She did love Drew. She wanted only to be in his arms now. Forever.

They could be together, but only in marriage would he have what he really deserved. To be respected again, admired. To become a duke one day.

Surely, she could bear to become a duchess one day, too?

But only for him. She'd never wanted to marry for a title, but she could wed the man.

Unfortunately, Drew had promised never to ask her to marry him again.

She winced inwardly. That meant that she'd have to make the proposal herself if she ever hoped her wish for his life to come true. She'd have to ask him to ask her somehow. She'd been so set against marriage for so long, believing she was unworthy of his love because of her past. But something had to be done to restore Drew's place in society. She'd never expected any harm to come to him because of her lack of faith in love.

Aurora hurried to help Drew put the chicken in a cage, and when it was secured to Drew's satisfaction and he stood back, she hooked her arm through his immediately. She wasn't quite sure how to start this conversation, but she had to trust she would find enough of the right words for him to understand she'd had a complete change of heart about love.

"I'd like to travel before we decide where to settle. What do you say to a trip to the north first?"

"I would always want your opinion on any property I considered buying for us. It will be your home. But it's quite a good idea to go north when the warmer summer months are ahead. Where would you like to visit first?"

"It's just over the Scottish border, I think."

He nodded. "Could you be more specific? There's a lot of farmland to the north of us."

"Let's start with Gretna Green."

Drew stiffened at her side. "That's a town. Why would we go there first?"

She gulped. "I'm quite fascinated by how anvil marriages are conducted."

"That's unexpected," he murmured—before spinning around to face her.

She could see the puzzlement in his eyes, and the hope he couldn't quite suppress. Aurora was unused to feeling nervous around him, and quickly slid into his arms and held him tight as she spoke, "Would it be so dreadful? I know you mentioned St. George's with all your family and friends present. But I've always expected the roof to cave in on me should I ever step onto hallowed ground, and your father doesn't like me."

"I'd protect you from him. I'll be right by your side the whole time," Drew promised as his arms tightened bit by bit around her, holding her fast against him. "Marriage is forever, you know."

"So are you and me," she promised, smiling up at him. She rubbed her palms over his chest possessively, fingers spread as she caressed him. "This is forever. *Us.*" She drew back a little more to look up into his dear face, and said the words that had terrified her for so long. Words she'd denied him so many times before. "I'd be honored to be your wife, my lord."

Drew's whoop of joy brought an immediate smile to her lips, but a scream burst from her throat the next moment as he tossed her up into the air without warning and held her high above him. But she knew he would never let her fall.

When he brought her down, he spun them around and around in the courtyard, laughing and clutching at her. His face wreathed in smiles so wide, she thought she might cry again. But this time it would be for joy, because they were in love.

She hugged him tight, secure in the knowledge that at last she'd found herself a man she could count on to hold her heart. She knew his promises wouldn't be broken. He would never take his love away.

Drew required a marriage to ever be content. There was no greater gift she could give him than surrendering her heart and soul to his boundless love.

Epilogue

They said marriage changed people.

Drew wasn't sure if that was true of him and Aurora.

Well, yes, they had changed, mellowed together, committed to mutual goals…but that was well before matrimony had occurred in their case.

They had always been well matched as lovers though, and now three months on they were much the same. Finding any excuse to linger in bed. He was happy, and he was certain Aurora was, too.

Once she'd made up her mind, she had committed to a life with him. Despite the burden of becoming a countess, too, she had also worked on making sure her matchmaking business thrived. With his blessing, and occasional participation too.

He told her he loved her every day, kissed her goodbye when he went out, and he always came back at the time he promised, or sent a note to explain any delay, to dispel any lingering fears she might still harbor about the possibility of abandonment.

Aurora had good reasons not to trust that happiness was meant to be hers, after all. He'd experienced that fear, too, having lost his first wife and child unexpectedly. So, he did all he could to forget those darker days and tried to help her do the same.

Aurora's love and trust had made his happiness possible.

That was not to say he was blissfully wed all the time. Oh, no, he'd discovered they did hold a few opinions in opposition, especially the methods they used when dealing with family matters.

Today was one such example.

"Have you come to disinherit me at last?" Drew asked as he stared at his sire. Northport had shown up, uninvited, but clearly spoiling for a fight judging by his scowls.

The duke's lips pursed a moment. "Where is this woman you are rumored to have married?"

"Never far away," he promised, hoping Aurora would actually stay away to avoid meeting his father, since he seemed to be in a bad mood. Northport had not disinherited him still. That he'd come to Drew now to complain about being the last to hear of his marriage amused him immensely.

The duke's scowl darkened as he looked past Drew's shoulder.

Drew turned to see his wife stroll into the room. Dressed in blue and smiling, and his breath caught.

"Darling, you should have told me we had a guest," Aurora murmured.

She linked her arm through his and gazed up at him with such a besotted expression on her face, he started to feel a blush coming on. "Father, I trust you remember my wife, Aurora."

"Yes," Father said slowly. "We've met."

Aurora's face changed as she whipped around to face the duke. "The drawing room. Now. She's expecting you—but don't think she will forgive you as easily as you expect."

"How dare you," the duke sputtered, obviously surprised by Drew's wife's abrupt change in demeanor and by her words as much as he was. Few women ever dared tell North-port what to do. Clare had and it seemed Aurora would too.

"Oh, I dare, your grace," she warned. "I know your character now. And so does she."

She was Juliette. His father's spurned mistress. Juliette was living with them now as a guest and had been since just after their marriage and return from Scotland. He'd brought the woman back to London because they still hadn't found anywhere they wanted to settle down.

Juliette's arrival had been a tearfully emotional reunion, especially when she'd seen them so happy together at last.

Aurora stared Drew's father down now as he remained silent, watching them both with suspicion. Drew hid a smile, proud of her. She was formidable when she wanted things done her way. She'd be more than a match for his father and his attempts at manipulation in years to come.

"Go immediately, if you believe there is any chance she'd take you back after you broke her heart." Then she said softly, "Believe me, I know exactly how you're feeling right now. You should not delay. You may never get this chance again."

To Drew's surprise, Father turned on his heel and stalked from the room without a word.

Aurora shook her head and muttered, "About time he came to his senses."

Drew was surprised. "I thought he'd come about us. How did you know he was looking for Juliette instead?"

"I have my ways."

He folded his arms over his chest. "Do tell?"

"Matchmaking is all about instinct." She shrugged and stretched up to kiss his cheek. "Northport broke with Juliette about the time he threatened you with disinheritance, telling Juliette he was setting a bad example. Then you married me, and I thought, if he had any love in his heart for the woman at all, he would need some excuse to seek her out again. So, after reminding him earlier in the season of what a fine woman she was, desirable to other men, too, I asked Scarsdale to make some offhand remark right in front of him about her being back in London, here with us, to see what he would do. He might love her after all. But I didn't expect him until tonight or tomorrow, at the earliest."

Drew laughed softly and put his arm about his clever wife. "If you can pull this off, I'd be surprised."

"It's up to Juliette now," she replied with a sigh. "She needs to put him in his place and make sure he knows how lucky he really is just to breathe her same air again."

He went to the doorway, listening, but then turned back to see his wife slipping away into her study. She had endless meetings now with new friends and old, who came to her constantly for advice about their hopes of making a marriage.

After the scandal, after news of their anvil marriage had been spread about, they had been swamped by well-wishing friends. Aurora accepted everyone's congratulations at face value. People formerly offended wished them well, too. Aurora liked to believe they saw how much they loved each other.

Drew was certain they came around only to get a closer look at their marriage.

But their marriage had wiped away the stain on Aurora's reputation, and that was what he'd hoped for most of all. She was popular again, and that pleased him immensely.

As for himself, he kept to a smaller circle than before on purpose. Most often he found himself in the company of Aurora's friends and family. Berringer, Wharton, Scarsdale and of course Wade.

Many in their closest circle knew some version of the truth about their slow journey to the altar. Drew, however, kept the specific details firmly behind his teeth. Aurora's painful past, the cause of their scandalous arrangement, would never be his story to tell.

He picked up the day's mail from the hall table and flicked through the envelopes. All were for his wife.

Drew sighed and went to his wife's door. He knocked, and she jumped almost out of her chair. Her appointment book fell to the ground.

Drew rushed to pick it up for her. "I didn't mean to startle you." He earned a smile for his apology and offered one his own. "Am I disturbing you?"

"Always, but I don't mind in the least." She sucked in a breath. "I'm afraid we have much to discuss, my lord, and before my next appointment arrives is as good a time as any."

He raised a brow. "What will it cost us this time?"

Her lips pursed and she set aside her appointment book. "Oh, many thousands of pounds I suppose, in the end."

Drew groaned and sank down into the chair before the desk. "Aurora, you are positively vague sometimes, but who is it really for? A male or female friend in need?"

"I can't tell you that."

He raised a brow at her reluctance to confess the details. "I probably won't say no, but I absolutely insist upon knowing where our money is going."

She winced. "I should be able to tell you in…oh, six or seven months?"

He scowled. "That's too long to wait."

She circled the desk, sinking into a chair by his side. She fluttered her lashes at him. "Perhaps as long as seven to eight months. It depends. The timing of the arrival is completely out of my hands."

He groaned.

His wife was sometimes too careless with her generosity. Early in their marriage, she had expressed a desire to sponsor young ladies who had fallen out of favor, and in that regard, he'd been all for helping the women make a good match.

He understood where Aurora's deep-seated need to help others came from, and had promised to render assistance in any way he could. That dark place, the painful memories inside Aurora, still shaped so many of her choices and opinions about the chances of happiness for others. She wanted to prove to herself and these strangers that, even if damaged and distrustful, they still deserved a good life—and a love like theirs had become.

He bent to kiss her cheek, reconciling himself to the inevitable expense. "Where are they coming from? Do I need to make any arrangements?"

"Oh, not very far," she murmured, looking down at her hands in her lap as her smile grew wider.

"All right. I give up. You're set on testing me again today, I see," he complained. "I have no objection. You can have as much money as you need."

"I am *teasing* you, Drew, not testing you this time. I know you're here for me in ways no one else ever bothered to be. And I am telling you the truth, too. I don't know when or how much it will cost, or even what our child will be born as."

He blinked—and then gasped in shock. "You're having a babe?"

She nodded. "I did not do it on my own."

He grinned, but the shock of the news had caught him

unprepared for such a momentous announcement. "Are you sure?"

She waggled her hand. "Fairly certain. My breasts have become sore, and my waistline has expanded an inch."

He winced. "You might have merely gained weight?"

She gave him a long look. "I cast up my accounts this morning."

"There could have been something wrong with what you were served?"

"Before I'd eaten a single mouthful? Before the tray even arrived in my chambers? And it's not the first time. I don't think I am imagining this," she said with a raised brow. "I am with child."

He rubbed a hand over his mouth, trying not to shout out with glee.

"Don't be afraid," she begged, misunderstanding his gesture. "I know how much you wish Pip had lived."

"It wasn't to be," he murmured, touched by her concern for him. Pip hadn't survived his birth, along with his mother. He'd told Aurora how much that had hurt.

He'd looked forward to being a father, but his dream of a family had been ripped away in one night. He doubted he'd ever recover, doubted he could ever love again. And then he'd met Aurora and fallen in love with her. He considered himself very lucky indeed that she loved him back. He didn't like to think of what his life might have been like without her.

He glanced at Aurora now, and fear for her welfare ripped through his entire being. What if he lost her, too, in childbirth?

Aurora covered his mouth with her hands before he could voice any doubts out loud. "I know what you're thinking. I'm not going anywhere, and our child will live. You are stuck with me, with us, forever and a day, my dear husband."

He forced himself to push the fear aside for now and her hands slowly lowered from his face. But he would always worry. Privately, though, when Aurora couldn't read his mind with just one glance. "I'm so glad to have you in my life, and so happy with your news."

"I feel the same way." She kissed his cheek and stood, putting her hands on her hips. "Now I have much to do if I am to be ready."

"Ready for what?"

"Well, obviously the Duke of Northport will be joining us tonight. I want everything to be perfect for when we sit down together for our first family dinner."

She summoned a servant and issued a stream of orders for Cook and for the evening to come. Drew caught her hand when the servant was gone off to do her bidding. "How do you know Juliette will forgive him?"

"She already has, but we cannot let him know that yet. She's as much in love still as you were with me."

"No one could be that besotted," he joked.

"People should be." Aurora stood and drew him to his feet. She smoothed her hands up and down his chest. "You do want to be on better terms with the head of your family, don't you?"

"Of course, I do," he promised.

"Good then, I'll leave it to you to announce my condition after the dinner, and our mutual wish that they marry before he or she is born. I want you to turn to him and Juliette for support during my pregnancy when you begin to panic."

He dropped his head to rest against hers. "I gather you've given this some thought already."

"It is my fault the estrangement between you happened in the first place. It is essential that you make up well before our child comes. You miss him and I don't like arguments."

Drew wrapped Aurora in his arms. "I have missed him sometimes. He's impossible, but…"

"He is your family." She snuggled against him. "And you are mine. I want everything to go as smoothly as possible for the birth of our child, that includes making him marry Juliette. I need to know things are going well in the family, so you won't worry yourself sick."

Drew slowly slipped his hand between them and gingerly spread his fingers over her belly. There was no hint of a child quickening beneath his fingers, although Aurora claimed the signs were there. "When did you say dinner would be?"

"Oh, the usual time, I imagine. Why?"

"Just a thought. When is your next client to arrive?"

"At four. We'll give your father and Juliette some time to thrash things out before we tell him he must go, so I can use the drawing room for dance practice. He can return, resplendent, to propose, and tomorrow he can make arrangements to marry her by special license at the end of the week."

"You think of everything," Drew promised before he swung Aurora up into his arms and carried her toward the base of the staircase. "I want to see your naked belly."

"I somehow expected you might, so I had already planned to give you an hour to celebrate with me. But no more than that. I'm a very busy matchmaker, you know," Aurora said, and laughed as he hurried upstairs. She snuggled in his arms until they reached their bedchamber doorway.

She wriggled and he set her down on her feet. Aurora

smiled up at him, eyes dancing with wickedness as she loosened her gown and stepped out of it right there in the hallway. "As ever, I'm yours to love, husband."

She backed into the room and Drew followed, fighting to be free of his clothing. Once naked, he caught her up again and held her tight against his skin. "You're forever mine, too, Aurora, and don't you ever forget I'm keeping you."

She offered him a saucy smile. "Always and forever."

More Regency Romance...

Distinguished Rogues Series

Chills ~ Broken ~ Charity ~ An Accidental Affair
Keepsake ~ An Improper Proposal ~ Reason to Wed
The Trouble with Love ~ Married by Moonlight
Lord of Sin ~ The Duke's Heart ~ Romancing the Earl
One Enchanted Christmas ~ Desire by Design
His Perfect Bride ~ Pleasures of the Night ~ Silver Bells
Seduced in Secret ~ Yours Until Dawn

Wild Randalls Series

Engaging the Enemy ~ Forsaking the Prize
Guarding the Spoils ~ Hunting the Hero

Saints and Sinners Series

The Duke and I ~ A Gentleman's Vow
An Earl of Her Own ~ The Lady Tamed

Rebel Hearts Series

The Wedding Affair ~ An Affair of Honor
The Christmas Affair ~ An Affair so Right

…and many more

About Heather Boyd

USA Today Bestselling Author Heather Boyd believes every character she creates deserves their own happily-ever-after—no matter how much trouble she puts them through. With that goal in mind, she writes steamy romances that skirt the boundaries of propriety to keep readers enthralled until the wee hours of the morning. Heather has published over fifty regency romance novels and shorter works full of daring seductions and distinguished rogues. She lives north of Sydney, Australia, with her trio of rogues and pair of four-legged overlords.

Find out more about Heather at:
Heather-Boyd.com

facebook.com/HeatherBoydRomanceAuthor

twitter.com/Heather_Boyd

instagram.com/iheatherboyd

bookbub.com/authors/heather-boyd

goodreads.com/Heather_Boyd